THE TRUTH OF STONE

The Truth of Stone

A novel by

David S. Mackenzie

MAINSTREAM
PUBLISHING

First published in Great Britain in 1991 by
MAINSTREAM PUBLISHING COMPANY (EDINBURGH) LTD
7 Albany Street
Edinburgh EH1 3UG
ISBN 1 85158 343 2 (cloth)

British Library Cataloguing in Publication Data
Mackenzie, David
Truth of Stone
I. Title
823.914 [F]

ISBN 1-85158-343-2

The publisher acknowledges the financial assistance of the Scottish Arts Council in the production of this volume.

Designed by James Hutcheson, Edinburgh
Typeset in 10/12pt Baskerville from disc by Falcon
Typographic Art Ltd, Edinburgh and London
Printed in Great Britain by Billing & Sons Ltd, Worcester

THE TRUTH OF STONE

PART ONE

PART TWO

PART THREE

PART FOUR

For my mother
and in memory of my father

For their support and practical help
I would like to thank:

Jo Brown
Sigra. Pamela Falanga
Dennis Garwood
Rachel Mishan
Neville and Gabriella Rienzo-Clark

PART ONE

1984

STONE

THIS is the story of some things that really happened and of others that did not. In a way then, there are two stories but woven together so that it will be difficult for you to separate the fact from the fiction. It is difficult enough for me. Writing the fictional part is easy; it is the factual part that is hard. However, since I am committed to producing this hybrid does it really matter if I can no longer separate these two in my mind even before I start? I have a feeling that it does. I'm not sure why. Maybe I'll find out as I write it down. One thing is sure though; real people inhabit these pages and although most of them are now dead I have changed their names. I find it interesting that in trying to approach the truth I have to start off by telling lies.

Simon McAndrew lived in a tall, three-storey house next to the village shop. I refer to the village of Spaladale in the Highlands of Scotland, the village where my grandparents lived, where my mother still lives and where I spent part of my childhood. Simon's house is still there. It is built of sandstone and has a pitched roof of slate with a single sky-light window. Its shape is that portrayed in the early drawings of children – rather square, the front door centrally placed with a window on either side. There are two windows on the ground floor, two more on the first and two dormer windows above these which admit light to the attic bedrooms. The symmetrical arrangement of doors and windows is lost slightly as the sky-light, a small window, is set to one side. The house adjoins the village shop whose stone is white-washed. There is a distinct and very straight vertical line, white to one side and bare brown stone to the other, where the two properties meet. At the base of this line is the first post of the decayed and flaking green wooden paling which surrounds the tiny area of what was Simon's front garden, a now hopelessly overgrown and tangled mass of weeds.

I visited Simon's house once only, when I was about twelve. I wanted to know the meaning of a word I'd heard and my grandmother sent me over to see Simon because he had lots of books and was bound to have a dictionary – only necessary of course if he didn't know the word himself because he was regarded as a bit of a scholar. If I was twelve at the time then this would have been in 1967 when Simon was about seventy. He had been married but his wife Elsie had died. Or at least this is what I assumed then as Simon was referred to as a widower and I knew what that word meant. Later I was to learn that Simon's wife had 'disappeared'. Maybe she was dead but no one knew. It seems that one day in 1933 or 1934 Simon came home from his work – he was a clerk in a town a couple of miles away – and Elsie was gone. He contacted neighbours, relatives and eventually the police but there was no trace of her. The two people who told me the story of Elsie's disappearance – my grandmother and my mother – both recounted the rumours of the day which mainly centred on Elsie's likely elopement with a farm labourer from a nearby village. 'Elsie, you see, was younger than Simon' is a sentence I heard a few times and it was given as an explanation, almost a justification of Elsie's departure. The name of the farm labourer and even whether he disappeared at the same time as Elsie could not be recalled. This puzzled me and puzzles me still as surely these are facts upon which the whole thing hinges. To be fair, my mother would have been in her early teens when the incident occurred and her recollection of it has probably been shaped by the host of stories that no doubt circulated after Elsie's departure, and by time itself. After a while it is difficult to differentiate between what happened and what might have happened. It is a problem I'm very aware of, particularly in the writing of this story.

The immediate problem then, in 1967 or whenever it was exactly that I made my only visit to Simon's house, concerned the Salinas Valley in California. According to my notes, made in geography class, this valley produced vegetables and citrus fruits. I didn't doubt this for a moment. However, I didn't know what 'citrus' meant. I decided against asking Mr Salenson, the geography master, because he was a complete tyrant and I felt sure he would have belted me for my ignorance. I was staying at my grandparents' house at the time so I asked my grandfather first and when he could offer no answer, my grandmother. She suggested I should go along to Simon's house to ask him.

It is difficult for me now to describe exactly what Simon was wearing then but I have a picture in my mind of an old man in brown tweeds with a watch chain across his chest. He wore huge brown boots, I remember, or perhaps in this respect I am confusing him with old Mr McRitchie who lived next door to us. Mr McRitchie was related to one of my uncles, the husband of my mother's sister. He was a very old man who walked with the aid of two sticks. He used to wear plus-fours with thick green woollen stockings. He had big brown boots that turned up at the toes and had rows of square silver studs on the soles. Yes, perhaps he was the one with the boots, not old Simon, but the tweeds I am fairly sure of.

I have a photograph, taken in 1938 – the date has been written in ink on the back – which shows my grandfather, my great grandfather and Simon standing in the yard of my grandfather's smithy. At their feet sits a little terrier called Coogan. Simon is the lanky figure on the right. He is wearing a collarless shirt and a shapeless tweed jacket with one button tied. A watch chain emerges from inside the jacket, moves over the left lapel and into the top pocket where, presumably, the watch is located. The chain is too short and this configuration of watch and chain has bunched and creased the jacket by the lapel. In his left hand Simon is holding a pair of garden shears. The forefinger of his right hand appears to be bandaged. His attitude can be described as a gentle slouch. He is a head taller than both the other men and is leaning forward slightly towards the camera. His eyes seem to be screwed up against the sunshine – there is a clear shadow of Coogan the terrier at the base of the photograph – and this has resulted in the definition of a crease in the skin of his cheek, running from eye to chin.

Simon's moustache, fairly trim in 1938 but bushy and drooping in later years, his height, his leaning pose and that long line of shadow upon his face give him the spare and craggy look that I remember from that day in 1967 when I made my only visit to his house. And he was wearing brown tweeds. (And brown boots.)

It was an old musty house full of heavy dark furniture. On hearing my request Simon hobbled through to the front room where he opened a glass-fronted bookcase and extracted a dictionary. He said nothing as he put on his wire-framed spectacles, carefully fitting the thin springy metal of the legs over his ears. He began to flick through the pages. I had followed him from the hall unbidden and I stood in the doorway of the front room in an awkward silence that was only disturbed by the turning of the pages. I was not sure if I should remain standing or sit down or even if I should have moved from the hallway at all. It was clear that I had interrupted him and he wanted to deal with me as quickly as possible.

'Citrus,' he said at last, peering through the tiny round lenses, ' . . . the fruit of the citron.' He snapped the book shut and unhooked the spectacles from his ears. As he replaced them in their case whose brown cover had worn away at the edges to reveal the dull grey of the metal beneath, I was already backing towards the door saying thank you and thank you again and again to hide my confusion. He said a brief goodbye and the front door slammed behind me. Anyway, I thought, relieved to be outside again away from the close disagreeable atmosphere of Simon's house, anyway, that's what it is, the fruit of the citron. But what's a citron?

Simon's house has stood empty now for the sixteen years or so that have passed since his death. On my intermittent returns to the village I have seen how the garden has overgrown, the rose bushes at the front become a hopeless tangle and how the house itself has decayed. The tiny offset sky-light window is broken and someone has jammed a small piece of hardboard behind it in a vain attempt to keep out the rain. The only adornment visible from the street now is a vase in the left front window which no one thought to remove. There were flowers in it once and they have been reduced to a jumble of dried stalks. Apart from whoever it was who tried to repair the sky-light window no one has been inside the house for years.

I discovered the photograph of Simon, my grandfather and great-grandfather (and the little dog called Coogan) some years ago in a tea chest in the smithy. My grandfather was the village blacksmith and his smithy, unused since his death in 1971, stands at the back of the house that he bought in the early twenties. Since 1971 the smithy has served merely as a store, or more of a junk room to be accurate, the old forge now cluttered with mouldy suitcases and cardboard boxes. The place on the floor where the anvil stood is still marked and the twisted broken ends of the bolts that secured the heavy mechanical hammer are still there but most of these things are hidden. An old sofa, a kitchen table, a sideboard, step ladders, boxes of paints and the discarded ends of rolls of wallpaper used not recently but two or three decorations ago, these together with a large collection of smaller items now clutter the dark interior of the smithy. My brother and I have occasional clearouts to reduce the rubbish into more manageable amounts. Three years ago, when we were engaged in another cleanup, I found this old photograph and my brother found an old curling brush and a curling stone.

Curling is played in winter on an ice rink. I suppose it resembles, in a way, green bowling, except that rather than rolling a bowl across grass you slide a heavy curling stone along the ice towards a target at the far end of the rink. The stone itself is a sort of flattened globe of granite with a handle sticking out of it. The underside is highly polished to ensure a smooth slide along the ice. Because the stone is so heavy it can slide a long way with the slightest push. In fact the delivery of the stone by the player is a graceful business, ballet-like. Some time passes before the stone is released and the player slides along with it in a gentle and poised follow-through.

Accuracy in curling depends on careful judgment of line and strength of delivery. If the stone has not been pushed hard enough and doesn't seem likely to reach the target circle which is visible beneath the ice then a little outside help can be used to speed up its progress. This is where the curling brush comes into play. Other members of the team use their brushes in vigorous strokes to polish up the ice ahead of the stone. This is quite legal, in fact an integral part of the game.

I don't know the scoring system nor the finer points of the game and I haven't taken the trouble to find out. This is partly laziness, I suppose, but anyway these aspects are unimportant to the story. Important are the curling stone and brush found in my grandfather's smithy.

The brush was more of a broom or besom – stiff fibres bound tightly round the end of a pale whitewood walking stick. I say 'was' because it is no longer a brush. Apart from the fact that no one in the family goes curling any more the head of the brush was so worn down that it would have been useless for its original purpose. I had the idea of cutting away the fibrous stump and turning the brush into a walking stick proper. I put a rubber tip on the end and now stride along with it when I am out with the dog, occasionally swishing at ferns and decapitating wild flowers.

Unfortunately such a seemingly innocent transformation from curling brush into walking stick was not a good move. Mother expressed displeasure when she found out. In fact she was rather upset about it. The curling brush had been presented to my grandfather – not the blacksmith but the other one, my father's father – when he had won some major competition back in 1932. In fact a little brass ring encircles the stem just below the curve of the handle and it is engraved with my grandfather's name, the competition and the year. My mother's objection to what I had done lay not in the fact that something of value had been damaged – after all the brush had lain in a corner of the smithy, completely forgotten, for more than fifteen years. Nor was the problem to do with the idea of a family heirloom or anything like that. It concerned the past. In our family, as in many families I suppose, you are not allowed to tamper with the past. The alteration of such an insignificant item as an old curling brush was not a desecration, a violation, nothing as strong as that. No, it was just another example of the chipping away of memory, the fading of a person, of what that person had been, through the casual alteration, years later, of something that had belonged to him and had been held dear. I suppose we want to cling to these things more and more as we get older and suddenly here was one summoned up from long ago, a sort of surprise bonus ticket back to a person and a place and a time long lost. Unfortunately I had not recognised that these things do not have to be made into something practical in order to be valuable. By making the curling brush into something useful I destroyed it.

There was still the stone of course, but no engraving here. Mother struggled to remember who the stone had belonged to. My grandfather's stones had been passed on, after his death, to an uncle of mine. So who had been the owner of this stone? It was all so long ago. To my mother's surprise and perhaps more so to my surprise, it was I who remembered. On this occasion I managed to conjure up the past unaided. Not very far back in the past of course, but it was all locked in with my childhood, with my grandfather, with Simon McAndrew and with a small meek man called Donald McPhail.

Donald was his real name; McPhail was not. I should point out too that although there were, and still are, a lot of Macs and Mcs in our village, not everyone is a Mac or a Mc. Donald McPhail will probably be one of the last I will mention. From now on I will begin to favour Munros and Campbells, Murchisons, Urquarts, Mathesons, Tuachs and Keddies. Maybe a Menzies or two will appear, and a Finlayson. There are plenty of names to choose from, spread about the village as in almost any village in the Highlands. When my mother and father were children the names didn't change much because people stayed. The same family of Andersons or Stuarts or Eliots farmed this or that land for years and years. Only the generations changed. These days things are a little different.

To me Donald McPhail was Uncle Donald although he wasn't my real uncle at all. He was a contemporary of my grandfather and of Simon McAndrew and was therefore classified by me, when I was twelve, as old. He too had a moustache but it was very different from Simon's. Whereas Simon's was rather ragged and drooping, Donald's was small and neatly trimmed. He was a much shorter, slighter and more stooped figure than Simon. Furthermore, he was not a fan of tweed. I distinctly remember a dark blue serge suit. Well, perhaps again this is one of those strange fixations of memory. However, I can see him in contrast to Simon. Simon's colour is brown; he is a craggy, unkempt, shuffly, baggy-kneed sort of person. Donald, in spite of his stoop, is blue, smart, dapper, with black polished shoes. Perhaps I am being unkind to Simon. After all, he had no wife to impose order upon him whereas Donald's tiny birdlike wife, whom everyone referred to as Mrs Donald, was a tyrant about the house. Everything had to be neat, tidy and sparkling clean, including her husband.

I have two main memories of Uncle Donald himself – no, I must include a third, the day when I saw him for the last time. The first of these concerns several visits to his house when I was six or seven. I remember sitting on his knee while he sat at the small pedal organ in his tiny sitting room and tried to teach me some simple tunes. Unlike my experience with

Simon's house which was restricted to that one awkward visit, my trips across the road to Donald's house occurred frequently, but they have all merged into one in my memory. His lessons, as I suppose they could be described, were a failure inasmuch as I learned nothing. It wasn't until I was nine or ten and I was introduced to the Misses Reid, two elderly spinsters who were both piano teachers, that I acquired any skill at the keyboard. As I sat on Donald's blue serge knee while he sat on a piano stool before the pedal organ I realised that as far as the production of music was concerned Donald was much better at it than I was, so why not just listen to him playing? It seemed rather illogical that I should be guided towards making so many unruly sounds when Donald could be playing beautifully, as he always did. What usually happened was that Donald would spend two or three minutes trying to induce me to play a few notes, while he pedalled away at the organ bellows on pedals that were some considerable way below my feet. But he would give up this unequal task soon and accept my pleas for him to play. By the time that Mrs Donald appeared from the kitchen bearing a tray of queencakes and rockbuns that she had just baked, the lesson had been abandoned and the recital was under way.

Uncle Donald may not have taught me to play the organ but I grew to understand certain things about our relationship and about endeavour and reward. I would not have been able to explain it in such terms then but I understood that the attempt at a lesson was necessary if then I was to hear Donald play. Consequently I gave it a go even though I knew it was really bogus, a gesture to ensure that Donald played for me and that Mrs Donald came through later with the cakes. I suppose this is my earliest memory of what could be called cheating, a kind of pretence. One thing was sure though; I enjoyed Donald's playing. Looking back on it, I can see that Donald had my education at heart because music was not the only thing he tried to teach me about. It was Donald who told me all about newts.

You will probably accuse me of rambling, of presenting you with something that is without shape, that is little more than a jumble of memories. I can't deny that there is some truth in this. After all, we have jumped around from citrus fruits to curling stone, from brown tweed to blue serge, from organ playing to newts. Don't despair however, because the newts are important. Everything ties together. There are links which bind people and things and places one to another and the chain is a mischievous one which loops back upon itself and back upon itself again to create a multitude of interdependencies. To take just one example, that of the brush and the stone, we find that the brush was presented to my grandfather by the local laird, as I have already mentioned. This laird owned most of the surrounding countryside and most of the village too. His property included the wood above the village, lots of farmland and a couple of quarries. From one of these quarries was taken the granite which was shaped into two curling stones that once belonged to Donald McPhail, one of which has been lost and the other found, after an abandonment of fifteen years or so, in my grandfather's smithy. I remembered that the stone had belonged to Donald because it used to sit outside his front door at the foot of the right-hand doorpost. On that day, in 1969 or 1970, when I was thirteen or fourteen, on that traumatic day (for me also) when Donald and his wife left the village forever, he gave the stone to my grandfather. It was one of those completely useless but very important gifts. My grandfather thanked him for the stone and carried it home, a little unsteady under the weight of it, took it to the smithy and placed it on a window ledge for a year or two from where it was later consigned to a far-off corner.

But curling stones come in pairs. I have already mentioned the fact that Donald had once had two but one was lost. There was a little concrete ledge at the foot of each doorpost at his house where the two stones had been sited. In fact I can just remember where the other one had sat, by the left-hand post, because the circle of dark red painted concrete was the brighter there where the stone had covered it. It had been there for a long time but nevertheless it was so long ago since it had disappeared that Donald couldn't remember what had happened to it. I think I asked him once but I can't remember what he told me. This second, missing stone is important however, and I am going to try and find it. There are buildings where I could look, I suppose, but nobody left alive who could give me any help as to its location. There is one chance though, and this possibility concerns the newts.

The newts lived in Loch Craig and I was introduced to them by Donald. He took me for a walk one day up to the loch which was situated in the woods above the village. It was a small loch, less than fifty yards across, with one or two little streams running into it and out from it. It was full of newts. Donald, I remember, placed his highly polished black shoes very carefully as we stepped round the loch and across the rickety planks that served for bridges over the tiny streams. There were newts everywhere and frogs too and he trod carefully so as not to step on any. I was more concerned about Donald himself. He was quite an old man and I was afraid that his efforts on behalf of the little creatures around us would land him in the water and perhaps me as well. We all survived. I returned home in wonder, determined to find out all about newts. I spent an afternoon in the library reading about them and making drawings of them copied from photographs.

The newts were there in their hundreds and thousands in spring and early summer. They were there all the time, I supposed, but in winter you couldn't see any at all. I learned that they hibernated like frogs. In winter Loch Craig was often covered with ice. Spaladale is in the northern Highlands where winters can be severe. When Donald was young and my grandparents were young, Loch Craig in winter was where you went to go skating. It was also where you took your heavy granite curling stones to go curling.

So, is this where the other curling stone is, lost through a crack in thin ice one March day in nineteen something or other when the thaw had set in but the village curling enthusiasts were taking a chance on just one more match? It's a nice thought. It would be suitable, another example of the neat looping of history, a connection between Donald, his stone, the newts, me, the laird, the quarry and the loch (on the laird's land, inevitably). Bear with me. You may be right. We will find the stone yet.

Did you notice that when I wrote about Loch Craig I used the past tense? This was not because I was talking about a time long ago but mainly because Loch Craig isn't there any more. Loch Craig has gone. In the early seventies it was filled in, mostly with rubbish, levelled over, covered with earth and flattened and that was that. No more newts, no more frogs, no more rickety planks across little waterways, no more skating, no more curling. In fact there were two lochs side by side, only a hundred yards apart, Loch Craig and another whose name I've forgotten. It was smaller than Loch Craig but in fact my recollection of it is rather hazy. My mother remembers this second loch, quite well it seems, but she too has forgotten its name. How is it possible, I wonder, to forget the name of such a thing, not just a thing but a place, something of life which played such a part in the childhood and adolescence of so many? I don't know. Maybe somewhere in the village there are people still alive who skated there in the thirties and forties, who went curling there until the curling club disbanded in 1952. Surely there are. If so, I don't know them and neither does my mother. And if she doesn't know them maybe there are none after all. Both lochs were filled in. I have consulted old maps but neither loch was big enough to be registered. It is as if they had never existed at all.

But they did exist. They existed and they were destroyed. That they existed has just been drawn to everyone's notice. (Are you ready for this?) A few weeks ago work began on some building development in the wood above the village. As digging started the huge mechanical shovels came across debris, rubbish, the tin cans, old bottles, plastic containers and chicken bones of the nineteen sixties. Someone remembered something. Oh yes, there was a pool here once and it was filled in years ago.

Work continued, a sort of unwitting post-historic archaeological dig – marmalade jars, milk bottle tops, prams, bedsteads, the chassis of old cars, bicycle wheels, old notebooks, broken records, a million modern artefacts without value. Then, two or three days later, underneath all the rubbish, resting on the bottom of the former loch, a curling stone was found which was made of grey granite.

And why should a curling stone be noticed among all this detritus? Perhaps because it had aged well, still looked shiny and new? No, that wasn't the main reason. The main reason was that not far away from the curling stone was found the badly decomposed body, a skeleton more or less, of a woman. She had lain there for many years and identification was difficult. It took a long time to decide who she was but she was finally identified as Simon McAndrew's wife Elsie.

PART TWO

1917-1934

PHOTO ONE

July 1917

THE children in the front row are sitting cross-legged on the grass. The second row are on individual chairs and behind them stand the remaining children. The first and second rows have their hands on their laps. Those in the third row grasp the backs of the chairs in front of them except the boy on the far left whose left hand is visible on the shoulder of the boy in front. His right hand is by his side. The children are ten or eleven years old. All are smiling.

On the right stands Mr Dunglass, the headmaster. He is wearing a dark three-piece suit. His shirt has a high collar. His tie is black. He has long grey sideburns and is bald-headed. He is not looking towards the camera but seems to be concentrating on something off to his left, across the line of focus.

Miss Ingram is on the left with her left hand on the back of the chair at the end of the middle row of pupils. Her slim attractive figure is apparent from the cut of her long dark skirt. There is a large brooch at the throat of her high-necked blouse. She is not smiling. Her face is serious. She appears concerned that the right impression should be given.

Elsie is seated third from the left in the middle row. Her long fair hair is tied in two bunches. She is wearing a smock dress with a frilled collar. She is sitting very correctly, with knees together. Her feet are not visible.

'They don't even look like shoes, do they?' Archie said. He held the two shiny black leather shoes up by their laces so that the others could see.

'This one does. It's that one that's a bit funny.' Daisy Mitchell pointed to them in turn. It was the left shoe that they found peculiar. It was shorter than the other and wider at the toe. Daisy reached for the shoe and took it from Archie's grasp. Two or three heads craned in to look as she turned the shoe over in her hands and examined it. Suddenly she dropped it as if it were diseased. 'Ugh! It's so ugly!' she said.

Daisy was eight and a half, Archie nine. They were standing with a few classmates in the playground of their school. A game of tag was in progress on the playing field itself, half an acre of grass fading into bare earth as it neared the grey granite school buildings. The owner of the shoes was involved in this game, running back and to in stocking soles.

Hamish Campbell, ten, picked up the shoe that Daisy had dropped.

'I don't like it. It's horrible!' Daisy said and she made a face.

'What can we do with them, then?' Hamish asked. He looked round the group with a glint in his eye.

'Tie them together,' Archie suggested.

'Naw, that's too easy.'

'Not if you put lots of knots on them. She won't get them out before we get back.'

'That's not fair,' Daisy said.

'Who asked you, anyway?' Archie said. He reached forward and gave Daisy a push which sent her backwards. She stumbled and fell over onto the grass. She got up quickly.

'You're a menace, Archie Sandison,' she said. 'Pushing girls around!'

Archie had not intended to knock Daisy down but he would never admit this. 'Serves you right,' he said. He took the other shoe from Hamish and began to knot the laces together.

At eleven o'clock the janitor appeared at the rear entrance to the school and rang the handbell that signalled the end of playtime. As the pupils lined up in their classes Elsie McKillop ran over to pick up her shoes. She could run quite quickly despite her slight handicap. She discovered that her shoes had been tied together with five or ten knots on the laces. She didn't care. She decided to leave the shoes outside in the hope that Miss Ingram would not notice her stocking soles during the next lesson. She could pick the shoes up later and she would have all of lunchtime to disentangle the laces.

Unfortunately Miss Ingram did notice.

'Put your shoes on, child,' she said to Elsie five minutes into the lesson. She turned back to the blackboard where she was in the middle of writing up some problems of arithmetic. A little buzz went round the classroom. Most of the children who had not been involved in the tying of Elsie's shoes already knew what had happened.

There were thirty-five children seated at tiny wooden desks on a bare wooden floor. The classroom itself had a very high ceiling and windows set up high in the walls. The room was full of light but the children, looking up, could see only sky. Round the walls, below the windows, were pinned examples of the pupils' work, mostly sprawls of paint on stiff coloured paper.

Miss Ingram was thirty. She had been working at the school for six years. She came from a village twenty-five miles away and so was regarded as a foreigner. She was a pleasant looking woman who dressed well, usually in grey or brown, and was always neat and tidy. Her long brown hair was parted in the middle and gathered into a bun at the back. She was unmarried and lived with an aunt in a village two miles from the school. She was of the opinion that most of the people in these parts were rather common and their children could be described as unfortunate. Still, she did the best she could under the circumstances.

In spite of her condescending views Miss Ingram was well aware of the various forces at work in her classroom. She knew who were the reliable pupils, who were the trouble-makers and who were the dolts. She could identify the bright pupils too, one of these being the unfortunate Elsie. She was conscious of areas where she had to tread warily for fear of upsetting her pupils. The children might only be eight or nine years old but they knew where they stood in the hierarchy that was largely created by themselves and had little to do with their teacher's opinion of their academic abilities. They could see who was reasonably well off and who was poor – nobody was rich. The poorest of the poor were the tinker children who turned up to school in little more than rags. The fact that some of them were quite bright did not matter much; they were tinkers and it showed. One of the things that made it clear they were tinkers was the fact that they had no shoes.

The question of who had shoes and who had not was therefore a delicate one. Miss Ingram knew that if she had said anything to Tommy Carterson or Ian Chattan she would have blundered and invited the ridicule of the other pupils directed not only at Tommy and Ian, who rarely wore shoes, but also at herself for assuming that the two tinker boys were as well shod as the rest of them. These two sat together, spurned by the others most of the time because they smelled a little in winter and quite a lot in summer. In her more human moments Miss Ingram felt rather sorry for these two children and wished there were something she might do for them. She decided usually that her concern was misplaced; their case was hopeless. She preferred to stick to her job which was to try as best she could to instil some basic education into them. She was able to admit, somewhat to her surprise, that the Carterson boy appeared to be quite intelligent. This did not really seem right.

Telling one of the children to put on his or her shoes was therefore a command to be given with care. Miss Ingram had to remember which of the pupils had shoes but disliked wearing them and which did not wear shoes because they had none.

Of course Elsie was different. The problem with her left foot meant that she had to wear a surgical shoe, built up at the heel slightly and shaped to fit the ugly contours of her foot. It was not strange that Elsie disliked her shoes; what seemed unusual was the fact that she appeared to be far more mobile when not wearing them. However, Miss Ingram had no qualms about ordering Elsie to put on her shoes. The headmaster himself had taken an interest in Elsie and had asked Miss Ingram to keep an eye on her.

After she had spoken to Elsie and then turned back to the blackboard the whispers that went round the class alerted Miss Ingram to the fact that something wasn't quite right. She turned to the class again. 'What *is* the matter?' she asked sternly. Her eyes travelled from the boy on her far left, little Hugh Sinclair, round to the right where Daisy Mitchell was sitting, twisted round in her seat in quiet but excited conversation with Alec Manson.

'Daisy Mitchell!'

Daisy jerked back in her seat and faced the front.

'Have you anything to say?'

Daisy got to her feet. 'Please Miss, no Miss.'

'Then be quiet.'

'Yes, Miss.' Daisy sat.

Miss Ingram's eyes fell on Elsie.

'Elsie, didn't I ask you to put your shoes on?'

Elsie rose. 'Yes, Miss.'

'Then why have you not done so?'

'Shoes are outside, Miss.'

A few of the children giggled behind their hands.

'Silence!'

Miss Ingram left her stance at the front of the class and made her way down the central aisle to where Elsie's desk was situated. Elsie remained standing.

'And why are they outside?'

'Left them there, Miss.' More giggling.

'Well, you had better go and get them. Now.'

'Yes, Miss.'

Elsie left her place and made her way to the door. After she had gone Miss Ingram addressed the rest of the class.

'Whatever it is that some of you find so amusing, we'll soon get to the bottom of it. Would anyone care to volunteer any information?'

Blank stares greeted this request.

'Diane, what about you?'

Diane stood.

'Well?'

'Don't know what you mean, Miss.'

There was more giggling but this stopped abruptly when Miss Ingram gave the class one of her looks.

'I mean, do you know why everyone should find it so funny that Elsie left her shoes outside?'

'No, don't know, Miss.' She sat down and fixed her gaze on the floor in front of her desk before another question could be fired at her.

'Mabel?'

'No, Miss.'

'Archie?'

Archie Sandison got to his feet quickly and stood at attention. 'No, Miss.'

Miss Ingram was quite sure that this boy knew something about it, probably all about it, but of course she could prove nothing. She kept him standing there, however, for half a minute or so before motioning to him to sit down. She wanted to make it plain to him that she knew he was lying and that the very next time he erred she would punish him severely.

'My, my, what a lot of ignoramuses we have here today.'

Miss Ingram turned her attention to the blackboard again. 'Now copy these down and get on with it or we'll never get finished.' She resumed her task of writing up mathematical problems. For a minute or so the only sounds were those of the teacher's chalk on the blackboard and the squeak of chalk against individual slates as the children recorded their work. The noise stopped abruptly when Elsie returned with her shoes. She stepped across to her desk, her limp only just perceptible.

'Put them on, Elsie, and then do these sums.'

'Yes, Miss.'

Miss Ingram turned back to the board, consulted her notebook and raised her hand to write down the next problem. She was interrupted by renewed whisperings and stifled laughter. She turned and showed that for the first time irritation had changed to anger.

'What *is* going on!'

The children, aware that the new tone in her voice was the first danger sign, were immediately quiet and suddenly found their slates totally absorbing. All the children pretended very hard to be working at their sums, all except Elsie who was struggling to slip her feet into her shoes without untying the complicated knot that bound the laces together. There was a little free play and she reckoned that with a bit of a push she could do it.

'Elsie, are you ready, child?'

'Yes, Miss.' Elsie stood and beamed in triumph. She shuffled her feet slightly to indicate that she had finally managed to cram them inside her shoes. From where Miss Ingram stood, on the raised platform at the head of the room, it was not possible for her to see Elsie's feet and even if she had been able to she may not have noticed that her shoes were, in fact, tightly tied together. None of the children responsible for the knotting of the laces sat near Elsie and they assumed that Elsie's stance indicated that she had somehow managed to disentangle the laces. Only Agnes, sitting next to Elsie, and Ian and Michael on the other side of the aisle could see clearly what was going on.

Miss Ingram became a little calmer.

'All right, Elsie. Sit down and get on with your work.' Her voice was quieter with even a hint of friendliness in it.

'Yes, Miss.'

'The rest of you, do the same.' Sharper tones returned.

For the next five minutes the only sound in the classroom was again chalk upon slate. Elsie was quite good at sums and despite her trip out of the classroom to collect her shoes she was one of the first to complete the exercise. She laid her slate flat on top of her desk with the chalk beside it and folded her arms. Across the aisle Ian gave Michael a nudge and nodded over to Elsie.

'Watch this,' he whispered.

Miss Ingram was now seated at her desk leafing through the storybook she was going to read from when the arithmetic lesson was over. She failed to notice Ian as he leaned across towards Elsie's desk. Because of the number of desks in the room the central aisle was quite narrow. Ian had little difficulty in grabbing Elsie's piece of chalk. He tossed it a few feet up the aisle in the direction of the teacher. She may not have seen what happened but the sound of the chalk landing on the bare floorboards alerted Miss Ingram to the situation. She stood up and walked round her desk to the top of the aisle.

'Whose chalk is that?' she asked. She was using her stern tones again.

Elsie rose.

'Please Miss, mine Miss.'

'And how did it get there, Elsie?'

'Please Miss, dropped it, Miss.'

'Dropped it or threw it?'

Silence. Elsie fixed her attention on a wide groove in the floorboard near where her chalk lay.

Miss Ingram knew what Elsie was doing. She was doing what all the children did: protecting her persecutors. No child would tell tales on another. It was an inviolable law which most of the teachers, including Miss Ingram, found understandable, in a way, but very irritating. Miss Ingram also knew that she would be drawn into this subterfuge. Pressing Elsie to tell who had grabbed her chalk would inevitably lead to her having to punish Elsie because she knew Elsie would not tell. On the other hand, an inquisition among the rest of the class into who really had done it would probably lead nowhere. Further, if she were able to find out the truth things would not go well with Elsie because it would be shown that she had lied about dropping the chalk and Miss Ingram, to save her own face, would feel obliged to punish Elsie in some way. The other children, in particular the child who was guilty, would feel let down and might take out their irritation on Elsie.

These considerations passed through Miss Ingram's mind as they had done many times before and she decided, as on most of these occasions, that it was not worth making a fuss.

'All right, Elsie,' she said, and her voice betrayed a feeling of resignation, 'pick it up and finish your work.'

Elsie did not move.

'Come on, Elsie, get your chalk and finish up.'

'Already finished, Miss.'

'Good, but come along and pick up your chalk.'

Although the chalk was only a few feet from where Miss Ingram herself was standing at the head of the aisle, she was not about to pick up the chalk on Elsie's behalf. Neither would she ask another pupil to do it now that she had asked Elsie quite clearly, three times, to do so. Although she had an inkling that something was going on which she did not know about, she allowed her pleasant tones to take on a harder edge.

'Elsie, the chalk.'

Elsie began to move out into the aisle. She was frightened. She knew she should not have allowed anyone to play around with her shoes. The fact that someone had done so revealed that she had taken them off during playtime, something expressly forbidden by her mother despite her pleas that the shoes hurt her feet. However, even now she clung to the idea that if she took tiny steps she might just be able to reach the chalk and pick it up. She took four or five very small sideways steps to reach the aisle from her initial position behind her desk. She then began to move forward like some kind of trapped mechanical doll. Miss Ingram watched Elsie's clockwork progress in astonished silence. A few giggles started up and the children farthest away from Elsie stood and craned their necks to see. Within a few moments all were laughing. Something close to pandemonium broke out with children actually leaving their seats and crowding over to watch Elsie. Only Elsie and Miss Ingram were apart from this, Elsie because she was concentrating grimly on the task she was required to do and Miss Ingram because she was transfixed by what was happening before her.

Suddenly breaking from her trance-like state Miss Ingram yelled for silence. It was the first time she had actually shouted in the classroom.

The children had never seen her so angry before. They darted back to their seats and were instantly quiet. Only the strange shuffling progress of Elsie could be heard. Miss Ingram stepped forward. 'Oh, Elsie . . .' she began but before she could reach her the child overbalanced and fell with a clatter to the floor. She twisted an ankle while doing so and burst into tears.

Miss Ingram knelt down and gathered Elsie into her arms. It was something she had never done. Generally she did not like to touch the children. She stood up and held Elsie tightly to her. She walked to the door where she turned and over the head of the sobbing child she shouted at the class: 'You disgusting little creatures!'

PHOTO TWO

September 1917

THE photo is taken in a studio with the three subjects positioned in front of a screen. The screen depicts the garden of a large country mansion. An avenue with statues can be seen. The statues seem to grow out of a profusion of flowers. One end of the mansion appears on the left. In the far distance there are mountains.

Peter McKillop is standing behind and slightly to the left of the chair on which his wife Jean is seated. Their daughter, Elsie, is standing close by her mother who has her right arm round the child's waist. Peter McKillop has one hand lightly on his wife's shoulder, the other on his daughter's. All three look towards the camera. Only Elsie is smiling. Her left foot is hidden by the folds of her mother's wide skirt. At the base of the photograph the bottom edge of the screen can be seen. Lush vegetation gives way to black and white squared linoleum.

New sounds began to reach Elsie.

Lying in bed in her room on the first floor she would examine the world through the sounds that reached her from outside, from below and occasionally from above. In the mornings there was the call of birds. The regulars, the blackbirds, sparrows and thrushes, were easily recognisable. So were the intermittent visitors such as the rooks that flew down the coast to forage along the shoreline and the gulls which made the reverse journey, heading inland to the rubbish dump by Killail or to McAllister's fields when the ploughing started. In the autumn geese would pass overhead. They flew high but in such numbers that there was no escaping their strange tumbling call. Once or twice Elsie had heard the raucous cry of ravens.

Elsie's room had a window to the front of the house, overlooking the main street of the village, and another to the rear which gave onto the back garden and the playing fields. From her bed in the centre of the room the passage of birds overhead could be detected by the movement of sound from window to window. At times she imagined that the birds themselves stayed still and the house moved beneath them, making its way up the hill to the woods or down through the fields to the banks of the river Spala.

The early morning sounds included the noise of Mr Fraser the milkman and his horse and cart from the dairy at Ardallt. On Thursdays he would be followed by Mr Spivie the fishman whose progress up the main street was chronicled in his shouts of 'Fresh herring! Fresh herring! Fresh herring!' as they grew in intensity from the bottom of the village and then faded away again once he had passed below Elsie's window and made his way round the corner and up the brae.

At night the sounds were more sinister and Elsie was sometimes afraid. She knew what the owl looked like which lived in the big horse-chestnut tree at the foot of Mr Craven's back garden for she had seen it a few times. This did not diminish the little tremble of fear she experienced when she heard its eerie hooting late at night. The attic rooms above her head were closed off from the rest of the house but mice nested there and she could hear their occasional scratching and the tiny scrape of their claws upon the bare floorboards.

In the evening the noises from downstairs were mainly from her mother moving about the house clearing away the tea things or preparing the fire to heat up the iron. Lately, however, she had begun to hear strange new sounds. These were loud harsh sounds and they always involved her father.

Elsie did not understand the words used but they would wake her late at night or very early in the morning. At first there was usually laughter and singing. There would often be several voices together. These would separate at the front door of the house. Her father's voice then reached her from inside the house, travelling up the stairs and slipping by the edges of the ill-fitting door of her room. The other voices remained outside and their owners took them off down the village street until they faded away completely in the night.

When her mother's voice was heard for the first time, her father's singing stopped. There was a period of strident tones from her mother and no sound at all from her father. Then her father spoke and it was always a quiet sound at first but building slowly, getting bigger and bigger until he was shouting loudly, bellowing the words out.

Elsie huddled down beneath the covers when the sounds began and found that if she put her hands over her ears and started singing too then she could keep most of these sounds away. She sang the nursery rhymes she had learned in school and some psalms too that they sang in church on Sunday. She would sing until she was sure that the noise from below had stopped or until she fell asleep.

But one evening it was different.

Things started in the familiar way with singing and tramping of feet, laughter and loud conversation in the street. Then there was the silence that followed the closing of the front door. She heard her mother's voice, then her father's and as they both got louder so she retreated beneath the bedclothes and began to sing. This time however, she could not blot out the noises from downstairs. She sang louder and louder but the shouting and yelling were inescapable.

Suddenly there was a huge crash as something heavy fell over and glass was broken or rather smashed on the floor. Elsie stopped singing and felt her heart beating wildly during the few seconds of absolute silence that followed this awful noise. Then she heard something she had never heard before. It was a high-pitched, thin sound. A few moments passed before Elsie realised that this strange new sound was coming from her mother. She wasn't crying exactly; it was a sort of desperate wailing. After another few seconds it broke up into large gulps or sobs. Elsie had never heard her mother crying like this. She began to cry as well.

There was the sound of footsteps on the stairs. Elsie knew it must be her father because the steps were heavy and uneven. She wondered why he was coming upstairs because when he quarrelled with her mother he usually stayed downstairs and fell asleep on the sofa or sometimes on the rug in front of the fire. She realised that this time he was coming up the stairs to see her. She started to feel afraid.

'Leave the bairn alone!' It was her mother's voice, shouted from the foot of the stairs. 'Don't you dare touch her!'

'I'll take my hand to you but not to her so don't worry about that,' came the reply.

The door opened. Elsie tied herself in a ball below the covers. She heard her father fumbling to light the paraffin lamp. When he had succeeded the room was filled with light. Even beneath the heavy quilt she was aware of this.

Her father's hand was on the bedclothes. 'Elsie, where the devil are you?'

She pushed her head out from under the covers but held them tightly against her throat.

'Oh, there you are. Well now.'

She was still crying. Her father drew a chair over to her bedside and perched himself precariously upon it. He leaned over at an awkward angle. He looked very untidy and dirty and he had a black eye. He placed a hand on her shoulder and she shrank back.

'Don't be afraid, Elsie, it's only your Da.' His voice was slow and strange as if he was half asleep. Elsie could smell his breath as it reached her in waves. She could not have put a name to anything he had drunk but the smell nauseated her. 'Are you going to give your Daddy a kiss?' He leaned forward. Terrified, Elsie raised her head and pushed her cheek up against his. 'There we are, see!' he said and sat back in the chair. He almost fell over while doing this and spent a few moments trying to restore his balance.

Elsie's mother appeared at the door. 'Are you all right, Elsie?' she asked.

'Of course she's all right. Why wouldn't she be all right?' There was no venom in his voice, just befuddlement.

'She needs her sleep.'

'So do I, woman, so do I. But Elsie and me have got to have a little chat, man to man. Man to . . . ' He burst out laughing and Elsie thought he might fall off the chair. 'No, no, no,' he went on, 'I can't say that, can I? No, no. But Elsie, Elsie, are you listening?'

Elsie looked to her mother who gave a little nod. She was still by the door, monitoring what was going on. She seemed calmer now and dry-eyed.

'Are you listening, Elsie?'

'Yes.'

'Good girl. Now, it's like this, Elsie. I'm going to go away for a while. Yes, Daddy's going away. Just for a while. Now I know you'd like to come too – you would like to come, wouldn't you, Elsie?'

Again Elsie was guided by her mother's nod. 'Yes.'

'Of course you would. But I think it would be better if you stayed here with your mother. She'll take better care of you than I can. What do you think? Is that the best idea?'

Elsie was still lying flat in bed with the bedclothes tight to her chin. 'Yes,' she said.

'I thought you'd say yes, Elsie. You're a good girl. Yes, you are. And a very bonny one too. I don't care what anyone says, Elsie. No . . . ' He reached out an unsteady hand to stroke her hair. 'Don't care one bit for what anyone says. So there.' He turned in the chair and looked towards his wife. 'Elsie's bonny, isn't she?' he asked.

'Of course she is.'

'There, you see Elsie, your mother and I agree on one thing at least.' He got to his feet and looked down at the small, frightened child. 'Goodbye, Elsie,' he said quietly and tears spilled from his eyes. Unable to say any more he turned for the door and fell over the chair he had just been sitting in. He landed full length on the hard floorboards with his head by the door. He made one pathetic attempt to rise and then collapsed. Within moments he was sound asleep.

Jean McKillop stepped over his motionless body and took Elsie from the bed. She picked up the confused child and carried her through to the other bedroom. When Elsie was safe in bed she returned to throw a blanket over her snoring husband.

Elsie slept with her mother that night. She slept fitfully and dreamt of her father's soiled jacket and of his black eye. When she woke in the morning her mother had already risen. She went downstairs expecting to see her father too but he was not there. He had gone and she would not see him again for another ten years.

PHOTO THREE

June 1925

THIS is a postcard. It was available for purchase in the village shop in Spaladale throughout the twenties. Mr Gould, the shopkeeper, bought in two hundred of them in 1921. Sales were slow.

The photograph is of Spaladale Parish Church. It is not an imposing building, being rather squat with neither spire nor tower. The square base and thin gothic windows suggest a Victorian school rather than a church. At the apex of the roof, twenty feet or so above the lintel of the front door, there is a tiny open belfry. The bell-rope hangs down the outside and is looped through an iron ring set into the sandstone wall by the front door. The front door is closed. The church appears to be situated on a grassy knoll split by the gravel path that leads back down to the main road. To one side of the path there is an elm tree whose branches reach up beyond the roof of the church into the pale brown sky.

Elsie had been to church every Sunday for as long as she could remember but she realised, as she approached the brown sandstone building next to the church, that she had never been inside the manse. The gravel path that led up to the manse was an offshoot of the main one to the church door and Elsie was conscious of how exposed she was. If she was on this branch of the path there was only one place she could be going to. Anyone watching from the road or from the manse itself knew her destination. There was the gravel too and the sound it made, her feet crunching down upon it in uneven rhythm as she approached the heavy brown front door. She imagined that this would alert the Reverend Murdoch in his study or his strange little wife in the kitchen to the fact that someone was about to arrive. Elsie kept an eye on the windows waiting for the slight movement of a curtain but she saw nothing.

In fact there was no immediate response to her ring. Elsie considered turning for home but she was determined to see this business through. It had taken a major effort to steel herself for this visit and she didn't want it all to go to waste. Besides, she imagined that if she started trudging back down the drive now the Murdoch household would burst from the front door to pursue her and drag her back up to the manse. She raised her hand to ring the bell again and as she did so the door opened.

Mrs Murdoch, the minister's wife, was the plainest, drabbest woman Elsie had ever seen. Her short blonde hair was parted in the middle and fell to just below her ears. It appeared to be shaped not by any attempt at style but by the lankness of the hair itself. Her face was the colour of paste and her expression one of vague unease. Elsie had rarely seen her smile. Her clothes were dark and heavy and seemed to be so all year round. Elsie tried to imagine Mrs Murdoch wearing a red dress or perhaps a light blue headsquare; it was impossible. When she answered the door she was wearing a white apron, speckled with flour, over a brown woollen jumper and a black skirt. Her sleeves were pushed up above her elbows revealing hands, wrists and forearms that were red from work at the sink. Elsie was struck by the fact that her hands displayed more colour than her cheeks.

At first Mrs Murdoch did not seem to recognise Elsie. In fact they had only met once or twice. Elsie shuffled slightly on the doorstep as she asked to see Mr Murdoch. A quick downward glance from Mrs Murdoch betrayed her. 'Elsie!' she said in surprise. 'Elsie, how nice to see you. You'd better come in.'

It was Elsie who blushed however and immediately got annoyed with herself. She felt that already she had lost a point. She stepped up into the hallway and followed Mrs Murdoch into the sitting room. She was shown to the settee.

'Is it church business you would be wanting to discuss?' Mrs Murdoch asked. She had caught up the hem of her apron and was wiping her hands on it.

'Well . . . ' Elsie began, not too sure how to answer this question. In a way it was church business.

'With church business,' Mrs Murdoch explained, 'the Reverend would probably prefer to see you in his study where he has his books to hand and all the church records, you see.' She seemed to be making an effort to appear concerned and interested but her enquiry only distanced her.

'It's . . . well . . . personal.' Elsie said.

'Just a moment, then.' Mrs Murdoch left the room.

Elsie began to think that she had made a terrible mistake in coming to the manse. Probably the minister's wife could not help it but she was an awkward, off-putting woman. As for the Reverend I. T. Murdoch, he was a bit daunting too. If the living room had been nearer the front door Elsie reckoned she might just have tried to sneak out. It was unlikely though. She heard Mr Murdoch approaching and composed herself for the encounter.

As he entered she got to her feet.

'No, no, no, Elspeth, sit down, sit down,' Mr Murdoch said, rushing over and taking her by the hand. 'Just you sit down and make yourself comfortable.' In sharp contrast to his wife Mr Murdoch was wearing a broad smile. He was a tall, bald-headed man of about fifty-five with a ruddy complexion. He was dressed in his usual clerical outfit of dark suit and dog collar. Elsie wondered whether he ever felt relaxed enough to wear something else.

The Reverend Murdoch seemed strangely animated. Elsie supposed her unexpected visit suggested to him that she wished to join the Bible Class or perhaps attend the confirmation group. If so, he was about to be disillusioned. He sat down opposite her.

'And what brings you here, young lady?' he asked. He was beaming And Elsie was struck again by the contrast with his wife. 'Would you be wanting to join the Bible Class?'

'As a matter of fact, Mr Murdoch,' Elsie began, 'that's not what I wanted to see you about.'

'No? Well, I did mention it to your mother just last night. I thought perhaps she had said something to you about it.'

'No, it's not that.'

'Oh.'

'Actually, Mr Murdoch, now that you mention it, it has something to do with last night itself.'

'You mean the prayer meeting?'

'Yes, that's right.'

'Your mother was there as she is every Wednesday evening.'

'She was.'

'And I hope that one day you might consider joining us on Wednesday evenings too. I know your mother would like that.'

'Would she?'

'Oh, I'm quite certain of that, Elspeth, quite certain.'

'I'm not so sure of that now, Mr Murdoch, not so sure at all.'

'No?' Mr Murdoch looked rather perplexed. 'That's a most unusual thing to say, Elspeth.' He shifted position in his armchair.

Further conversation was suspended as Mrs Murdoch entered bearing a tray with cups of tea and a plate of cakes.

'You got here just as I took them out of the oven,' she said, with not a trace of pleasure in her voice nor displayed upon her face. 'They're as fresh as fresh can be.' She drew a small table over by Elsie's chair and laid the tray on it. Mr Murdoch got up and offered Elsie a cake. Elsie disliked being waited on. She took one with a muttered thank you. Mr Murdoch replaced the plate on the tray, took his own tea and went back to his seat.

As his wife withdrew, Mr Murdoch returned to the question of the Bible Class. He seemed to have forgotten both Elsie's comment about her mother and the fact that the subject of the Bible Class had already been raised and, in Elsie's opinion, dealt with.

'There's no higher study, Elspeth, than that of the Lord's word. There's many a man will testify to that.'

Elsie was unable to reply to this. She took a sip of tea.

'Yes, there's more truth between the covers of that black book than in all others combined. I can testify to that one myself, Elspeth. Oh yes. Yes indeed.'

Elsie placed her cup and saucer on the broad arm of the settee. 'I wanted to talk to you . . . ' she began.

'Feel free, Elspeth, feel quite free. It is part of my pastoral duty to minister to the needs of others, to listen and perhaps offer a little advice. Just you tell me what's on your mind.'

'Well, it's my mother . . . '

'A fine lady, Elspeth, none finer in the village. You can take my word for that.'

'I know that, Mr Murdoch,' Elsie said, unaware of the rather deflatory nature of her remark. 'It's just that last night . . . '

'Yes?'

' . . . last night . . . ' This really was a struggle. ' . . . When she came home from the prayer meeting she was . . . well . . . upset.'

'Upset?'

'Yes. Very upset. I haven't seen her in such a state for years.'

'My dear Elspeth, I'm so sorry to hear that. Of course I will have a word with her . . . '

'No!' This was close to being a shout.

There was a moment of shocked silence. Elsie had not intended to speak quite so sharply. 'I mean, I don't think that would be a good idea. She wouldn't talk about it and I would get into trouble for coming here behind her back.'

'But Elspeth, I assure you . . . '

'The reason I came to see you,' Elsie went on – she was under way now and determined to go through with it – 'the main reason is to ask you what you were discussing last night that got her into such a state.'

'I see. Well now . . . ' Mr Murdoch sank a little deeper into his armchair. 'If I remember correctly we were discussing the commandments in general and more specifically the nature of sin.' He composed himself, fingertips together across his chest and Elsie saw the signs that he was settling in for a sermon. This had to be prevented at all costs. 'Sin is a terrible thing, Elspeth, a terrible thing . . . '

'Is my mother a sinner?'

Mr Murdoch's eyes moved swiftly from a distant corner of the ceiling to Elsie's face. At that moment he knew he had misjudged her. He was not accustomed to such direct questioning and it was not to be explained away as the naïvety of the young. Elsie was a young woman now, he could see that. He sat up in his chair. 'We are all sinners, Elspeth.'

'But some more than others.'

'Yes of course. There are degrees in everything.'

'And is my mother a bad sinner, Mr Murdoch?'

'Elspeth, you're asking very grown-up questions for such a young girl.'

'I'll be eighteen at my next birthday, Mr Murdoch. I'm not a child any more.'

There was a long period of silence. Mr Murdoch remembered that he had reflected on Elsie's advance towards adulthood only a few moments before. 'I can see that,' he said at last. 'I can see that clearly.'

'So please tell me, Mr Murdoch, what has my mother done wrong that is such a terrible, terrible sin?'

Mr Murdoch's feeling of discomfort increased. He was used to being asked questions but interrogation was something else altogether. He felt at a disadvantage. This young girl was forceful and tenacious.

'Tell me, Elspeth,' he said and for the first time his voice was steady and serious, 'where did you or your mother get this idea that she is such a terrible sinner?'

'I believe it was from you.'

'From me?'

'I don't think it could be anyone else. Considering that it all came about at last night's prayer meeting it must have been something you said.'

'Oh, I doubt that, Elspeth, I seriously doubt that.'

'What did you say, then?'

'To your mother?'

'Yes. About sin.'

'I read the word of the Lord, Elspeth. The Lord is very explicit about sin. Just a moment.' He rose and stepped over to a sideboard where a Bible lay. He picked it up and returned to his seat. He began leafing through it. 'Remember please that I was talking to a group of people, members of the congregation, not directly to your mother or anyone else in particular.'

Elsie did not reply to this immediately. There were a few moments of silence as Mr Murdoch continued to search for an appropriate passage from the book before him.

'My mother married in June,' Elsie said at last.

Mr Murdoch looked up from the Bible. He had an inkling that he was not going to get off lightly in the exchange that would follow. 'Did she now,' he said.

'And I was born in September.' She paused. 'Is there sin in that?'

'Ah. Well now, the Bible . . . the Bible is very specific on this point.' He broke off to find the relevant text. 'As we read in Galatians, yes, the works of the flesh are manifest . . . and numbered among them is . . . is . . . immorality. "They which do such things shall not inherit the kingdom of God." Now of course in all things there is forgiveness from the Lord if we are truly penitent, Elspeth, if we are truly sorry for what we have done. Make no mistake about that. There are no bounds to the love of God . . .'

'Did you read that text last night?'

Mr Murdoch shifted in his chair once more. He was no longer smiling – this had stopped some time ago – but there was still a high colour in his cheeks. 'I believe I did, Elspeth, I believe I did. But we must all be aware of where we stand. I make no apology for that. We must not be kept in the dark. The Lord came to bring us light. If we sin and go on sinning there is no end to it. As we read in Exodus chapter thirty-four, the Lord will visit the iniquity of the fathers upon their children and their children's children even unto the third and fourth generation. We have to take care, you see. The devil is quick to take advantage of our weaknesses.' He placed the Bible on the arm of his chair. 'If we do not cherish the Lord we become tainted with sin, tainted . . . '

'Am I tainted?' Elsie interrupted.

'What's that you're saying, Elspeth?'

'What about me? Am I tainted with sin?'

'We . . . we are all tainted, Elspeth, all of us. You are tainted, I am tainted, all of us are. It's inescapable.' It was a struggle but Mr Murdoch seemed to regain his composure a little. He realised he had been speaking too quickly. He sought to slow things down. 'Yes, it is clear that we are all tainted with sin.'

'But some more than others.'

'Why yes, as in all things, there are degrees. Of course.'

'And am I tainted more than others?'

Mr Murdoch began to feel acutely uncomfortable again. Why could this woman, this child, not leave well alone? 'Your situation, Elspeth,' he said at last, and he found himself avoiding her gaze, 'your situation . . . is . . . unfortunate, most unfortunate. The Lord . . .'

'You mean because I am the result of a sinful act?' Elsie interrupted again. She found it quite easy to look directly at the flustered minister sitting opposite her.

'Now, Elspeth, you are being very bold to come here and ask such questions . . . '

'I want to know.' Her voice rose slightly. 'I need to know and I think I have a right to know. It's my life after all.'

'Prayer, Elspeth, prayer is the solution. Prayer is the solution to most things, all things . . .'

Elsie ignored this remark. 'And this is the reward, is that right?' she asked, moving her left foot forward. She pointed down at the highly polished misshapen leather toe. 'This is the reward for my mother's sin, is that it?'

Mr Murdoch's face was bright red. 'The Lord . . .' he began, ' . . . the Lord . . . chooses in his infinite wisdom to . . . to . . . remind us of our carnal nature. If we err, he . . . he . . . rebukes us . . . he punishes us . . . but repentance, Elspeth, repentance brings the full wonder of his glory. He is quick to scold, yes, quick to bring down his wrath upon us but much more hasty to accept us back into the fold when we repent of what we have done . . .'

'And should my mother repent for that?' Elsie surprised herself by the vehemence of her words. 'Is she responsible for that?' She pointed at her foot. 'And what's more to the point, should I repent because of that?'

Mr Murdoch found himself embarrassed and irritated in equal measure. He became aware that he was actually beginning to sweat. Never in his thirty years in the ministry had he been so pressurised by one of his parishioners. He could not speak but stared at Elsie in confusion. Why didn't she just accept the situation? He saw that the high flush on her cheeks was that of indignation.

'Elspeth,' he began at last, knowing that he was floundering, 'Elspeth . . .'

But she interrupted him by rising to her feet. 'I think I'd better go now,' she said. Her face was calm, impassive; her voice less strident but still abrupt.

Mr Murdoch rose quickly. In his haste he knocked over the Bible perched on the arm of his chair. It landed awkwardly, face down, open. He picked it up immediately, straightened the pages and closed it tight. He moved over to the sideboard and replaced it on the exact spot from which he had taken it earlier.

Elsie was already by the door leading into the hall. Mrs Murdoch stepped through from the kitchen. 'I hope you've had an enjoyable little chat,' she said and perhaps through a huge effort of will something close to a smile appeared on her face.

'Thank you for the tea,' Elsie said coldly as she walked past the startled Mrs Murdoch towards the front door. Mr Murdoch hurried after her, ignoring his wife. Outside, on the doorstep, he tried desperately to recover the situation.

'Elspeth, I can understand why you might feel bitter,' he said bleakly.

'Can you now?' She turned to face him. 'Tell me then, what have I to be bitter about?'

'Well . . . that is . . .' He was struggling again, still unable to say anything directly about her disability. He tried but he could not bring himself to name it. Again, Elsie intervened.

'If I am bitter, Mr Murdoch, I am bitter because of the way my mother has been treated . . . by you and your church. You'll not be seeing me in church this Sunday.' She paused. 'Nor any other Sunday again, for that matter.'

She set off down the driveway before he could think of any reply.

PHOTO FOUR
September 1926

THE college buildings are seen in the background but the picture is filled by the main entrance with its pair of wrought-iron gates. The sandstone pillars to which the gates are hinged are eight feet high and set fourteen feet apart. Each gate is about six feet high by seven wide. In the centre of each one is a plaque bearing the names of college tutors and administrators who died in the Great War. The gates are heavy enough to be supported by rollers but the scrolls of iron seem almost fragile.

A young man stands at the left-hand pillar. His stance is three quarters to the camera but his head is turned to face the viewer. He looks slightly awkward in his suit with its tiny high lapels. Perhaps the starched collar of his shirt is choking him. The suit trousers are about an inch too long with a fold or two above the turn-ups which rest snugly on the tops of his heavy black shoes. The man is in his early twenties, his greased fair hair already beginning to recede. Both hands are occupied holding a tweed cap which he seems anxious to put back on his head. His is a slight figure; he looks rather shy, as if he wants to be elsewhere in more comfortable surroundings and in more comfortable clothes. His name is Will and he is the blacksmith who made the gates.

Elsie came out of class with her head spinning. It seemed to her that Mr Fraser, the tutor in Office Practice, had tried to cram everything about correspondence, filing, office etiquette, message taking and so on into this one lesson, the very first lesson of the college term. She wondered if every lesson would be like that. Jane Spence said no. Jane was the girl with freckles and long red hair who had sat next to Elsie at the same desk during Mr Fraser's class. Elsie had liked the idea of sitting beside someone. It reminded her of school. However, the desks were quite different. They were tables with separate chairs, chairs you could actually move around, not the fixed flap seats that Elsie knew from school. Still, two to a desk was nice, particularly as her companion, Jane, was so well-informed. She said that Mr Fraser, or Jock as he was known, tried to pack as much into each lesson as possible which meant that he frequently repeated his points later on. He seemed to like talking and did not like to be asked questions.

'How do you know all this?' Elsie asked.

'My sister Alison came here three years ago. She told me all about it.'

'And did she like it? How did she get on?'

'Oh she's in Glasgow now and doing quite well. Works in a big office for a whisky firm. I don't know if she liked college much but she likes her job fine.'

'Is she married?'

'No, not yet. Says she wants to wait a while.'

'Oh.'

They were walking along a corridor making for their next class, typing, which was due to start in three minutes' time. Elsie desperately wanted someone to say that Mr Fraser's lesson was not typical. After typing she had shorthand and that was only the morning. She had two more classes in the afternoon. She had found the first one so intense that she wilted at the thought of four more like it.

'They're not all like that, are they?' she asked Jane.

'Like Jock? Oh no. Miss Pringle's a bit of a taskmaster, though . . .'

'Miss Pringle?'

'Shorthand.'

'Oh, yes.' Elsie drew her timetable from inside the cover of one of the books she was carrying under her arm. She had copied it neatly from the big blackboard in the main hall. 'And Mrs Mowat?'

'Typing. She's fine. I mean she actually smiles. There's no one who's really bad. That's what Alison told me, anyway. And Simon's nice.'

'Who's he?'

'Simon McAndrew, Economics. We've got him at three.'

Elsie consulted her timetable again. 'Three o'clock.' She sighed. 'To tell you the truth, I'm not sure I'll make it that far.'

Jane laughed. 'Of course you will. It's always like this on the first day. Come on or we'll be late for typing.'

'Now don't worry, girls,' Mrs Mowat said in a soft but clear voice. 'They look horrible brutes of things but you'll be typing out letters on them in no time at all. You'll see.' She smiled at the class, taking in all of them in a sweep from left to right. 'What you have to remember is that Rome wasn't built in a day, now was it?' There was a general murmur of agreement and one girl said 'No, Miss.' Laughter followed this and Mrs Mowat smiled again. She was a large woman in her early fifties dressed in a white blouse, green cardigan and brown tweed skirt. She wore thick stockings and heavy brown walking shoes. Her greying hair was very neatly done up in a bun at the back. She gave the impression of being tidy and organised but not fussy. The girls felt at ease with her.

'During this lesson we'll just learn a little bit about the machine itself,' Mrs Mowat continued, 'how to look after it and keep it clean. I'll also show you the correct way to load a sheet of paper. It sounds very simple but I can assure you it's very easy to get it quite wrong. I think we'll wait until the next lesson before we actually start to type.' This brought a sigh of relief from one or two of the girls. 'I thought you'd be glad to hear that,' Mrs Mowat added. Laughter followed.

'What do you understand by "Economics"?' Simon McAndrew asked. These were his first words to the class after they had settled at their desks. The question was met with blank stares. Although his manner was not intimidating, the girls were not used to answering this type of question, especially from someone they had never seen before.

'Oh, come now,' he said when the silence had lasted for about ten seconds. 'Someone must have an opinion at least.' This was another novelty: asking for an opinion. Some of the girls did not look at him, afraid that they might be singled out for an answer. But Simon McAndrew had no intention of putting such pressure on an individual. However, he was determined to get some kind of response from the girls. He was a man of about thirty, tall, good-looking. His brown hair was wavy, parted high on the left and heavily greased. He had a small neatly trimmed moustache much lighter in colour than his hair, tending towards red. The collar of his white shirt was narrow and stiffly starched; the edge of a gold stud was just visible above the tiny knot of his black tie. The jacket of his dark grey three-piece suit was quite long and as he walked back and fore in front of the class he occasionally fixed his hands on his hips and so flicked the jacket back as if he were wearing tails. Everything about him was clean, smart and in order except for the fact that he was wearing brown shoes.

'I'm sure that you've heard people discussing the "economic situation", haven't you?' he asked as he paced across the room. 'Everyone seems to blame everything on the "economic situation". And then they blame that on the War.' He made a gesture towards the ceiling. Someone sniggered. This was ignored. Having reached the far wall and so the end of his short walk he turned and began to stroll slowly back, looking straight ahead and talking rather as if he were discussing the point with himself. 'Of course the War is the result of the "political situation" and then the whole argument is usually turned on its head when people say that of course this "political situation" is so bad because of the "economic position".' There was a little light laughter at this. Simon stopped his pacing and turned to face the class. His left arm was across his chest with his left hand tucked under his right upper arm. His right hand supported his chin. His right forefinger played with his lower lip. One or two of the girls found this absent-minded stance rather amusing but they suppressed their laughter.

'I may say,' Simon went on, 'that most of the people who talk about the "economic situation" don't know what they're talking about. It's a pity because, as usual, it means that more and more people get misled.' He was silent for a few seconds before continuing. 'Of course you are probably asking yourselves what all this has got to do with learning to be secretaries. So far I have mentioned politics and the War and . . . well . . . what has that got to do with you? That, in turn, brings me back to my first question. If we can answer that one maybe we can see the relevance of the subject to our own study. So . . . ' He released his right hand from its role supporting his chin and folded his arms across his chest. ' . . . So . . . would anyone care to try and answer that first question?' He leaned forward and looked from left to right at the faces before him. 'I expect you've all forgotten the question already,' he said. There was laughter at this. 'Well then, I'll repeat it. What do you understand by the word "Economics"?'

Although the girls were much more at ease now few felt inclined to offer an answer. However, one hand did go up, very slowly.

'Yes.'

Linda Gordon, seated at the back, rose to give her answer. 'It's . . . well . . . it's got something to do with buying and selling, sir.'

'It certainly has, yes. Thank you.'

Linda sat down.

'And what is your name?'

She got to her feet again. 'Linda Gordon, sir.'

'Well, thank you, Linda. You've got us off on the right lines, certainly.'

Linda sat down again.

'Oh, by the way, girls, I'm quite happy for you to remain seated when you ask or answer questions. I expect you to do a lot of talking so I don't want you to be up and down like jack-in-the-boxes. Now, any other offers on "Economics"?'

This time several hands rose.

'That's better! Right. What would you like to say?' He gestured towards a girl two rows back on the left. She rose to reply, remembered Simon's instruction about not needing to get up and she sat down abruptly. Everyone burst out laughing. The girl smiled to hide her embarrassment. Simon, also smiling, took control. 'Now come along girls, that's a little unfair.' The laughter subsided. 'What's your name, please?'

'Elsie McKillop, sir.'

'Right. Well then, Elsie, what is your opinion about "Economics"?'

'It's all about money, sir.'

Simon's eyebrows rose in surprise. There was silence in the classroom for a few moments. 'Well now, Elsie,' Simon said after considering her reply. 'Well now, that was short, direct and almost exactly right. All about money. I don't think we could have a better starting point than that. Very good. Of course now we have another question. Can anyone tell me what the next question is?'

No one could.

'It's tricky, isn't it,' Simon said, smiling. 'First I ask you to answer a question and then I ask you to ask a question. Well, I'm afraid it will be a lot like this in this class, so get used to it as quickly as you can. Just for the moment though, I'll tell you what the next question is. The next question is: What is money?'

Questions and answers flowed after that and the fifty-minute lesson was quickly over. Elsie had enjoyed it. She felt more confident now than she had earlier in the day when she had been disheartened by the first lesson and had questioned her own ability to keep up with the course work. She decided that her first day had been a success.

No one had said anything about her foot.

PHOTO FIVE
April 1927

THE photograph is the last one taken of Jean McKillop, Elsie's mother, before her illness. She is sitting, in profile, on the bank of the river Spala with her hands clasped about her knees. She seems unaware that the photograph is being taken. She is looking out across the river towards the hills to the south. The sleeves of her blouse are rolled up, almost to her elbows. Her hands hold her checked tweed skirt in place over her knees. Her ankles and a few inches of calf are revealed.

In the background on the far side of the river and upstream of where Jean is sitting someone is fishing. He is caught in the act of casting a fly upon the water with his body leaning forward and his right arm stretched out. Only the butt of his rod is visible so the surreal and somewhat unnerving impression is given that he might be a runner in a relay race about to hand on the baton although he is standing in two feet of water and several yards from dry land.

The photograph could be posed but somehow you know it isn't. Jean appears to be day-dreaming.

'He's upstairs with her now,' Elsie said.

'He is?'

'I wouldn't have let him in if it was up to me but mother wanted to see him so I just told him to go upstairs by himself. I've got nothing to say to him.'

Elsie was talking to Jane Spence and the person they were talking about was the Reverend I. T. Murdoch. When he had heard of Elsie's mother's illness he decided to make a visit, even though he knew he would get a frosty reception from Elsie herself. The bedroom was directly above the living room where Elsie and Jane were sitting and they could hear the low tones of the minister as he talked to Elsie's mother. At one point his voice became deeper, more sonorous, almost as if he were chanting. Elsie raised her eyes to the ceiling and pressed her hands together to mock the minister. The Reverend Murdoch had begun to pray.

'How is your mother?' Jane asked.

'Not well at all, I'm afraid. The doctor says it's a stroke. She's lost all feeling on her left side, can't move her left leg or her left arm and she can't speak properly. The doctor says it will all come back, but slowly. It will take a lot of time, it seems.'

'I'm sorry to hear that, Elsie,' Jane said. She had her red hair tied in a pony-tail and had a bonnet, rather like a wide-brimmed boater, which she had removed and placed on her lap. 'Who's going to help you out, then?'

'Help me out?'

'Yes, help you look after your mother.'

'No one, as far as I know.'

'No one?'

Elsie shrugged. 'Not as far as I know.'

'But there must be someone, surely.'

'No, I don't think so. My mother's got a brother somewhere but they've lost touch. When my father left us his side of the family just sort of drifted away. Anyway, the only one of those we really got on with and who looked after us to a certain extent was my grandfather, old Mr McKillop, and he died four years ago.'

'Oh.'

'I mean we've got neighbours of course – Mrs Anderson is very good to us and Mrs Campbell too – but it's not the same, is it?'

'Well . . .'

'I mean, looking after my mother is going to be a full-time job and I'm afraid that I'm the one who's going to have to do it.'

'You mean you're going to give up college?'

'I haven't any choice.' Elsie gave the impression that she had reasoned it all out and come to the only conclusion possible.

Having made this decision she had further determined not to be miserable about it but to accept the situation with good grace. This was not easy.

'Oh, Elsie, that's awful.'

'Don't get me wrong, Jane. I care for my mother. It's just that it's all come at a bad time – as if there's ever a good time for illness.'

They sat in glum silence for a few moments. Jane turned her bonnet over and over in her hands and tried to think of a way out of the problem. Above them the minister's prayer seemed to have ended; they could hear footsteps and the creak of floorboards as Mr Murdoch took his leave and prepared to descend. When he reached the tiny front hall he called through to the living room, 'Well, goodbye then, Elspeth.'

'Goodbye, Mr Murdoch,' Elsie said. She made no attempt to rise and see him out. The front door closed and then a few seconds later they could hear the squeak of the front gate.

'I think you're a bit hard on the man, Elsie,' Jane said. She had seen Elsie in determined or even stubborn mood before but this was never edged with rudeness. Elsie's farewell to Mr Murdoch had been delivered coldly, almost sternly.

'Not at all. You don't know him as well as I do. Christianity is supposed to be a loving religion and he's loveless and insensitive. It's a bad state to be in if you're a minister of the church.'

'But he cares, doesn't he? After all he's here visiting your mother when she's sick.'

'He's just obeying the rules, Jane. He's doing it because that's what a minister's supposed to do. He's not doing it because he really wants to.'

'How do you know that?'

'I just know,' Elsie said and that was the end of that discussion.

Elsie went upstairs to see her mother. When she returned Jane was leafing through her notes from college. 'I can bring you the notes from every lesson,' she said. 'I mean, even if you have to stay off for a couple of months you can still do enough to keep up with the work.'

'I doubt it,' Elsie said. 'Anyway, it's going to be more than two months, I'm sure of that.'

'Oh.'

'Come into the scullery while I make some tea.'

They moved from the living room into a small dark kitchen dominated by a black cooking range with a coal-fired oven. A kettle sat on the hob, the water already simmering. Elsie prepared the tea in a small teapot and laid out a tray to take up to her mother. Jane took no part in this activity.

'One of the first things I've got to do,' Elsie said, 'is sort out the back room. I'm going to clear it out and turn it into a bedroom. Then I can move mother downstairs. Getting up and down those stairs is difficult.' She stepped across to the larder, opened the door and searched inside.

'I imagine it is,' Jane said, not sure if Elsie was referring to her own difficulties with the stairs or her mother's.

Elsie returned to the kitchen table and put some scones on a plate. She looked at Jane. 'I'm talking about my mother. I can manage the stairs fine,' she said.

Once again Elsie's tone had an aggressive edge to it and Jane was taken aback. 'It wasn't clear from what you said,' Jane said quietly, just a little hurt.

'I'm sorry, Jane, I shouldn't have snapped at you . . .'

'I'm on your side, Elsie, just remember that.'

'I know.' She abandoned the tray and took Jane's hands in her own. 'I just get so fed up at times.'

'Elsie, It's only natural that you feel like that. I understand, really I do. I mean, I'd be just as fed up myself. And I'd be fed up with the stairs too.'

They both smiled at this. When the tray was ready they left the kitchen and passed through the living room. As they reached the bottom of the stairs the squeak of the gate could be heard and then the doorbell rang. Elsie looked at Jane and shrugged. She was not expecting a visitor at that time. Jane took the tray and went upstairs. Elsie answered the door.

Her visitor was Simon McAndrew.

He was wearing a mid-brown jacket and plus fours, both in tweed. He had cycled over to Spaladale from Auchendale and his bicycle was propped against the green paling that ran round the edge of the tiny front garden. Elsie was so surprised to see him that she did not know what to say. It was Simon who spoke first.

'I hope you don't mind my calling by, Elsie,' he began. 'I . . . I heard your mother was unwell and then of course you've had to miss classes . . . I just thought I should pop over and see how things were.'

'But of course, come in, come in,' Elsie said as she recovered from the shock of seeing someone she associated with college here, at her front door. She had never seen Simon McAndrew anywhere else and she had never seen him in anything but his grey suit. As she led the way through to the living room she wondered how different he would be out of the classroom.

'How is your mother?' he asked when they had sat down.

'Not very well, I'm afraid.'

'Oh, I am sorry.'

Elsie went on to explain about the stroke her mother had suffered and her partial paralysis. She outlined what the doctor had said about her chances of a full recovery. Simon expressed his sympathy.

'Will it be some time, then, before you'll be back at college?' he asked.

'I don't think I will be back, Mr McAndrew,' Elsie said. 'I've written to Mr Docherty about it.' Mr Docherty was the college Principal.

'Oh, surely not, Elsie. I mean, you were doing so well, so very well. In fact, I thought I'd bring these over to help you out a little . . .' He drew out a small wad of folded papers from an inside pocket. 'These are notes on my lessons of the past week or so. I'm sure the other teachers would oblige in the same way too, given the circumstances.'

Elsie was not at all convinced of this. The idea of Mr Fraser making up notes for an individual student was a little far-fetched. But she thanked Simon for his considerate gesture. 'It was good of you to think of it,' she said, 'but honestly it seems unlikely that I'll get back to college. I'll miss it, of course, but there just isn't anyone else to look after my mother.'

'I see, I see.'

Silence followed. They could hear Jane moving about in the bedroom upstairs and the intermittent clink of crockery.

'Do you have a typewriter?' Simon asked.

'A typewriter?'

Simon's innocent question was a big mistake and he realised this as soon as it had left his mouth. Anyone with half an eye could see that the living room was clean and tidy but the standard of furniture was modest. How could a woman and a teenage daughter with no man to support them afford to live, far less afford a typewriter?

'I mean, do you have the use of one?' he asked or rather stammered through his blushes. But the damage was done.

'No I don't,' Elsie said and her manner was at best cold.

Instead of letting the matter pass, Simon tried to redress the balance by explaining, 'I mean, of course, that if you had the use of one . . . well . . . you could do some practice. I'm sure Mrs Mowat . . .'

'Mr McAndrew,' Elsie interrupted, 'I understand perfectly what you mean and I have to say now that I don't want to put anyone to any trouble . . .'

'Oh, I'm sure it would be no trouble . . .' he insisted.

'But you can't speak for Mrs Mowat.'

'Mrs Mowat would be delighted to help, I'm quite sure . . .'

'I would prefer you not to approach her.'

'But Elsie, it's absolutely no trouble at all, really.'

'I appreciate that, Mr McAndrew, and I'm grateful for your concern. I am. But I don't want to put anyone out. I don't want any special treatment.'

'But, Elsie, these are special circumstances.' By this time Simon was on the edge of his chair and arguing vehemently.

'Not so special around here, I can assure you.'

'But . . .' Either he thought better of his next comment or realised its futility in the face of Elsie's stubborn resistance. He sank back in his chair.

There was an awkward silence. Simon had come determined to convince Elsie to continue her studies. Elsie felt that perhaps she had gone too far and would appear ungrateful if she did not explain her position a bit more clearly. They both began to speak at once:

'Elsie . . .'

'Mr McAnd . . .'

This lightened the atmosphere. Both smiled self-consciously.

'I'm on your side, Elsie. I want you to understand that.'

'I appreciate that, Mr McAndrew. I do.' Elsie noted that she had heard Simon's phrase, exactly the same phrase, from Jane earlier on. Perhaps they were both right, perhaps she was being too hard on them and a bit too hard on herself.

'I understand what you're saying, Mr McAndrew,' she said. 'I understand, really I do but . . . well . . . I don't think I can do both, I mean I can't look after my mother and do my college work at the same time. One or the other would suffer. Of course I don't want to give up college, not at all, but I feel I must make a clean break, a complete break. It's no good trying some sort of half-way answer. I don't want to neglect my mother . . .'

'No one's asking you to neglect your mother, Elsie,' Simon said. 'No one could possibly ask you to do that. It's just that it seems such a waste . . .'

'I agree. I'm sure Mr Docherty isn't too pleased about someone wasting a place on his course.'

Simon decided there was no irony in Elsie's voice in this last sentence. It was difficult to tell, however.

'I was thinking of it from your point of view, Elsie, not a waste of a college place but a waste of someone who clearly has a great deal of talent.'

Elsie looked directly at him and he blushed. She dropped her eyes again. 'It's good of you to say so, Mr McAndrew, but my mind's made up and there it is.'

'I see.'

A few moments passed in silence and then Simon rose to his feet. 'I think I'd better go,' he said. 'Yes, I think I'll be away. Give my regards to your mother.'

'I will.'

They reached the front door. Elsie caught a glimpse of Jane at the top of the stairs. Jane glanced down at her and then quickly disappeared back into the bedroom.

'Well, goodbye then, Elsie,' Simon said. He opened the front gate and stepped out onto the street. He reached for his bicycle. The lecture notes were still in his hand. 'Ah . . . I don't suppose you'll be needing these,' he said, apologetically. He began to cram them back into his inside pocket.

'I'd like to read them, actually,' Elsie said in what Simon took to be a genuine voice. 'And thank you for going to all that trouble.'

'Trouble? No trouble at all, Elsie,' he said. 'No trouble at all.' He handed over the small wad of papers.

'Thank you,' Elsie said. 'Thank you very much.'

Simon wheeled his bicycle round and set it in the direction for home, back to Auchendale.

'I . . . I'd like to visit you again . . . if I may,' he said.

'Of course,' Elsie said. 'Please come round, any time.'

'I will then.' He smiled. 'I mean, I'll come round again maybe in a few days . . . or so. Yes. Goodbye then, Elsie.'

'Goodbye.'

She watched him mount the bicycle and set off, none too steadily, towards Auchendale. It was a long way, twelve miles or so and as she went back inside the house and climbed the stairs to join Jane in her mother's room Elsie realised she had not offered Simon McAndrew anything to drink, not even a cup of tea.

PHOTO SIX

June 1927

THIS is a photograph of her father that Elsie never saw. It is a studio portrait, full length, in front of a rural backdrop. The photographer has taken some care to ensure that the floor of his studio and the scene against which the subject stands are not incongruous. Peter McKillop could be on a country path. He faces the camera with his right hand resting on a rustic bench. He is very well dressed, the trousers of his black suit displaying razor-sharp creases – the left trouser leg at least, as the end of the bench hides his right leg. He is showing just enough shirt cuff below the cuffs of his suit jacket. He appears to be wearing cuff-links and a tie-pin is visible exactly half way between the top of his waistcoat and the full Windsor knot of his dark tie. He is wearing a bowler hat. The formality of his dress and the correctness of his posture add to his stern demeanour.

Several moments passed before Elsie realised that the tall man in the grey suit who was standing on the far edge of the small crowd was her father. Her immediate surprise was not how he had changed since they had last seen each other ten years before but that he was there at all. Who had contacted him? Who had told him to come?

Then she looked at him more carefully. His hair was beginning to grey at the sides but he still looked lean and strong. She thought that perhaps he had lost a little weight. He was very smartly dressed, his dark grey suit clearly new or at least seldom worn. His black shoes were highly polished. He was standing very straight with his hands behind his back. His head moved very little but Elsie could see that he was scanning the crowd. Their eyes met in one long rather empty look. After that both turned their attention to the Reverend Murdoch who was conducting the service.

Elsie tried hard to ignore the minister's words. She hated every moment of this service. She knew that most of her grief had already gone so she was calm and unafraid. She was even able to reflect wryly that it was her mother's death that had brought her face to face with her father again and that now they stood almost opposite one another, separated by the grave into which, in a few moments, her mother's coffin would be lowered. She wondered if her father could remember what his wife had looked like, whether he still had a photograph of her.

The Reverend Murdoch's voice droned on. Elsie looked round the twenty-five or thirty people standing at the graveside. Her neighbour, Mrs Campbell, was there and Nurse Gordon. Mrs Mowat from the college was standing near Betty Munro, one of Elsie's former classmates. Jane Spence was at Elsie's side. There were no other women. Simon McAndrew was opposite Elsie, close to where her father was standing. The rest were distant relatives and a few neighbours. There were three or four people Elsie could not recognise.

The minister's voice stopped and there was some fluttering of Bibles. The twenty-third psalm had been called for. Those who had brought psalm-books looked it up but only from habit. The books were opened at the correct page but were not consulted as everyone knew the verses by heart. Mr Murdoch led the singing. Elsie mouthed the words.

Findocht Cemetery was situated on a gentle rise which led to the side of a steep hill called Fiuran although it was known locally as The Sma' Ben. Its shape resembled the curved outline of the upturned hull of a wooden boat – a long central ridge with steeply sloping sides. Bracken covered the lower slopes and a stand of pine trees could be seen near the top. Some of the trees had suffered badly in the winter storms of three years before and had many lower branches missing. A few of the trees were completely dead, reduced to their trunks only which were whitening slowly in the summer sun.

The Sma' Ben dominated the landscape. The air was clear, the sky almost cloudless. The cemetery itself was well kept, the grass a lush green, the gravel paths tidy and weedless. As she pretended to sing Elsie wondered at the fact that the dead had so much more beauty around them than the living.

The psalm came to an end and Mr Murdoch called out the names of eight people each one of whom would take a cord. Elsie had decided who the eight would be but now regretted that her father would not be one of them. If she had known he was coming she would have arranged it. But she realised that this would have been something close to forgiveness and this was not what she wanted to display.

A couple of distant uncles, a cousin, Mr Campbell from next door, Mr Murchison the postman, Alec Gould the owner of the local shop and Simon McAndrew were seven of the eight who took cords. Elsie was the eighth. It was a little unusual for a woman to do this but as Elsie was the closest relative there was little choice. The undertaker and three assistants raised the coffin from its position over the grave and slipped the wooden struts from underneath it. The coffin, slung on tapes, was lowered gently with guidance from the cords. When it rested on the floor of the grave the tapes were drawn out from beneath but the cords tossed in on top.

Elsie willed herself to remain dry-eyed. She also shut out the final few words that Mr Murdoch had to say as he threw a handful of earth onto the coffin lid. There was some movement among the small groups of mourners and Elsie realised with relief that the ceremony was over. People slowly drifted towards the cemetery gate as the grave-digger and his mate moved forward to begin filling in the grave.

Ignoring Mr Murdoch Elsie walked purposefully to the gate to accept condolences as the mourners left. A small table had been set out with glasses and malt whisky. Mr Campbell was in charge of this. Most of the men accepted one dram before leaving. It had been made clear that there would be no gathering at Elsie's house; the funeral arrangements ended here.

Elsie was standing with Jane Spence and Mrs Campbell as her father approached. He was walking slowly at the side of the Reverend Murdoch and they were in earnest conversation. The women fell silent as the two of them drew near. They stopped a few feet away and Elsie's father said, 'Hello, Elsie.'

'Hello.' She found it difficult to look at him.

'I'll come and see you a bit later on.'

Elsie managed to lift her eyes to his waistcoat with its gold watch-chain, his black tie and then his face.

'Why?' she asked.

'Well, we have a few things we'll need to talk about.'

'I'm not so sure we have.'

The minister interrupted at this point. 'Oh come now, Elspeth my dear,' he said. 'Your father has come all this way from Glasgow, after all.'

'Is the distance important?'

'It's a long way,' Mr Murdoch said, thinking this was a suitable reply.

'You arrived a bit too late,' Elsie said, looking directly at her father.

'I didn't know Jean was ill,' he explained.

'How could anybody tell you? Nobody knew where you were.'

'Your mother knew.'

'Did she now.' Elsie did nothing to disguise the sarcasm in her voice. 'She had a stroke. She was paralysed down one side and couldn't speak properly. She could barely recognise me, let alone remember you.'

The Reverend Murdoch clearly found this exchange embarrassing, as did Jane Spence and Mrs Campbell.

'Don't be so hard, Elsie,' her father said.

'Hard? Hard? If I'm hard it's you who's made me hard. You've a nerve reproaching me for being hard.'

Mrs Campbell put a hand on Elsie's arm. 'Elsie, Elsie, don't upset yourself, eh?' She shot a glance at Elsie's father. 'Let's just leave it at that.'

'Yes, Elspeth,' Mr Murdoch said. 'You've had a very difficult day, after all. Mrs Campbell, perhaps you'd be kind enough to take Elsie home.'

'I don't want to go home,' Elsie said.

Jane recognised that Elsie had entered that mood where she would stubbornly refuse all offers of help and advice, especially if put in the patronising manner of Mr Murdoch. 'I'll walk with you,' she said and Elsie nodded her consent.

In the short silence that followed, Elsie and Jane turned to go but Elsie's father still had more to say.

'I have to see you, Elsie,' he said in a firm voice.

Elsie turned back to face him. The others expected some sort of rebuke to be made but she surprised them. 'If you must,' she said. Then: 'But tell me one thing.'

'What's that?'

'How did you find out? Who was it who told you to come?'

He motioned towards the minister. 'Mr Murdoch here managed to find out where I was.'

'You!' Elsie flashed a look of scorn at a rather sheepish Mr Murdoch.

'Elspeth . . . Elspeth . . .'

'You're never done, are you, never done meddling in other people's business.'

'Oh Elsie, shush now.' This from Mrs Campbell.

'Come on, Elsie,' Jane said quietly.

Mr Murdoch took on a lofty, somewhat hurt look. 'I did my duty, Elspeth,' he said in as dignified a manner as he could.

'Your duty to whom?'

'To your father . . . '

' . . . As he did his duty to my mother ten years ago, is that it? Don't talk to me about duty.' She turned away sharply and walked purposefully out of the cemetery gates. She allowed Jane Spence to take her arm.

Perhaps it was this last exchange with Mr Murdoch that convinced Elsie's father that visiting Elsie would not be a good idea. He wrote a letter instead and had the good sense to have it delivered by Mrs Campbell, not the minister. Mrs Campbell persuaded Elsie to read it and sat down opposite her as she did so. In fact Elsie read it twice, very carefully, before folding it up and replacing it in the envelope. She sat back in her chair and there was silence between the two women for a few moments. Then Elsie took out the letter again and handed it over to her neighbour. 'Please read it,' she said, 'and tell me what you think.'

'Elsie, will you be of a mind to listen if I do tell you what I think?' Mrs Campbell held the letter, still folded, in her hand.

'I will, Mrs Campbell, I will, I promise you.'

'Maybe I should say nothing, Elsie, but you're awful hard on folk you think are interfering in your affairs.'

'Only Mr Murdoch, I can assure you, only him. He's got such a way with him. He just makes my blood boil.'

'I can't say I like the man overmuch myself but he does his best.'

'Well, his best isn't very good. That's all I can say.'

Mrs Campbell ignored this remark. 'I just don't want you to turn on me when I've read this letter . . .'

'Really, Mrs Campbell. I won't. I promise you that.'

'All right then.' She unfolded the letter and read it out loud quite slowly:

'"My dear Elsie, I do not expect you to like me for what I did ten years ago or even to understand why I did it. I hope however that one day you might find it in your heart to forgive me. The purpose of this letter is not to explain my action either although I would say only one thing, that I am mostly to blame for what happened but not totally.

'"Anyway, Elsie, what you feel about me is unlikely to change, I suppose, as we will probably not see one another much in the future. I regret this and would point out that you will always be welcome in my home should you ever wish to visit me or even stay with me. I'll put my address on a separate sheet of paper so that you can contact me if you want to.

'"No, Elsie, the main reason for this letter is not to review the past but to look forward to the future. The last few years have changed me in many ways and have been very good to me, in fact. The result is that I am now quite well off, or at least I'm doing a bit better than average. I thought of making you an allowance of so much a month as I had been doing for your mother (although I feel sure she never told you about this, did she?). However I thought you would probably reject this and I can understand why you might want to do so.

'"Then I hit upon a way of giving you something that you could not reject, you could not give back. The house, Elsie.

'"I have paid off the outstanding balance of the mortgage and had the house put in your name. This means that at the very least you have a place to live, free. You will find the deeds deposited with McMahon and Fraser in Strathinver. The house means much more to you than it does to me, though I was happy there for a time, I will grant you that. Anyway, Elsie, it is yours now and you can live in it or sell it or do what you want with it. I do not expect you to accept it for my sake but do it for your mother. After all, she would have liked to see you with a bit of security, I am sure of that. Your loving father, Alec McKillop."'

'Well,' Mrs Campbell said when she had finished reading. 'Well.'

'Does it surprise you?' Elsie asked.

'I don't know what to think, Elsie, I really don't.'

Neither spoke for some time. Elsie rose and slipped through to the kitchen. Mrs Campbell began to reread the letter. She was still reading it when Elsie returned a minute or two later with a pot of tea and cups on a tray.

'What would you do in my position, then?' Elsie asked as she passed Mrs Campbell a cup of tea.

'What can you do?'

Elsie took her own cup and sat down opposite Mrs Campbell. Bright sunlight filled the small living room. The day of the funeral, the day before, had also been sunny but today there seemed to be a new intensity to the light. As she sat in the armchair and pondered her reply Elsie thought that she might have felt differently about her father's letter if it had been raining or if it had been late evening and the world outside quite dark.

'Not much, I suppose,' she said at last and with the words came a feeling of resignation. She did not like the way the house had come into her possession but as there was little she could do about it she might as well accept the situation.

'Precisely what I've just been thinking myself,' Mrs Campbell said. 'There's nothing you can do about it so you might as well take it with good grace.'

'Oh, I don't know about good grace. I'll take it but that doesn't mean that I have to like the way it was given to me or even the person who gave it.'

'You'll at least write the man a letter, surely.'

'I doubt it.'

'Oh Elsie, I think the poor man deserves that, at least.'

'Why is he suddenly a "poor man", Mrs Campbell?'

Mrs Campbell sipped her tea. 'He's making an effort, Elsie.'

'Is he? Well it's a pity he didn't make more of an effort ten years ago before he ran off.'

They fell silent. Elsie rose and walked over to the window. She looked out onto the bright street through the stems of a potted geranium positioned on the window sill.

'So you think he's a nice man, Mrs Campbell.'

'Nice enough.'

Elsie remained by the window, her back to the room.

'Nicer than he was ten years ago?'

Mrs Campbell turned in her armchair to catch sight of Elsie in order to determine whether the question was straightforward or just sarcastic. As all she could see was Elsie's back it was impossible to tell.

'People change, Elsie.'

'You're too trusting, you know, far too trusting.' Elsie turned and faced her visitor. 'You don't know what my mother went through because of that man.'

'But you can't remember much of that, surely.'

'I'm glad I can't. But I can remember enough.'

She came away from the window and sat down again.

There was silence for a few moments and then Mrs Campbell said: 'You've got to look to your own future, Elsie.'

'What do you mean by that?'

'Well, what do you think you're going to do?'

'At the moment I haven't the faintest idea.'

'Have you given any thought to getting married?'

'Not much, really.'

'Well, you should maybe be thinking about it a bit more.'

'Should I now.'

'Particularly as you have the house . . .'

'What's that got to do with it?'

'Well, you've more of a start if you've already got a house. You can see that, surely, can't you?'

Elsie rose. She walked over to the kitchen door and then back again. It was a matter of four or five paces. She turned and repeated the procedure. Mrs Campbell looked on, rather puzzled.

'Do I limp much, Mrs Campbell?'

'What's that, Elsie?'

'Do I limp much? Watch me again.' She walked to the kitchen door and back for a third time.

'I think you're just trying to make fun of an old woman,' Mrs Campbell said and she turned away in a huff.

'Nothing of the sort. You've known me for years, haven't you. I just want to know if you can still see it, if you still notice it.'

Mrs Campbell's head moved slowly round until she was facing Elsie again. Clearly unhappy with the request she paused for some time before replying.

'You've always limped, Elsie, there's no sense in denying it.'

Elsie sat down.

'And what did that little business prove?' Mrs Campbell asked.

'Oh, I don't know,' Elsie said. 'Maybe I've never really faced up to certain things . . . well no, that's not true exactly . . . I've never accepted them. Up to now I've always thought that was a good thing. Maybe I'm wrong, in a way. I don't know.'

'I have no idea what you're talking about, Elsie.' Mrs Campbell looked as if she was out of sorts again. She drew a handkerchief from her sleeve and blew her nose.

Elsie said: 'The house makes me more marriageable, doesn't it, all things considered?'

Mrs Campbell raised a hand to remonstrate but Elsie cut her off before she could speak. 'No, don't get upset, Mrs Campbell. I'm not angry with you or anyone else and I don't want to offend you; that's the last thing I want to do. No, it's just that I realise that whatever my feelings are, other people believe – and I don't blame them, really – that not many men would want to marry a cripple . . .'

'But, Elsie, I've never thought of you as a cripple.' Mrs Campbell's tone was indignant.

'Don't take me the wrong way, neither have I, but that doesn't change the fact that most people see me that way. They wouldn't say so, not even perhaps to themselves, but at the back of their minds they've . . . I don't know . . . they've classified me.'

'Oh, you're exaggerating the whole thing.'

'Am I? Are you sure? Can you honestly say that it didn't flit through your mind that my chances of finding a husband are greatly improved now that I've got the house?'

Mrs Campbell blew her nose again and pushed her handkerchief back into the cuff of her cardigan. 'What you're saying goes for anyone, Elsie. Any girl's chances of marriage are improved if they're a bit better off than most. Surely you can see that.'

'That doesn't mean I have to like it.'

'Nobody's saying you have to like it and nobody's saying that a man will be attracted only by your money or your house or whatever. I'm just saying that it helps, it might help. What's wrong with that? That's the way things are so why not take advantage of them.'

'I suppose you're right, Mrs Campbell.' Elsie sighed. Any anger she might have felt had gone. Mrs Campbell rose and made for the front door. Elsie followed.

'You've been a great help to me, Mrs Campbell, over the years and especially over the past few days and I've maybe not shown my appreciation very well but I'm grateful to you, I want you to know that, I really am.'

Mrs Campbell ignored this but decided on another word of advice. 'When you get a man, Elsie, just make sure you get one that doesn't drink.'

PHOTO SEVEN

October 1927

THE scene is the tiny forecourt of the Ardallt Registry of Births, Marriages and Deaths. Seven people are standing on the even flagstones. Simon is wearing a three-piece tweed suit. Elsie is in white. Her dress is ankle length with very full skirts. She has a veil and a spray of what appear to be carnations. A little alteration was necessary to the dress which is the one her mother wore when she got married in 1908.

Simon's parents are on the left. They are very neat and proper and rather forbidding. On the right stands the portly figure of Mr Bethune, the registrar, and next to him Simon's brother Alec who is tall and thin. Mrs Campbell, wearing a grey coat and a very small black hat, is on Alec's left with her arm through his. She is a tiny frail looking figure whose head does not reach Alec's shoulder.

The photograph is indistinguishable from thousands of other group photos taken after a wedding. All are smiling except Mrs McAndrew, Simon's mother.

Elsie was not really surprised when Simon McAndrew proposed to her two months after her mother died. During those two months he visited her five or six times and on two of these occasions they went cycling together in the country. She found him rather shy and bumbling, a curious contrast to the confident, organised teacher she had known at college. She felt that she intimidated him a little; he had been within earshot when she had had her altercation with her father at the funeral. He knew she was a forthright young woman and perhaps he was just a little afraid of her.

On the day when he had actually got round to the proposal itself he had been much calmer, much more in control, and Elsie liked that. She felt that it was the important things that he approached with care and preparation. However, she decided to test his nerve a little and said that she wanted some time to think about it. She asked for a week and when that was over she asked for three days more. On the tenth day after the proposal she said yes, an answer she could have given at the very beginning because she had never had any intention of turning him down.

In the short period of their engagement Elsie wondered why it had been so easy to agree to marry Simon. She valued her independence but she did not enjoy living alone. She had got a job in a draper's shop in Ardallt within two weeks of her mother's death. Although she had the house she had no income and there was no question of her returning to college. She took the first job that she was offered and she hated it. It wasn't just that her brief time at college had raised her expectations beyond the humdrum routine of arranging shelves and organising stock; she did not get on very well with the other shop girls nor with the manager. Again, the fact that she had little in common with them had nothing to do with it – she had precious little in common with Mrs Campbell but they got on very well – she just did not like them. The other girls resented her intrusion into what was a well-established circle and the manager was bossy and overbearing. Also the pay was barely enough to live on.

She certainly did not want to become a housewife straight away but marriage would at least allow her to look around and find something more enjoyable. This was her reasoning at least. It would take the urgency out of the need to earn a living.

Elsie also realised that she liked Simon. She did not love him, whatever that word meant, but she felt that this was not necessarily a problem. She was rather sceptical, anyway, about the notion of romantic love; she decided a much more practical approach was needed. Simon was intelligent, well-educated, had a good job and was reasonably well off. And he didn't drink.

They decided that a long engagement was not a good idea. In fact they were married within six weeks. Elsie was adamant that a church wedding was out of the question; she was appalled at the thought of being married by Mr Murdoch. This did not please Mrs Campbell and some of Elsie's aunts expressed surprise if not displeasure. Simon was indifferent to this question. His family found it unusual but raised no objection. Elsie's decision did not prevent anyone from wishing them all happiness. Wedding presents began to arrive.

Elsie wore white but only because the long skirts of the wedding dress hid her feet. She had a veil, a bouquet, a silver horse-shoe for luck and she was wearing something old, something new, something borrowed and something blue. She regarded these things as sheer nonsense but she agreed to them all. After her refusal to be married in church she felt obliged to accept everything else she was asked to do; it was a small price to pay.

It was a distance of about two hundred yards from the Ardallt Registry Office to the Glencairn Hotel where the reception was to be held. As the day was fair the wedding group made their way on foot. Mr Bethune had completed his official duties for the day and so was able to join them. An elderly, rather fat gentleman, he was happy that the pace was not brisk. As she was supported by Simon, Elsie's walk was slow, deliberate and could perhaps have been called stately. She maintained a dignity which was remarked upon by the onlookers who halted their business and came out of the shops to watch her as she passed. There were encouraging words from those who knew the couple and one or two had rice or confetti ready. With Simon's arm tightly around her, Elsie waved with her free hand and smiled through the pain she was experiencing in her attempt to walk straight and true without the slightest hint of a limp.

In the foyer of the Glencairn Hotel she stood with her husband and greeted each one of the forty-seven guests as they passed through to the dining room. Fifteen minutes later she almost cried out with relief when at last she was able to sit down and rest her feet. She knew that a bigger test was to follow later.

Simon's brother Alec was best man. His short speech contained old jokes that everyone had heard before. This did not diminish the laughter that greeted his stories. As he spoke, Elsie sifted through the small pile of telegrams that had arrived. Hoping that the action went unnoticed she removed one and slipped it under the table mat of her place setting. The telegrams, when they were announced, were the usual mixture of sentiment and homely advice. Alec sat down to warm applause.

Simon's speech was also short and direct. He allowed himself to linger, in the traditional way, on the opening of 'On behalf of my wife and I . . . ' which received hoots and whistles and applause. He went on to mention Elsie's mother, though not her father, and his own family. He thanked everyone for their presence and their presents – the only joke he attempted – thanked Elsie for agreeing to marry him and sat down looking quite relieved.

Following this an uncle of Elsie's made a somewhat emotional speech, though mercifully short, and the guests were then invited to repair to the bar while the floor was cleared for dancing.

Twenty minutes or so later the dance band – accordion player, fiddler, double bass and drummer – played the first chord of the first waltz. Simon and Elsie danced elegantly and apparently effortlessly to the amazement and pleasure of the guests. Mrs Campbell burst into tears. However it was the only dance that Elsie allowed herself. She retired immediately to a side room where she slipped her shoes back on. She had danced in her stocking soles and taken the chance that her wedding dress would conceal this subterfuge.

Back in the function suite she sat quietly at the side, politely declining any further invitations to dance. Simon sat beside her; he did no more dancing either. At one point a waitress approached and handed Simon an envelope. It was the telegram that Elsie had removed from the pile. The waitress had discovered it while clearing up. 'It's from my father,' Elsie said as Simon was about to take it out of the envelope. 'Oh, I see,' was all he said and he handed it over to Elsie without looking at it. No more was said on the subject.

The honeymoon was five days in a boarding house on the West Coast. Elsie said she enjoyed the wild landscape and the walks along the sea shore and she did, in a way. However, the thrill of being in a new place wore off quickly. She had wanted the new experience of marriage to begin in familiar surroundings; here there were too many new things at once and she felt a bit lost. It struck her that she had never before spent even one night away from her home in Spaladale. Day trips to Strathinver had been her longest journeys up to that time. Now she had crossed the whole of Scotland from coast to coast and she could hardly believe it. She found herself in a strange house and in a strange room where she was almost afraid to touch anything lest it break. She was in a strange bed too and it was a bed she had to share with someone else. Suddenly she realised she had given up privacy for ever. There would always be someone very very near her for the rest of her life. She had to share everything with him, even her own body.

Simon was not fumbling or shy when it came to sex; he was strong and confident. The act did not disgust Elsie as she thought it might but she did not really enjoy it at first. She was surprised at how Simon approached her, surprised at how much he seemed to know. She reflected that this was her own naïvety. Simon had clearly taken women to bed before. She wondered how many but never even contemplated asking. On the third night of their honeymoon, after rather laborious sex, Simon said something to the effect that it would get better. She despised him for that comment then but the next day resolved that indeed it would get better; she would see to it. That night she tried to respond to him with passion and it was better, she was sure. If only she could love him then it might all become completely right.

Back home – and home was now Elsie's house in Spaladale – adjustment to married life took Elsie a long time. She enjoyed having someone to care for, someone to look after and be looked after by, but there were times when she felt Simon to be almost an intruder. Here was someone who now sat in the corner where her mother used to sit, who spread his newspaper out over the dining table after supper where Elsie used to lay out her books. It was true she no longer went to college but she knew that there had been a subtle shift in things, even tiny things like that, which had once been open to her and now were not. They had been married for two weeks when she caught herself thinking: 'Well, after all, it is my house.' When she realised what her thoughts had been she made another resolution. She determined to share everything, to go at this thing called marriage wholeheartedly. She had been petty, she decided, understandably petty perhaps but petty nevertheless. She would be a good wife to Simon.

For it was clear that Simon had resolved to be a good husband to Elsie. She felt that perhaps the little tokens of affection – unexpected flowers and other gifts – would disappear after the first few weeks but they did not. Simon was generous towards her and tended to be frugal towards himself. He told her exactly how much he earned – this was something that not many husbands did – and his housekeeping allowance to her was more than ample.

At weekends they spent time together cycling in the country. As the year wore on and the autumn became winter they began to go for rambles in the woods above the village. Elsie enjoyed walking as long as no great distance was involved. They strolled among the bare trees when the first light snowfall of winter came and they were there at the side of Loch Craig when the curling club had their first match of the season. The game attracted Elsie. She felt that skating would probably require more time and perseverance than she was prepared to give it but curling looked enjoyable and relaxing. Both she and Simon joined the club.

Being members of the club opened their eyes to the fact that they had rather cut themselves off from village life. During the first few weeks of their marriage they had been very wrapped up in the new experience, wanting no company but each other. Also, because Simon did not come from the village he knew hardly anyone there, other than their neighbours the Campbells. Through the curling club they met up with couples of all ages including several of their own age. They met Donald and Heather McPhail for the first time. Here was a couple in their early thirties with whom they immediately got on well. They met regularly to play foursomes and would go back to Donald's or Elsie's house for tea afterwards.

This little social interchange threw up one small problem. Simon could not bring himself to say 'my house' when talking of where he lived. He felt it would be unwise to refer to it as Elsie's house so he tried, wherever possible, to say 'our house'. Sometimes he hesitated and stumbled over the words. Elsie became aware of this.

One day she went in to McMahon and Fraser in Strathinver and changed the ownership of the house. She wanted it to be in Simon's name. Mr McMahon advised against it but it was hard to dissuade Elsie. Eventually she agreed to put both names to the house, to have joint ownership. Mr McMahon saw no need to make any change at all but he was able to see that his point of view was a legal one and Elsie's was not. He agreed to the change and wished Elsie well. Elsie did not tell Simon what she had done until three weeks later when they happened to be talking about the house. She wanted to slip it into the conversation as if it were something of minor importance. Simon was surprised at the news but decided that Elsie did not want a fuss. He thanked her, rather formally, for her consideration. They went on to discuss one or two things that needed to be done to the property.

Elsie decided she had done the right thing. She had recognised that the success of this business of marriage depended on sharing. Because the house was now 'their' house, even although it was she who had arranged this, she felt that everything was now settled fairly. She asked herself if she was happy and she supplied the answer yes.

After this small affair of the ownership of the house was resolved, Elsie felt she was free at last to concentrate upon her marriage and to enjoy it. She felt that she could reasonably admit to being happy. She had a thoughtful and caring husband whom she was growing to love and she found that the role of housewife was one that she took to much more readily than she had expected. Her circle of friends was growing and she enjoyed her new interests, such as the curling club, very much.

Six or seven years later Elsie was to look back at this time and wonder if it ever existed. With a little effort she might have been able to calculate that this period of happiness lasted for perhaps two or three months.

PHOTO EIGHT

February 1928

THE photo shows the front view of a tall, three-storey house built of sandstone. It has a pitched roof of slate with a single sky-light window. Its shape is that portrayed in the early drawings of children – rather square, the front door centrally placed with a window on either side. There are two windows on the ground floor, two more on the first and two dormer windows above these which admit light to the attic bedrooms. The symmetrical arrangement of door and windows is lost slightly as the sky-light, a small window, is set to one side. The house adjoins the village shop whose stone is carefully pointed. There is a very straight, whitened, vertical furrow where the two properties meet. At the foot of this line is the first post of the new wooden paling which Simon built round the tiny front garden soon after his marriage to Elsie.

Elsie was three months pregnant when she miscarried her first and only child. She emerged from a short but serious illness to discover not only that she had lost the child but the operation which had served to save her own life had also ensured that she would have no more children. She found it difficult to understand how much this could upset her. Only a year or so ago she had been single, free, independent and not particularly interested in marriage. Her ideas had changed and Simon had helped to change them. Having decided to marry she was determined to succeed at this new life and take on whatever it demanded. Now she had been deprived of one of the central roles of marriage and she felt very bitter about it.

She left hospital after ten days but needed a couple of weeks of convalescence before she could take on the housework again. During this time Mrs Campbell looked after her and even through her depression Elsie realised once again how fortunate she was to have such a caring neighbour. In spite of that, she longed for someone of her own age to talk to. Heather McPhail from across the street visited her regularly but though she had a certain warmth there was no real understanding. Elsie wanted someone like Jane Spence, her friend from college, but Jane was now in Glasgow with her sister.

Simon assured Elsie that his main concern was her health. Of course he was upset that she had lost the child and of course it was a blow that there could be no more children but she was the most important thing to him and he was glad above all else that she would be well again soon. The question of children was less important.

Simon told her this many times during her convalescence. At first she was reassured but then she felt that Simon's attempts to convince her were really attempts to convince himself. She began to disbelieve him, mistrust the apparent sincerity of his assurances. She found it hard to blame him, however. If his hurt at realising he could never be a father was as great as hers at her loss of motherhood then she felt able to forgive him a great deal.

Three weeks after Elsie's return from hospital Simon got home one evening to announce that he had lost his job. Elsie was in the scullery when he arrived. He called her through to the sitting room, sat her down and told her, quietly, that he had been dismissed.

The idea was so strange that Elsie found it difficult to respond. At last she said: 'From the college, you mean?'

'Where else? It's the only place I work, isn't it?' He had given his words an edge of irritation which he immediately regretted. He went over to Elsie and took her hands. 'I'm sorry,' he said. 'It hasn't been a pleasant day.'

Elsie grabbed his arm tightly. 'You don't really mean it, do you?'

'Oh yes,' he said. 'I'm afraid so.' He gently disengaged her fingers and sat down opposite her.

'But why?'

'That's the amazing thing,' he said. He leaned back in his chair and raised a hand to stroke his chin. 'Yes, that's the most amazing thing . . .'

'What do you mean?'

'Well . . .'

'They did give you a reason, didn't they? They must have given you a reason.'

'Oh yes, they certainly did.' He had an expression of wry, resigned amusement on his face. 'They gave me the sack because they said I had been "carrying on" with one of my students.'

'What?'

'Taking advantage of . . . my position at the college to . . . how was it put? . . . ah yes . . . "force my attentions on one of the students in my charge". I think that's what Docherty said.'

'Docherty accused you of that?'

'Oh yes.' Simon linked his fingers across his chest and smiled at Elsie. She could not understand his manner at all.

'Why are you smiling?' she asked. 'It's all some kind of joke, is that it?'

'No.' Simon shook his head and the smile left his face. 'No, it's not a joke. I've been sacked and . . .' He paused and looked directly into Elsie's startled face. '. . . The reason Docherty gave for sacking me is quite true.'

Elsie found it hard to take all this in. 'You mean . . . you have been involved with one of your students?'

'Oh yes,' he said quite confidently. 'Yes, I have, for some time.'

'What!'

'Guess who.'

Elsie stood up. Suddenly she was angry. 'Simon! How can you sit there and admit such a thing and then . . . turn it into a game, a silly game!' She was near to tears.

Simon rose and placed his hands on Elsie's shoulders. 'It's you, Elsie. You're the one. You're the student I've been carrying on with.'

'Me?'

'That's right.'

'But . . .'

'. . . We're married. I know. I'm afraid that's just too simple an answer.'

'But it's the truth . . . I mean . . .'

'Look, sit down again and I'll explain, or at least I'll try to.' He pressed her back gently into the chair and sat down opposite.

'I said that to Docherty. "But we're married," I said. It seems that that's not the important point. In getting to know you I had abused my position as a teacher in the college.'

'But, when you started coming here . . . I mean, visiting me here . . . I'd already left the college. I wasn't a student any more.'

'Yes, I pointed that out as well but it made no difference, no difference at all.'

'But this . . . it's just not fair. They can't sack you, just like that.'

'I'm afraid they can. Remember, I was only a temporary appointment.'

'Temporary? But that doesn't mean anything, does it?'

'Oh yes, I'm afraid it does. It means everything in a case like this. It means that they can get rid of me even without an excuse simply by saying that they've found someone more suitable to take over the vacancy on a permanent basis.'

'And have they found someone?'

'I've no idea. Probably not. I'm afraid my face didn't fit. Something like that, anyway. Docherty or someone else high up just wanted me out.'

'But what an excuse.'

'Well . . . ' Simon shrugged.

'And why did it take them so long? I mean, we've been married for six months now. Six months.'

'Oh, I know that. I got some half-baked excuse that Docherty heard about it quite late on, then he had to talk to the Board of Governors . . . they had to meet a couple of times . . . and so on. It all takes time and . . . well . . . six months can go by just like that.'

'Pathetic,' Elsie said and there was a hard edge of resentment in her tone. 'What a pathetic excuse.'

'Yes, well, I didn't quite say that to Docherty.'

'No?'

'No . . .'

'You should have. You should have told him to his face . . .'

'What I did say was that his delay in sacking me had worked out very conveniently for the college. I mean, they'll have my services for another month which takes them to the end of the academic year and then, if they haven't got anyone in mind already, they've got most of the summer to find a replacement. Even if I walked out now it wouldn't be too bad for them as the bulk of the exams are over. There's not a lot of teaching left. Yes, Docherty worked it out very neatly, I'd say.'

'And I used to like that man.'

'So did I. Yes, so did I. I never thought he could do anything like this.'

'No.'

'No.'

They sat in silence for a few moments. Simon seemed resigned to what had happened; he had already worked out most of his anger and hurt. Elsie was still trying to take in the situation.

'But what about the other teachers? Won't they support you?'

'Perhaps. Up to a point. Actually they were a bit subdued when I went into the staffroom and told them what had happened. I got the impression that maybe they knew before I did. Strange. I suppose I should have taken better care of myself.'

There was silence for a while. Simon, looking less agitated but still very tired, seemed as if he might drop off to sleep. Elsie was thinking hard about ways to help her husband. Suddenly rousing himself from his daze, Simon said: 'What am I going to do, Elsie?' The apparent indifference he had shown earlier was gone and his tone betrayed not so much anger as the helplessness he felt.

She looked at him in astonishment. It was the first time he had asked her for advice. She saw the strain in his face.

'Is there anyone who can help you?'

'I doubt it.'

'What about the Board of Governors? Can't you approach them?'

'I don't know. Probably not.'

'Who are they, anyway?'

'I'm not sure.' He got up slowly and stepped over to a small bookcase to the right of the fireplace. He drew out a slim red volume which was the Year Book of the college. He flicked through the pages. 'Here we are,' he said. 'Well, we've got Provost Strachan of Strathinver, Lord Castledhu, Jameson . . . who's he?'

'Probably Jameson from the distillery.'

'Oh yes . . . Jameson . . . and McArthur the MP . . . it's quite an impressive list, isn't it . . . there's Docherty himself, of course . . . and . . . and . . .'

Simon suddenly burst out laughing. He sat down in his armchair again and continued laughing and shaking his head in disbelief. Elsie looked at him as if he was mad. After a few seconds he passed the book over to her, holding it open at the appropriate page.

Elsie looked at the page for several seconds before she found the name that had caused Simon to laugh. Her reaction would never have been the same as Simon's. A year or two before she would have let her anger prick her into action; she would have taken up the challenge that the name offered and set about in determined fashion to right the wrong that had been done. Perhaps it was her recent illness that had drained her of energy. Perhaps she had already grown to depend on Simon and had relinquished part of her fighting spirit. This time, for reasons she was not sure of, she burst into tears. The name of the last member of the Board of Governors was the Reverend I. T. Murdoch.

PHOTO NINE

February 1928

THIS is another wedding photograph. Only the bride and groom are in the picture. Both are in their early forties. They are dressed formally, he in a morning suit and top hat, she in a calf-length dress, though not white. The photograph is in monochrome so it is not possible to detect that the wedding dress is in fact pale blue. The bride is also wearing a short jacket in dark blue and a small pale blue hat with a light veil. She is smiling and appears to be very happy. The groom looks more serious. His stance is positive and solid as if he is quite comfortable in his formal suit and special situation.

The photograph was taken a month or two after Elsie's mother died. Elsie herself never saw it. The man in the photo is her father.

Looking back at that time from a time much later on, Elsie would be able to trace the beginning of the decline of her marriage to that one moment when she read the Reverend Murdoch's name in the college Year Book. She was convinced that he was responsible for Simon's dismissal. Simon told her that it really was most unlikely. After all, Mr Murdoch was only one man among several and anyway, they had no proof that he had attended the relevant meeting of the Board of Governors. It was coincidence, purely coincidence that they had once again stumbled upon the name of Elsie's least favourite person. This was why Simon had merely laughed when the discovery had been made.

Elsie would have none of this logic. She was sure that Mr Murdoch was the culprit and her hate for the man grew. The only difference was that this time, in contrast to what had happened a few years before when she had gone to the manse to confront him about her mother, she could do nothing. She wanted to be able to fight; she wanted to embarrass and humiliate the man as she had done before but she lacked the strength. Physically she was weaker since her miscarriage but something else was gone too. She felt angry and frustrated and hurt but she was weary as well. She realised that some of the fight had gone out of her.

One thing that she did manage to do, however, was to persuade Simon to go and see Mr Murdoch. It took considerable effort on Elsie's part to get Simon to do this and she only succeeded when she threatened that if he did not go, she would go herself. In fact, she had no intention of carrying out this threat but she presented it convincingly enough to ensure that, a couple of evenings later, Simon set off up the hill to the manse.

He left immediately after tea, at about six o'clock. Elsie had pressed upon him the need to be firm, to find out the real reason for his dismissal and to make it plain to the minister that he felt he had been treated unfairly. She had little hope that Simon would do any of this because he lacked the necessary determination. He had already resigned himself to the loss of his job. Elsie reflected that the gentleness of Simon's nature was one of the things that had attracted her to him. There were situations, however, where she wished he could be hard-headed and less willing to compromise. As she watched him turn the corner by the McPhails' house she believed that he would be back, probably quiet and dispirited, within an hour.

It was nearly nine o'clock when Simon returned. He had been talking to the minister for the better part of three hours. Elsie could not believe that he had stayed so long.

'What on earth did you talk about?' she asked.

'Well, he's a very interesting man, Mr Murdoch, very interesting.' Simon sat down in his usual armchair. He seemed to be in a serious, reflective mood.

'Interesting?'

'Yes.'

'I think that's the last word I'd use to describe him,' Elsie said. She was still unsure of how to react. Simon did not appear to be upset in any way yet he was sombre, introspective. 'He's also the last person I'd want to sit and chat to for two and a half hours,' she added.

'We didn't really chat,' Simon said.

'Didn't you?'

'No.'

'Well, what did you do?'

'Oh, I don't know . . .' He shrugged and then shook his head. 'We talked about a lot of things . . . education, the Church, the War . . . did you know he was an army chaplain in the War?' He looked up at Elsie when he said this. She moved over to the chair on the other side of the fireplace.

'I'm not sure,' she said. 'Maybe someone told me once but I forget. Is it important?'

'Perhaps not . . . well, yes, yes, I think it *is* important.'

'Why?'

'Because I'd always thought of him as someone who'd never left home . . . you know, someone whose whole world was confined to Spaladale, Ardallt and Strathinver.'

'I don't see what difference it makes,' Elsie said.

'Maybe it doesn't, maybe it doesn't at all. It's just that . . . well . . . he's been involved in unpleasant things, terrible things, and that must give him a different perspective.'

'Perhaps.'

'I'm sure it does.'

'But what about the job?' Elsie asked. 'You did ask him about that, didn't you?'

'Oh that. Well . . .' Simon looked as if he had forgotten that tackling Mr Murdoch about his dismissal was the main point of his visit. 'Yes, I asked him . . .'

'And?'

'Well, first of all, he said he'd no idea I'd been dismissed.'

Elsie laughed. 'As if we can believe that!'

Simon's face was still serious. 'Well, I do, as a matter of fact.'

'What!'

'He said he missed the last two meetings of the Board and was a bit out of touch with what was happening in the college. Anyway, it was an unwritten rule that his influence extended only to the teaching of religious studies. He plays no part in the day-to-day running of the college. He had no idea I'd been fired.'

'Well, even so . . . even if he was telling the truth . . .'

'Elsie, he's a minister, after all,' Simon interrupted.

'So? Are ministers any more truthful than anyone else?'

'I should hope so, yes.'

'I doubt it. I doubt it very much.'

'You really don't like that man at all, do you?' Simon asked.

'No, I do not.'

'But I can't understand, Elsie. Why are you always so bitter about him? He really brings out the worst in you, doesn't he.'

'Yes,' she admitted. 'He certainly does. I just can't get over how he treated my mother and how he interfered when she died.'

'We talked a bit about that,' Simon said.

'Oh, did you indeed.' There was more than a hint of resentment in Elsie's tone.

'Elsie, please don't get upset. He's trying to do his best . . .'

'But who's he doing it for? Have you considered that?' She was angry now and her cheeks were flushed.

'For you, Elsie. For you and for your mother and for your father too.'

'Well, that's easily taken care of, isn't it. My mother's dead, my father's down in Glasgow somewhere – he could be in the moon for all I know or care – and I certainly don't want any of whatever it is that Mr Murdoch is offering.'

There was silence for a few seconds. Simon thought of talking it through with her, saying how hard it was to reconcile this bitterness with the real Elsie. But he knew that such a comment was pointless. When she was in this mood she was quite intransigent; arguing with her would only make matters worse. Still, he could not leave the subject entirely.

'His one hope is that he'll be able to get you and your father together again, on friendly terms at least.'

'Never.'

'Did you know that he was responsible, in part at any rate, for your father's recovery?'

'Recovery? Recovery from what?'

'His drinking.'

Elsie was quiet for a moment. She could see her father again, very drunk, sitting on a chair at her bedside, explaining to her, in slurred tones, that he was about to go away for a while. She remembered seeing him fall from the chair and pass out on the floor. She could remember the next morning, finding that he had gone. The house had become quiet and peaceful after that.

'I don't know what you mean,' she said with no more anger in her voice. 'What on earth could Mr Murdoch have done to stop my father from drinking?'

'Well, he went down to Glasgow to see him, for one thing.'

'You're not serious.' She was genuinely surprised.

'Oh yes. It must have been shortly after he left here. Let's see . . . when was that?'

'About ten or eleven years ago. I was nine, I think.'

'Do you remember any of that?'

'I remember all of it.' Elsie leaned back in her chair. She was unable to sustain her annoyance with the minister or with Simon. She seemed to relax but this was caused by resignation rather than a feeling of comfort.

'I'm sure it wasn't very pleasant, Elsie.'

'It wasn't. It was awful.'

'I'm sorry.'

'Well, we can't change it now. But tell me, how did he know that my father was in Glasgow?'

'Oh that was the easy part. It seems that your father wound up in court a few times for drunkenness and one of the court officers – maybe even one of the magistrates, I can't quite remember what he said – noticed that your father came from Spaladale and knew that one of the local ministers had connections with this part of the world. This minister was approached and he in turn got in contact with Mr Murdoch.'

'It all sounds a bit too easy to me.'

'Well, I thought so too but anyway, that's what happened. Mr Murdoch decided he would go to Glasgow and see what he could do.'

'So he went all the way down there to try and save my father from drink.'

'That's right. He went down several times.'

'Several times?'

'Yes.'

'I find that hard to believe. I mean, if he'd done that, surely we'd have heard about it.'

'Oh, he liked to keep these things fairly quiet.'

'Well, he succeeded.'

'Yes, I suppose he did.' Simon paused for a moment. 'He did tell your mother, of course.'

'What?' Elsie sat up. 'He couldn't have.'

'He did, I'm afraid.'

'But . . . well, she would have told me. I mean, she told me everything.'

'But not this, I'm afraid.'

Elsie said nothing. The minister had certainly been in contact with her father at least once because it was Mr Murdoch who had fetched him up from Glasgow when her mother had died. She wondered how much more she could believe. It was true also that her father had seemed in good health and comfortably off when he had come north for the funeral. He was well-dressed, smart and gave the impression that the bad times were over. But she still could not be sure what part Mr Murdoch played in all this. She hated the way he interfered in her life and here was evidence that he had been more involved than she had thought.

'Why?' she asked. 'Why did he take such an interest in my father – assuming he did, that is. I'm not convinced of that yet.'

'You still mistrust him, don't you, Elsie.'

'Yes.'

'Well, I think that's a pity. Anyway . . . your father . . . I don't know, exactly. Mr Murdoch said he detected some good in him, he felt that the drinking was the result of . . . what did he call it . . . some dissatisfaction with life . . .'

Elsie gave an ironic laugh. 'Well,' she said, 'I've heard some funny reasons for tippling . . . '

'Maybe Mr Murdoch was right, Elsie.' Simon's voice remained calm and quiet. Elsie looked across at him and, for the first time since their marriage, she regarded him as if he were someone quite separate from her. She suddenly understood that something had shifted between them, that she was losing this argument, if indeed it was an argument, and that Simon had decided to take Mr Murdoch's part in this. She knew that nothing she could say would change his mind and for a moment or two she felt very afraid.

'My father never went to church,' Elsie said at last. 'I don't even understand how Mr Murdoch got to know him at all, let alone interested enough to help him.'

'Your mother was the key to that, I'm sure.'

'But she would never have asked for help, especially for my father. I mean, after all, she was glad to be rid of him.'

'At first, yes.'

'What do you mean by that?'

'Well, it seems that a few months after your father left here your mother had a long chat with Mr Murdoch. He already knew a little about how your father was getting on down in Glasgow – a few weeks sober and then back on the drink and so on. Anyway, your mother agreed that he could come back if he managed to stay sober for six months.'

'What? Back here, to this house?'

'Yes.' Simon realised that Elsie's tone showed frustration and tiredness rather than anger. He decided to plough on. '. . . So Mr Murdoch went down to put this idea to him. He agreed to try but it was a couple of years before he had straightened himself out sufficiently to stay sober for more than a few weeks at a time. And by the time he'd done that, things had changed.'

'In what way?'

'Well, he'd moved in with a woman down in Glasgow and that was more or less the end of that, although he continued to maintain contact with Mr Murdoch.'

'Why did he bother with that, under the circumstances?'

'Well, he continued to support your mother . . .'

'Support?'

'Financially.'

'I don't believe it,' Elsie said quickly.

'. . . Right up until her death.'

'It's not true.' Her tone was quiet but firm. 'It couldn't possibly be true.'

'Elsie, how do you think you managed to live during those years? Where do you think the money came from?'

'I don't know and I don't care but it didn't come from him. Please tell me it didn't come from him.' Suddenly she was in tears. Simon left his chair and came over to kneel on the floor in front of her. She leaned forward and pressed her face against his neck. He put his arms round her and they held this awkward embrace for nearly a minute without saying anything. He rose slowly then and drew out the handkerchief from the cuff of Elsie's blouse. He dried her tears and comforted her until her sobbing stopped.

'I hate that man,' she said when her tears were almost dry. There was hardly any force in her voice at all. 'I hate that man.'

Simon wondered whether she was talking about Mr Murdoch or her father. He decided that what she felt could apply to both.

Over the next few months Simon was to meet Mr Murdoch several times. Although the minister failed to help Simon regain his college job, he did help him to find other work, although it took some time to do this and the eventual job was not really to Simon's liking. However, there were few jobs around and Simon was glad to have one at all. He was grateful to Mr Murdoch for his help. Elsie viewed this unusual friendship with dislike and refused to meet Mr Murdoch herself. Simon endured her expressions of ill-will believing that she would eventually realise that her criticisms were pointless. In time she did stop making comments about Mr Murdoch although Simon misread her reason for doing so. He believed she had accepted the situation but he was quite wrong. She had come to the conclusion that Simon had become so distant from her as to be unreachable. She realised this two months after Simon first visited Mr Murdoch at the manse. At about that time, Simon began going to church.

PHOTO TEN
March 1934

ABOUT thirty people, including half a dozen children, are grouped round a very handsome black automobile which is parked on the bank of a frozen Loch Craig. Some figures kneel beside the car; others stand to one side. One man, in plus fours and a deerstalker hat, is sitting cross-legged on the roof. A double row of curling stones is laid out on the white grass in the foreground. Behind the car, and on the other side of the loch, conifers are visible. Like the trees the mountains in the distance are covered with snow. The sky too is white; it is difficult to tell where the sky ends and the trees and the hills begin.

Simon and Elsie are both present though not standing together. Everyone in the picture is laughing.

Simon could not be bothered waiting for Elsie so he had gone on ahead with the excuse that he had to help Drew Mowat sweep the surface of the ice to prepare the rink. When Elsie arrived, fifteen or twenty minutes later, everyone was there and the first end was in progress. Two rinks had been marked and a mixed-doubles match had begun on each one. Elsie approached Muir Urquart, the club secretary, to find that she had been put down to play the second match on rink two, partnering Donald McPhail. Her game would begin in twenty minutes or so.

At such times Elsie found herself less and less inclined to join the other spectators although she felt she should be loyal to Simon and support him in his game. Three or four years before she would have done this, standing at the end of his rink, shouting for him to win. Now he was easily the best player in the club and had become arrogant about it. Some of the other members disliked his attitude but accepted him because he really was a good player.

Elsie would watch silently or, as she was doing now, drift off to the side and wander down the driveway towards the old castle, hearing the conversation and laughter from Loch Craig recede into the distance, muffled by the snow that coated the trees and lay undisturbed on the brittle winter grass and dead bracken. A hundred yards further on and the sound would be lost altogether.

She began to review her situation. This was something she often did while walking alone here in the woods by the loch. She thought over the last few years of her life, the six and a half years of her marriage, of how things had started out so well and then, slowly, deteriorated to the point where life was almost unbearable. She found it hard to believe that Simon could have changed so much. When they married he had been kind, thoughtful and very caring. He had looked after Elsie well and she, in turn, had tried hard to make their marriage work. She wondered how it could possibly have gone wrong after such a wonderful beginning but it had.

Of course when she examined things more closely she could see reasons for the problems. For there were reasons; she could count them up.

She knew that Simon blamed her for the loss of his college job. He would not have admitted this, perhaps even to himself, but she knew he was still bitter about this although it had happened six years ago. It probably would not have assumed such importance had he not found it very difficult indeed to get another job, even with Mr Murdoch's help. Three months passed before he got a position in a small business in Ardallt. 'Glorified clerk' was what he called himself and he hated every minute he spent at work. The pay was lower than he had been used to and this clearly rankled. If they had not had the house their financial situation would have been difficult.

And here was the second problem. Elsie knew that Simon resented the fact that no matter whose name was on the deeds of the house it was Elsie's house and he had not provided it for her. Again, this was something that was never discussed but Elsie knew how he felt. Sometimes when a bill arrived he might say 'Just as well we don't have to pay rent'. Once he had said 'Thank God your father gave you the house', and she knew it was a barbed comment. He probably did genuinely feel grateful for they could not have got by otherwise but at the same time his pride was hurt.

Consequently it was ironic that while Elsie had provided him with something that on one level at least he did not want there was something else he wanted very much but which she could not provide. Simon craved a son.

Again, this was something that was never discussed openly but Elsie knew that as the years went by and Simon saw the children of his friends growing up, he felt more and more that here was something fundamental that had been denied him. After her miscarriage Elsie had felt the same way but she had learned to accept the situation. She had argued it out: there was nothing she could do about it therefore there was no point in allowing herself to be overtaken by regret and self-pity.

There was also the problem of Elsie's foot. Simon had never made any unkind remark to her about her ugly, misshapen left foot but she knew it had become a barrier between them. They had only ever danced once and that was at their wedding reception at the Glencairn Hotel. It had required a great deal of effort on Elsie's part and she did not want to repeat it. They had gone to a couple of village dances but on both occasions Elsie had sat through the evening and refused all invitations to dance. Simon had danced quite a lot at first but then had begun to feel guilty about leaving Elsie alone. When the third village social came along they decided, independently of one another, not to go. It was a bit of a surprise and rather a relief to both of them to find that the other was in agreement. They never went to a dance again.

The church also played its part in separating Elsie and Simon. He was now an elder in Mr Murdoch's congregation; she refused to go anywhere near the church. Elsie found it hard to believe that the minister could influence her life so much. On the one hand he wanted to reunite Elsie with her father whom she never wanted to see again and on the other he seemed determined to prise away from her the only man she had ever been close to.

From about a year after their marriage things had steadily got worse. Simon was not the kind of man to get angry or even say hurtful things; he just withdrew. He found more and more excuses to spend time away from Elsie. When they were together the atmosphere was strained; they spoke to one another less and less. On an occasion such as this afternoon's curling match at Loch Craig they might arrive and leave separately. Unfortunately, the more this kind of thing occurred the more Elsie wanted to set herself apart and so found herself walking in the woods as she was doing now.

And in the midst of it all something almost unthinkable had happened. Another complication had come about which she could not have foreseen. Nor did she know what the outcome would be. As she turned and set off slowly back to the curling rink the only thing that Elsie knew for certain was how unhappy she was.

When she got back to Loch Craig her match was due to start. Simon and his partner had won their match easily and were now discussing their chances in the forthcoming regional championships. They were deep in conversation and Elsie did not interrupt although she would have appreciated a word of encouragement from her husband. He ignored her completely.

Someone called for light as Elsie and Donald McPhail prepared to play. Although it was not yet four o'clock in the afternoon there were heavy grey clouds in the sky and the light had deteriorated greatly.

Stewart Candless got into his car, a 1924 Métallurgique and drove it up to the edge of the loch. His father had bought the car several years before and was very proud of it, especially as it was the only one of its type in the county and one of only four cars in the village. It was certainly a fine looking vehicle and obviously well cared for. Stewart himself spent a lot of time polishing it and the cream side-panels and black top and wings gleamed as did the chrome of the headlamps and handles.

When driving in the country on sunny days Stewart affected the dress of the keen motorist – plus fours, hacking jacket, cloth cap, muffler and goggles. The goggles were a bit superfluous as the car was not a soft top but he liked to look the part. Besides, although he was only twenty-five he had enough money to pay for these whims. Several of the villagers reckoned he had more money than sense.

Stewart was much in demand when the curling club met because of what he was doing now, positioning the car at the edge of the ice so that when he switched on the headlamps he could flood the rink with light. Albert Sandison beckoned him forward and Stewart let the car move another few inches before he pulled on the handbrake. He turned the headlamps on and illuminated almost the whole of the loch. However, it was mainly the trees on the other side that benefited from the light; it did not strike the surface of the ice directly. Albert suggested that a foot or two further forward would create the desired effect by bringing the front wheels over a low ridge by the edge of the loch. Stewart eased off the handbrake and revved the engine before engaging the power needed to push the car up this little rise. As he reached the top and the nose of the vehicle began to move down the other side he slowed down until he was just inching forward. At Albert's command he yanked the handbrake. The lever snapped off in his hand.

Later in the evening as he warmed himself by the fire with his feet in a tub of hot water Stewart Candless was to ask himself why he had not had the presence of mind to apply the footbrake. He could not remember. Perhaps he had braked but too late.

The car rolled forward quite quickly and Albert just had time to jump clear as the front wheels came in contact with the ice, slid along the top for three or four feet and then crashed through. Shouts went up and one of the ladies fainted. Apart from the snapping and cracking of the ice the slide forward of the shiny black and cream vehicle was slow and graceful. When it came to rest the bonnet was submerged and for a few magic seconds there was a dull glow upon the ice as it was illuminated from below. Then the lights went out and as the darkness rushed back Stewart Candless could be heard shouting a very, very rude word.

He climbed out of the car through the window of the driver's door. He clambered onto the roof and sat down upon it cross-legged and facing the loch. Meanwhile, now that everyone had got back on land, curling was officially abandoned for the day.

The Métallurgique was lying, nose down, at an angle of five or ten degrees and the water reached the hub of the spoked rear wheels. The men on shore realised that getting alongside the vehicle would mean wading in the freezing water. After a brief discussion it was decided that McAllister's Clydesdales were needed. Albert Sandison was despatched to the farm while others went in search of ropes. A plank was found and placed on the rear bumper of the Métallurgique with the other end on dry land. Stewart Candless was invited to leave his vehicle which was filling with water rapidly. He declined. Still perched on the sloping roof with his back to land he folded his arms and announced to Loch Craig that he would be staying where he was until his vehicle was extracted from the water.

He was to remain in this attitude of piety for an hour and three minutes during which time he entertained the men – but principally the loch because he never once turned round to face land – with a potted history of the automobile, dwelling particularly on the Métallurgique itself.

'What good things have come out of Belgium?' he asked. 'How many even know where Belgium is? No, it is a small and fairly nondescript place but it is the home of the Métallurgique which has been made there since 1898. It will surprise no one to learn that earlier models were chain-driven but how many of you . . .' – he paused here but did not turn to face his audience – '. . . realise that there is not one model of Métallurgique with more than four cylinders. No, gentlemen, the emphasis was placed on efficiency and smooth running. The rule was that four good cylinders are better that six mediocre ones and this, if I may say so, is an idea that man could apply to other areas of life with profit.

'Spring coupling, gentlemen, may mean little to you but I can assure you that this innovation in the transmission makes for reduced shock, and very important it is too. But why, you may ask, did the manufacture of such stylish and elegant vehicles cease in 1929? Ah, who can say what the deciding factors were – competition from other makes of automobile or a general decline in sales (surely not!)? Whatever the reason we shall see no more new models of Métallurgique. This machine here, the 1924 model, is one of the best. Yes, gentlemen, this four cylinder, twelve horsepower, two-litre engine is one of the best engines Métallurgique ever made and right at this moment it is full of bloody water!'

He continued in this vein for most of the time that he remained on the roof of his car. However, in the last ten or fifteen minutes of his stay it was difficult for anyone to hear exactly what he was saying as his teeth were chattering with cold. Nevertheless he was resolute in his wish to stay with his vehicle until it was removed from the loch.

Where men had failed, McAllister's two Clydesdales made light work of hauling the Métallurgique out of the water. There was perhaps one moment of strain at the beginning when huge plumes of their breath were snorted into the frosty air and illuminated by the tilley lamps that some of the men had brought back from the village. Once the initial inertia was overcome however, the horses completed their work so quickly that Stewart Candless was very nearly toppled from his perch. He just managed to avoid a very cold bath indeed.

When the vehicle was on dry land again he slid down from the roof with as much dignity as he could find under the circumstances, these being that he was trembling all over from the cold and he had been sitting cross-legged for so long that he found it difficult to stand up straight. When he staggered up the loch bank he intimated that he would never again perform the lighting service for the curling club. In fact he wished to resign from the club on the spot. He would now join the shooting club and take up clay-pigeon shooting which was undoubtedly a much safer occupation. He bade everyone a goodnight and, turning down one or two offers of company to his door, set off homewards alone.

The women from the curling club had long since gone home. Elsie had stayed later than the others but as there was little she could do and as it became clear that Simon had decided to stay and help with the removal of the car from the loch, she began the walk back through the wood to the road that led down to the village. The sky was quite dark by the time she left the loch but the moon had risen and the moonlight on the snow was enough to illuminate her way. She was at the end of the track to the loch and just about to leave the wood when a male voice called to her.

'Elsie, over here!'

She turned and stepped away from the track towards the trees. A few moments later she was nearly knocked off her feet when the man who had called to her rushed forward and flung his arms around her.

PHOTO ELEVEN

March 1934

THE photograph is of a waterfall on the upper reaches of the River Spala. It is difficult to tell how far the water descends; it could be four or five feet or even double that. Certainly the stream is narrow here, narrow and violent. It is not clear whether the slight mistiness above the white water is the spray or just light hitting the camera lens. The slopes leading down to the water's edge are thickly wooded. There are no people in the picture.

The footpath by the side of the river was hard and rutted with a light skiff of snow masking the edges of brown earth and the puddles of ice. The bracken on the bank was flattened and crystalled over with frost, the rowan and birch trees bare. The river itself had a colour somewhere between silver and lead, lighter but no less menacing than the massive grey clouds overhead which promised that more snow was on the way.

Elsie stepped carefully. The path was uneven and treacherous and a stiff wind had sprung up so from time to time she had to fight to keep her balance. At one point, when she was a quarter of a mile from the village, she stopped. She found that she was struggling not to cry and she knew that what she should do now was turn back. The whole thing seemed hopeless. The bushes and trees by the riverside were leafless and gave her no protection from the wind. They also allowed her to be seen from the village. The snow hindered her feet and registered her passing. There was no mistaking the print of her left shoe so anyone could follow her. She wished it were summer with the bushes full of leaves to make her invisible and a warm sun instead of this heavy sky and snow. She felt very cold.

There may have been a moment when the idea of turning back nearly took over but it passed. Summer, winter, sun or snow, it didn't really matter. The truth was that what she was doing was wrong whatever the season but as she had set out to do it the mere question of the weather should not interfere. She drew out a handkerchief and blew her nose. She looked downriver towards the estuary and set off again. If only it wasn't so cold.

Her conversation with Simon the previous evening came back to her. He had just returned from the mid-week prayer meeting at the manse. Elsie had got used to this and to his absence on Sunday mornings when he went to the eleven o'clock church service. Sometimes he went to the evening service as well and, although she was disappointed that he should spend so much time on religious observance, she enjoyed having the house to herself. She had made it clear to him a long time ago that she would have nothing to do with the church and that she would prefer not to talk about religion in general or Mr Murdoch in particular. Simon usually respected her wishes but last night he had a message to deliver from Mr Murdoch.

'I have some news, Elsie,' he began.

'Oh, what's that?' She had been reading a book when he came in and had not noticed the seriousness of his tone.

'Elsie.'

She looked up. She could see from his face that something was wrong. She closed her book. 'What is it?'

'It's bad news, I'm afraid.'

'Bad news?'

'About your father.'

In spite of herself she could feel her heart beginning to race. 'Tell me,' she said.

'He had a heart attack on Monday and on Tuesday he passed away in hospital.'

Elsie said nothing. It was difficult for her to believe that this news could affect her but it did. She had tried to erase her father completely from her life, had refused to meet him, speak to him or write to him. She thought she had been successful in ridding herself of him and for years there had been hardly a mention of him. Now it was as if all this forgetting was lost. In astonishment she found that she was on the point of tears. Simon came over to her, got down on one knee by her armchair and took her hand. Such a show of affection was rare but she allowed him to take her hand and stroke it as if she were a child.

'I'm sorry, Elsie,' he said.

'It's all right,' she said. 'Don't worry, it's all right.' Already her voice, though quiet, was controlled.

'It's a bit of a shock, out of the blue like that.'

'Yes, yes it is. I suppose it was Mr Murdoch that told you.'

'Yes. He got a telegram this afternoon. He felt he should wait till he saw me this evening.'

'He did the right thing,' Elsie said, surprised that the minister had displayed such good judgment.

'Do you want to go down to Glasgow for the funeral?' Simon asked.

Elsie found that she took a long time to reply to this and she wondered why. Before she could speak, Simon added: 'Mr Murdoch has offered to make all the arrangements.'

'No,' Elsie said at last. 'No, I don't think so.'

'I rather thought you wouldn't want to.'

Elsie looked at him, wondering if there was an edge of censure in his tone.

'It's a long way,' he said, 'especially at this time of year. Still, it was good of him to offer, wasn't it.'

'Yes,' Elsie said. 'Yes, it was.'

Simon took a chance. 'He'd really like to speak to you himself, you know, Elsie. Just a little chat . . . I mean, he's been in contact with your father over the years and he knows a bit about what's been happening.'

'I'd rather not,' Elsie said calmly. 'I've tried to forget about my father and I don't really want to undo all that.'

'He was your father, Elsie.'

'But not a very good one.'

'Oh, Elsie, how can you say such a thing at a time like this.'

'Because it's true,' she said. 'I can't forgive him for leaving us like that.'

'It was a long time ago, Elsie.'

'Does that excuse him?'

'No, of course not, but he changed. He knew he'd done wrong and he repented. Yes, he repented.'

Elsie ignored the biblical word. 'If he changed,' she said, 'he did it when it suited him.'

'I think he genuinely wanted to make amends.'

'Well, I can't agree.' Elsie decided that she did not want to be drawn into another argument about her father. She hoped that this last statement would put an end to the subject. She was wrong.

'Is there no forgiveness in your heart, Elsie?'

She sighed. 'Why is it,' she said, 'why is it that you continue to believe that I'm in the wrong? I wasn't the one who ran away. I stayed here and tried to get myself an education. I gave it up to look after my mother when she got ill. Where was he then? Down in Glasgow with his fancy woman, that's where.' She had managed to work herself up into something approaching rage and once again Simon had to admit to himself that he had pushed the point too far. He decided to try and recover the situation but only managed to get himself into deeper trouble.

'I'm not saying you haven't had your share of misfortune, Elsie . . .'

'What exactly do you mean by that?'

'Well, your father leaving, your mother taken ill and you giving up college . . .'

'Yes, anything else?' She knew what was coming and Simon could see it too. He knew he was being drawn into another blunder but he was helpless.

'Well . . . you haven't been in the best of health . . .'

'I'm as fit as anyone you could care to mention,' she said. Her tone was sharp.

'Oh, Elsie, you know what I mean . . .'

'No, I do not. You'll just have to tell me.'

Simon got up. He had been kneeling by her chair long enough to become a little stiff. He rose onto his toes and then took a few steps on the spot to ease the circulation in his legs. Suddenly he realised what he was doing and he stopped abruptly. He knew that whatever he said there would be a row but he had gone too far to call a halt now.

'Your foot,' he said. 'At the very least it's a bit of a hindrance to you.'

'I can't deny that.'

'So, as I say,' Simon went on, feeling that this time he might be able to get away with it, 'as I say, you've had your share of misfortune . . .'

'I don't want your pity,' she said tersely.

'Oh, Elsie, it's not pity. I wish . . .'

'What?'

'I wish you'd let the Lord help you . . .'

'Do I need help?'

'We all need help, Elsie, all of us. If only you could see how easy it is to accept it.' He seemed to be pleading with her. He leaned forward and was about to reach for her hand again when she withdrew it abruptly from the arm of her chair. He resumed his awkward stance in front of her.

'You're beginning to sound like Mr Murdoch,' Elsie said.

She could remember little of their conversation after that. Simon had gone to bed early and was sleeping when she entered their bedroom later. When she woke he had already risen. She had cooked breakfast as usual but they had said little to each other.

He left for work without saying goodbye.

This had angered her. It didn't take much, she reflected, just a tiny expenditure of energy and breath. But he had been unable to do it. Then she thought that maybe he was the honest one after all, deciding that if he couldn't say something with feeling then he shouldn't say it at all.

It distressed her a little that he should be able to stick to her rules better than she could herself.

As she continued along the footpath towards the estuary the wind lessened slightly and this raised her spirits. She could see the whole estuary now from the wooded slopes of Tolraddy on the far side of the bay to the town of Ardallt which lay on a little apron of land wedged between The Sma' Ben and the sea. The main road from Spaladale to Ardallt was far to her left with fields between it and the path she was following. The path ran along the riverside all the way from Spaladale to the estuary and then curved inland to reach Ardallt as well.

At about the same time that Elsie set out from the village someone else had left the town by the estuary path. Elsie could now see this figure walking quickly towards her. It was Donald McPhail.

When they met they stood apart without touching one another. Donald was breathless. He undid a couple of buttons of his overcoat and pulled his watch from the top pocket of his suit jacket. 'Thirteen minutes, Elsie, that's what it took me, so twenty minutes is all I can spare.'

'Is that how it's going to be, then?' Elsie asked. 'Twenty minutes every couple of days or so?'

'Don't be like that, Elsie. We'll sort something out, I'm sure we will.'

'I don't know,' Elsie said. 'It's funny how you can look forward so very much to something and then it arrives and it seems scarcely worth the effort . . .'

'Elsie!'

'No, no, I don't mean about you, Donald. I mean it's such a short time and in such an awful place.' She gestured towards the cold landscape.

'I know it's terrible, it's awful, but for the moment it's all we've got.' He stepped up close to her and took her gloved hand in his. 'Let's not spoil it by quarrelling.' He kissed her very lightly on the lips. Elsie's sad expression hardly changed. 'I don't know,' she said.

He took off his gloves and stuffed them in his overcoat pocket then reached up to remove Elsie's woollen hat. Her long light brown hair spilled over the shoulders of her coat. He ran his hand from her forehead over the top of her head down her neck, following her hair with his fingers to the place where it ended half way down her back. 'I love your hair, Elsie,' he said. 'It's so beautiful.'

There was little opportunity for anything more intimate than talking and even that was accomplished with difficulty. Donald stamped his feet on the hard earth to try and warm them. It was not a suitable place for his town shoes. He put his gloves back on and even then breathed into his palms. Elsie was beginning to feel less cold. She also began to smile. She could not explain to him that suddenly she saw the situation as being quite absurd, a tryst on a cold river bank with a man who could not keep still and was hardly able to speak because of the cold.

'You have to go,' she said at last.

He consulted his watch. 'It's all right, I've got a few minutes yet.'

'Go,' she said. 'Go now.'

He looked at her with a mixture of disappointment and resignation. 'Maybe I better had go,' he said. He stamped his feet and buttoned his gloves. He paused for a moment, put off by the fact that Elsie made no move, no gesture to help him. He rushed forward, flung his arms round her and kissed her roughly. Elsie was unable to respond. When they broke apart he regarded her for a moment as if she were an example of some alien species. 'Thursday,' he said and Elsie said 'No.'

'Tomorrow then. Sharp isn't in the office in the forenoon. I could get off a bit earlier.'

'No, Donald, not tomorrow either.'

'Well, when, Elsie? After the curling on Saturday?'

'No.'

'Elsie . . .' He took a step forward.

'It's all wrong, Donald.'

'Oh, Elsie, come on, you're not feeling guilty about Simon, are you?'

'That's not what I meant, no.'

'Then . . .'

'It's wrong for us. It's just . . . wrong. It's . . . well . . . it's daft, just plain daft. Two grown people meeting for twenty minutes a couple of times a week, hiding from folk on the bank of a river. Can't you see that it's just stupid. I can't believe that this is happening, I really can't.'

'Elsie . . .' He stepped towards her again but then collected himself. 'Now I really do have to go,' he said.

'Then go.'

'But tell me when, Elsie. I've got to see you again.'

'Why?'

'I . . .' He was unable to complete the sentence.

'All this is making me unhappy, Donald.'

'Unhappy?'

'Yes.' Then she added: 'No, not just unhappy, depressed. I feel bad, as if I'll never get back to what I was before.'

'But you told me you were unhappy then.'

'I know. I was. But now it's worse.'

Donald did not have a reply to this. He saw that nothing he could say would change her mood. He was glad that it was she who broke the silence.

'You'll be late,' she said.

'Yes, I will,' he said quietly. He touched her arm but that was the full extent of the affection he was able to display. Elsie did not move.

He turned and set off back towards Ardallt. Elsie watched him go. She could follow his progress almost all the way to the edge of the town. She saw him stumble once and he fell to his knees. She smiled, thinking of how he would have to explain the dirt on his suit. Then she reproached herself for this unkind thought. Finally, when he was reduced to a tiny floundering stick figure in the distance she turned and set off back to the village. She felt less cold and when a skein of geese passed overhead she stopped and watched them for a full minute as they crossed the estuary and headed up towards the top of the village, over by Loch Craig. As she started walking again she derived some comfort from the fact that the arrival of the geese had distracted her to the extent that a minute or two had passed during which her mind had not been occupied by the dismal business of her meeting with Donald. She found such meetings sad occasions, almost pathetic, but with an aspect to them that came close to being ludicrous. Today it had been different. The sadness and the element of absurdity had both been present but there had been something else as well: despair. She had reached the point where she was so unhappy she was unable to distinguish which was worse: her life with Simon or her clandestine meetings with Donald McPhail. Before she had met him today she had been unsure about how things would go on. Now her doubts had been resolved and she realised what she had to do.

PHOTO TWELVE

March 1934

THIS is another postcard which could be bought from Mr Gould, the Spaladale shopkeeper. It looks like an aerial photograph but the legend on the reverse gives it away: 'Ardallt and Spaladale from The Sma' Ben.' The picture was taken in late summer or early autumn as the distant hills are purple with heather. The sky is deep blue and completely cloudless. The town of Ardallt, perched on the edge of the sea, and the small community of Spaladale, on the banks of the Spala River, are only just discernible. Above the village, on the right of the photo, there is a tiny silver dot which marks the existence of Loch Craig.

The ice was thin on Loch Craig. As she approached the bank Elsie could see that the tufts of grass which had been stiffened with frost overnight were becoming limp as the thaw set in and the temperature rose a few degrees. If it froze again tonight, she thought, this would be ideal. She realised that even at a moment such as this she was able to calculate and to plan. Then she wondered what was the point of this. She took a few steps round the edge of the ice.

All the whiteness had gone and the ice was nearly transparent. She reached the place where rutted tracks led down into the water. This was where Stewart Candless had slid into the loch in his Métallurgique a few nights before. The earth round about had been broken up by the horses from McAllister's farm. The hooves of the heavy Clydesdales had dug through the surface of the ground despite the frost. Although Elsie had not been present when the automobile had been dragged from the water the signs of the commotion enabled her to imagine the scene – the huge steaming horses, the exhortations of the men and the curious figure of Stewart cross-legged on the roof of his car. It seemed strange to think that so many people had gathered here, that so much noise and life and energy had been present where now there was complete calm and quiet.

Elsie turned and took in the view from the track by which she had reached the loch, round past the birch trees beyond which could be seen the top of the church belfry, on to a stand of pine on the far side of the loch, the broken fence that gave onto McAllister's land with the white hills behind it and then back round to the track again. There was no one to be seen. Elsie wondered if anyone had noticed her leaving the house. Mrs Campbell was away visiting her sister in Strathinver. She was fairly sure that her walk to the loch had been witnessed only by a few rabbits and a roe deer. She hoped she was right but really it didn't matter.

So many things could have been different. So many things, with just a little pressure one way or the other, would have led her to an altogether different destination. Instead of which she had been led here, a strip of frost-battered grass on the bank of Loch Craig where she was contemplating a truly ghastly act. Although she had made her decision and resolved not to change her mind at the last minute she began to tremble. Then she found that her legs had begun to move, almost as if unbidden, and she thought no, this is not what I want to do, even as she was in the act of doing it. She felt that her body was acting independently from her mind, determined to carry out its commission. She took her first few tentative steps out upon the ice and suddenly thought yes, this is what I want. She was about five yards from the bank when the first crack appeared on the flat, glazed surface of the loch.

PART THREE
1984

THE BUTCHER

OF course the whole thing is a pack of lies. Or fiction.

Certain things are still here: the curling stone; the brush, or walking stick as it is now; the old photograph, a little ragged at the edges, which displays three men and a little terrier called Coogan. Other things did exist but are no longer with us. Loch Craig existed, as did the newts, Donald's blue serge suit and Simon's dictionary. Elsie existed. Elsie lived but we know very little about her beyond a few basic facts: she married an older man who was rather irascible and treated her badly; she disappeared in mysterious circumstances when she was about twenty-six; her body was discovered a year ago on the bed of the filled-in Loch Craig. Consequently my life of Elsie is imaginary. Call it a fictional biography, a historical fantasy or just plain lies. However, there is one other thing that we know about Elsie for sure: she did have a club foot.

'Oh yes,' my mother said, 'Elsie had a club foot, didn't you know that?' I did not. Over the years we had often talked about Elsie and Simon and Elsie's sudden departure but my mother had never mentioned this most important fact. It was the misshapen left foot that helped the police to identify the body.

So it was my mother who pointed the police in the right direction. She read the newspaper report of the discovery of the body. A woman with a club foot. 'Now that could be Elsie McAndrew,' she said. 'With a club foot?' I asked. 'Oh yes,' my mother said, 'Elsie had a club foot, didn't you know that? It wasn't all that obvious, though.'

The body was identified then, but the cause of death was not. Accident, suicide or murder? The police could not say. How close was the body to the curling stone? The operator of the mechanical digger who unearthed both was not sure. A few feet perhaps, maybe more. There was no rope connecting one with the other but this might have disintegrated completely over the years. In fact the proximity of the stone might have had little to do with Elsie's death. In other words I was free to speculate and this is what I did. I decided on a story with some happiness – well, just a little – struggle, hardship, occasional success, ultimate failure, sadness.

I suppose I was a bit brutal to Elsie, a bit brutal to some of the other characters too, but realistic. There we are: realism based on lies, the truth approached through fiction. You can decide.

The one thing that drew me to Elsie was her disability. To explain why that aspect interested me particularly I have to tell you about the Butcher.

Mr Gillis was nick-named the Butcher because in summer he wore a white trilby hat which he hung on the back of the door of his tiny glass-walled office in the corridor just outside the gymnasium. Rather like himself, his office was unusual; it gave the impression of being an afterthought, a sort of architectural cul-de-sac. The corridor by the gymnasium was barely able to accommodate it; it forced those walking past to do so in single file. The walls were of glass from desk-top height upwards. This meant that Mr Gillis could patrol the corridor without leaving his seat. It also meant that the boys could see in and witness the general untidiness of his tiny room. Even more unusual was the door because it too was of glass. Mr Gillis had stuck a plastic hook near the top of this door on the inside and it was here that he chose to hang his white trilby. Boys approaching the gymnasium from the chemistry labs had a clear view of the door. They could also see the inside of the hat. This was not white. It was rather dark and greasy.

'Measuring will be on Tuesday and we'll leave the weighing till Thursday. Got that?' The Butcher gave us the impression that he was indeed talking about chunks of meat – sides of beef or lamb or perhaps great hams trussed up with string. In fact he was talking about us, the boys of class 3B. He was a large, barrel-chested man in his early forties, his black hair plastered to his skull with hair cream. We were standing around him in a ragged semi-circle in the gym at the end of our physical education period. It was the third week of our third year in secondary school. We were all thirteen or fourteen years old.

'If we do it that way, spread over two periods, we can get some games in each period. Right?'

A few boys mumbled 'Yes, sir.' Mr Gillis took a long look from one tip of the arc of boys round to the other. The Butcher image was maintained. We might have been livestock that he was assessing for slaughter.

'Any Fs this year, do you think?' he asked. His voice was loud and uncompromising. 'One or two maybe, eh?'

Some of the boys looked round at Alec Davidson, the smallest boy in the class, and sniggered. The bell rang to signal the end of the period but nobody moved. We had learned this at the very first lesson of the term – something most of the boys should have remembered from the previous year – when Mr Gillis had belted fourteen of us for setting off towards the door when the bell rang rather than waiting for his instruction.

'All right, then. Dismiss.' Once away from the gym and the deadening influence of the Butcher we felt released and began to caper along the corridor to the next lesson. Someone swiped one of little Alec Davidson's gym shoes and tossed it ahead to the front of the uneven column. Alec gave chase until it was thrown back over his head to be caught by one of the boys at the rear. Then he turned and began the hopeless task of chasing his shoe as it flew back and to above his head. Once he nearly caught it but someone pushed him out of the way at the last moment. He fell over and clouted his head against one of the heavy silvered cast-iron radiators that were to be found throughout the school. He burst into tears.

Two or three boys stood round him as he sat on the floor nursing the side of his head where a lump was rising under his probing fingers. The boys' attention did not spring from concern for Alec but concern for themselves if Alec was cut and needed to see the nurse. There would be hell to pay then and they knew it.

'Any blood, Alec?' one of them asked. This was Charlie McHugh, known as Snecky. The best footballer of his year he was also regularly in trouble with one teacher or another. He had once been suspended from school for a month.

'Hey, Alec, any blood?' Snecky repeated.

Alec, still tearful, examined his fingers and shook his head slowly.

'Nah, he's OK,' Murrick said. 'Come on.'

'Right.'

Alec was abandoned as the boys raced ahead to the next class.

'Hey, Alec!' one of them shouted from ten yards down the corridor. Still sitting on the floor by the radiator, Alec ignored this shout. The stolen gym shoe, hurled by Snecky, caught him on the side of the face.

Fifteen years or so after these events of my early life in secondary school it is hard to remember now how important all these things were. Mr Gillis, the Butcher, was a man to be treated very carefully because he put up with no nonsense, had a vicious temper and he bore grudges. Gym class was the place where we were most vulnerable. It was the place where we had to display our knobbly knees and pimply backs, our sometimes not very clean underwear and our sweaty socks. It was where physical prowess was under constant assessment and where a boy's self-respect could be built up or crushed. Alec Davidson, for example, was one of those who came off worst. It didn't matter that he was quite well built, had strong legs and could run quite fast; he was too short and that was that. He was the titch, the weed of the class, standing about four feet eight in his shoes and somewhat less barefoot. He was an F and the other boys never let him forget this.

I had only just joined the school as my family had recently moved into the area. All this talk of weighing and measuring and being an F or an E or whatever was new to me. It was Alec Davidson who explained. It seemed that everyone had to be classified according to height and weight so that they would compete against boys of roughly the same size in the school sports at the end of the year. The tallest, heaviest boys were in the A group; the next size down was B and so on until F. F was the group for the real tinies, the handful of Alec Davidsons who were mostly in first year. Alec had been an F in first year, an F in second year and he was worried – no, perhaps terrified is a better word – that he would end up an F even in his third year. Being an F in third year would be very close to hell.

At this time, when I was thirteen years old, I was about average in height and weight for my age and so would most likely be a C. This aspect of the annual weighing and measuring routine – the actual result – didn't really bother me much. However, as Alec explained to me in detail the procedures involved I began to realise that I could be in trouble, that I could be in serious trouble. It became clear that my enemy in all this business, the thing that could promote my own humiliation, was the Butcher's measuring rod.

I should explain first why it was Alec Davidson who exposed these mysteries to me. I didn't really like the way the other boys treated him. I was new at the school and still observing, still beginning friendships. Perhaps Alec noticed that I did not ridicule him as the others did. Anyway, we became friends of sorts. I didn't actually like him all that much. I suppose I felt sorry for him; I tried to like him. Also I didn't want to get too close to him because I felt some of his rotten luck might rub off on me. I didn't want the other boys to view us as being mates because then I would probably come in for abuse too. I think Alec realised this at the beginning. He knew he was an outcast and understood why others might be reluctant to befriend him.

Perhaps I exaggerate. After all, these things happened a long time ago. I couldn't tell then nor can I tell now exactly what went on in Alec Davidson's mind. However, I can remember clearly my own alarm, bordering on terror, when he told me about the Butcher's measuring rod.

This was a thin length of yellow wood, calibrated in inches, which was fixed against the one brick wall in his glass office. A short horizontal bar slid up and down the length of the rod. Mr Gillis seemed to delight in slamming it down on the top of the tousled head below. He would allow no cheating.

'McMillan, five foot three. Are your feet on the floor, boy? Flat on the floor?'

'Yes, sir.'

'Don't believe a word of it. Five two and a half. Next!'

No boy was happy with his measurement. Everyone reckoned the rod was wrong. After all, it did not stretch to the floor but started at three feet six and went up to seven feet. Who could be sure that it had been positioned correctly, that the first thick black line was exactly three feet and six inches from the green tiles of the floor? The tiles directly underneath seemed to be worn after years of having bare feet placed on them. Maybe the weight itself of thousands of boys over the last couple of decades had led to some sort of subsidence. These were some of the theories produced to argue that the rod was quite wrong. It was half an inch out at the very least. If only the bar wasn't brought down quite so hard on everyone's head. If you winced from the blow you might lose three quarters of an inch or more and it was no use arguing about it. All you earned for that was a belting. Mr Gillis never measured anyone twice.

There was the added problem that the whole process was very public. The boys lined up in the corridor by the glass office and looked in to see who was up against the rod. Mr Gillis seemed to take pleasure in shouting out the height of each boy. It was unfair. It was very unfair and for Alec Davidson it was torture. As I heard more stories about the measuring rod, not just from Alec but from other boys as well, I began to realise that it would be as big a problem for me as it always was for Alec. Perhaps it would be worse.

When I was seven I had an accident. I was knocked down by a car and very nearly died. There were several injuries and all healed up after a while. Except one. My right leg remained shorter than my left by about half an inch. Nowadays few people can detect this very slight disability although I tend to limp a bit if I get tired. Even when I was a schoolboy I was able to disguise it because my parents made sure that I had the best of footwear specially made to build up my right foot without making it obvious that this was the case. In fact, because only half an inch was involved it was impossible to see from the outside of my right shoe that it was different in any way from my left. You had to look inside the shoes to be able to judge the different thicknesses of sole and heel. Of course the main thing about the shoes was that I had to wear them all the time. In stocking soles or barefoot I had an obvious limp.

Of course it is easy to look back now and say, well, would anyone have noticed if I had left my shoes lying around the changing room instead of buckling them up inside my satchel when I changed into my gym kit for classes with the Butcher? And if anyone had noticed, maybe I could have just tossed the whole matter off in a casual way: 'Oh, that . . . it's nothing much . . .' No, it's too easy to forget that something which I hardly ever think about now was then a very great concern. I was aware what could happen, I could see that any weakness was pounced upon by the other boys and I knew that I wasn't big enough or belligerent enough to bully my way out of it. I saw what they did to Alec Davidson and I was determined to avoid such treatment. A lot of planning was required.

At gym lessons I needed to organise my changing routine so that I could take off my outdoor shoes, slip my feet immediately into my gym shoes and, even before I tied my gym-shoe laces, put my outdoor shoes into my satchel hoping that they would stay there throughout the lesson. This operation was tricky because there was the little matter of taking off my trousers and putting on my shorts. In fact I did both before changing my shoes – quite a number of the other boys pulled their trousers off over their shoes so this was not unusual.

Timing was the most important aspect of the procedure. I even practised a few variations at home to see if the system could be improved. However, it seemed to work, complicated or not. I could not decide if the fact that no one had discovered my secret was actually the result of my elaborate efforts or just the boys' lack of attention. I did not want to test this out so I took care to keep my changing routine sharp and exact.

When I heard about the business of measuring and weighing I realised that all the care and effort I had put into keeping my secret had probably been a complete waste of time. If the Butcher insisted that we attend the measuring process barefoot there were two problems. First, getting from the changing room to the glass office meant a barefoot walk, or run, of twenty or thirty yards. Without my shoes I had an obvious limp. I reckoned I might still escape detection, however, if I ran on my toes in a sort of hearty limbering up exercise. I practised at home, of course. Then there was the feet-flat-on-the-floor problem. It seems strange now, fifteen years on, that I should have been so conscious of this. Now I can put both feet flat on the floor and stand up straight without slouching or bending a knee or looking strained in any way. Perhaps it was different then; I don't know. Perhaps the discrepancy was more marked; I can't remember. Whatever the case, I believed that my disability was obvious and that was what determined my approach.

I decided that I would have to get to the Butcher's office first or at least early on in the queue so that I would be barefoot for as short a time as possible. I would run there, tiptoe across the green tiles and after measurement sprint back to the changing room to put on my gym shoes. There was the added complication that for the first time there would be a period of five minutes or so when I would have to shut inside my satchel not only my outdoor shoes but my gym shoes as well. I made sure that a couple of books were left at home so that there was more room. I had thought it all through; I reckoned I had covered all possibilities.

When the day came I had no time to think. I got to the changing room first and was already stripping off as the sixteen other boys in the class barged in flinging satchels and blazers everywhere and kicking their shoes off so that they landed underneath the slatted benches that ran along each wall. As I left the room at a trot everyone else was still pulling on shorts or even struggling with tightly knotted ties. I might even get to the office and be measured and out again before the first of the boys arrived. I prayed that Mr Gillis was on time and in a hurry to be done with his tedious task.

At the office door I found that I was second in the queue, not first. Somehow Alec Davidson had contrived to beat me to it. I thought that maybe he had had the same idea as me only for a different reason. He knew that he was the shortest in the class by about three inches and that Mr Gillis was considerate enough to bark out the height of each boy after measurement so that everyone in the class knew the awful truth.

As I got to the office I could see Alec poking his head round the open door. Mr Gillis was at his desk with his back to us. I heard Alec saying, in a voice that tried to be light and urgent at the same time, 'We're ready, sir,' and I heard the reply: 'Well I'm not. Just wait there.'

Mr Gillis continued writing and when Alec turned to me I could see the strain on his face. I had no time to feel sorry for him though because I was under considerable strain myself. I experienced the agonisingly slow passage of time and decided that I needed to go to the toilet.

The first of the other boys arrived and Mr Gillis was still hunched over his book. He glanced round quickly, saw only three boys and started writing again. A few more boys arrived and I began to realise the terrible blunder I had made. I had tried to be first in order to get it over with quickly but now it was clear that I would be under the gaze of most if not all of the class. If only I had been less impatient and tried to go last. I could surely have bluffed out the running; it was the standing under the rod that was the important part, the critical part; why hadn't I realised that? As the last of the boys arrived I thought that maybe I could just make my way to the back of the queue, or sprint back to the changing room on one pretext or another and conveniently lose my place in the line. In fact I was just about to do this when Mr Gillis decided he was ready. He got up from his desk and stepped over to the measuring rod. It was too late now for me to go anywhere. 'Right,' he said, 'let's be having you.'

Alec Davidson stepped forward like a condemned man. His plan had misfired as badly as mine. Instead of skipping through unnoticed he was now the focus of attention. He stood against the wall as sixteen pairs of eyes from faces pressed up against the office windows scrutinised him and saw, he knew only too well, a small, scrawny creature with spots breaking out over his face. He wore an expression of abject defeat and for a short moment my attention moved away from my own troubles and I felt sorry for him. The bar slammed down.

'Four foot nine. Next.'

Howls of laughter went up from the other boys. 'Another F, eh, Alec,' someone shouted. Mr Gillis, recording the information in his book, said nothing. Alec slipped by me and set off towards the changing room at a sprint. A shower of jeers greeted him from the queue and, as he passed the last boy, who was just out of sight of Mr Gillis, a foot shot out, caught him on the ankle and down he went, sprawling on the wooden floor. Another shout. Alec picked himself up and raced for the door. Someone, smiling, said 'Poor wee bastard,' and that seemed to be the extent of feeling for Alec.

'I said next.'

It was my turn. I tiptoed across the floor. This got a few whistles. Mr Gillis watched me and said: 'Very nice. Something wrong with your feet?'

I experienced a moment of complete terror in which my mind raced – I had been discovered after all; it was obvious that I had a limp; everyone could see it; they'd seen it all along and had chosen this moment to hit me with it, my weakest moment . . .

'The floor's awfully cold, sir.' Afterwards I couldn't believe I had managed to say this; I couldn't believe that I'd had the intelligence, the wit, the inspiration to come up with this perfect reply. Everyone laughed, including Mr Gillis. 'Oh well,' he said, 'we'd better measure you quickly then, hadn't we, in case your little feet catch cold.' More laughter. Then under the rod. Slam. 'Five foot two. Next.'

As I reached the changing room again my heart was thumping inside my chest. I'd made it but by the skin of my teeth. I sat down on the bench and leaned back against the wall. The tension had been unbearable, the relief was ecstasy. Then I noticed Alec at the other end of the bench. He was in tears.

'Gillis is a bastard,' Alec sobbed. 'And so's Snecky for tripping me up.' He took a handkerchief from the pocket of his trousers which were still hanging on a hook behind him. He blew his nose noisily. His tears began to dry. 'But for Christ's sake don't tell Snecky I said that, will you,' he said, suddenly afraid. I promised I wouldn't. The next boy returned from the office. We put on our gym shoes and trooped out to the gym in silence.

I remember the rest of that gym period very well indeed. We did some circuit training and finished off with a quick game of indoor football in which I scored twice in my team's three-one win. I felt great. I had successfully evaded detection; I had passed the terrible test of the measuring rod. I had also proved to myself that I could play football at least as well as the other boys, if not better. Back in the changing room at the end of the period Alec Davidson casually asked me why I always put my shoes inside my satchel during the gym lesson.

The question took me completely by surprise. After a moment's hesitation I blurted out, 'Tell you later.' This was not unreasonable as the changing room was the usual scrum of bodies with shirts, ties and the occasional boot flying through the air. The stale smell of socks and the constant din contributed to the normal post-gymnastic atmosphere. Steam issued from the shower room. Showers were not compulsory and in fact only a few boys took advantage of this facility. You can guess that I was not one of them. There was a great deal of laughter and shouting and hurried cribbing of the history homework for the next lesson. It was not a place for reasoned argument and Alec Davidson did not press his point further. I had earned myself a little more time to think.

Over the years since that occasion I have often wondered why I did what I decided to do. The precise reason escapes me now, lost perhaps in the flurry of activity that followed. Perhaps, suddenly, I was tired of it all – the painstaking care in fashioning this huge pretence about something that probably was not particularly important to anyone but myself. After all my care and attention to the tiniest detail of keeping my secret I decided to tell Alec Davidson the truth. Maybe I had meant to raise Alec's image of himself, show him that I was effectively placing myself in his power, giving him the responsibility that friendship demanded. As someone destroyed daily by the taunts and jeers of others he would now have the ability to destroy someone else in his turn. I felt it would bind us together.

When I first mentioned the subject of the shoes, as we were walking home from school that evening, he wasn't sure what I was talking about. As I blundered on in my explanation I realised he had forgotten all about it and if I had kept my mouth shut the problem need never have arisen. But it was too late, or perhaps I forced the confession out of myself, determined once and for all to rid myself of the burden of this secret.

Alec received the news in silence. When we reached the street corner where our ways separated I asked him not to tell anyone. He promised that my secret was safe. I smiled at him, a little uncertainly perhaps, and walked back home slowly.

The next day it seemed as if everyone in the school knew. The other boys in my class turned their fickle attention away from Alec and diverted it to me. Immediately I was 'Limping Jimmy' or 'Jimmy the Limp'. I pointed out that I did not limp or at least not so much that anyone had previously noticed. Oh no, they said, we knew. They were adamant that it had been clear all along, they'd suspected something from the start.

I was grabbed and my satchel torn from me. It was opened so forcefully that one of the straps broke. This did not seem to concern anyone. They were searching for the gym shoes. As we were not due for another lesson till the next day I wasn't carrying them with me.

There was a moment's hesitation before attention turned to the shoes I was wearing. Kicking and struggling I was forced to the floor and lay there, face down, while three boys sat on top of me and others pulled my shoes off. A scuffle broke out as boys fought to claim them. After a few moments a truce was arranged. The shoes were examined and the discrepancy between them noted. A cheer went up. Still pinned to the floor I was about to burst into tears of frustration when I was suddenly released.

I rose slowly. My attackers had scattered and I assumed that a teacher was approaching along the corridor. When I got to my feet I wiped a mixture of snot and blood from my nose and looked around. There was no one there; I had been released on a false alarm. I stuffed my shirt tail back into my trousers and tried to straighten my tie. My white shirt was soiled from its contact with the floor. I knew I looked a mess and I could not face going into class in that state. Besides, I had to get my shoes. These were nowhere to be found.

I picked up my satchel with its broken strap and walked – no, limped – to the window. The corridor was lined with windows overlooking a central quadrangle. From my second-floor vantage point I could see my classmates as they tumbled out into the quad playing catch with my shoes. I looked down in misery tinged with the first real touch of hatred I had ever felt. Alec Davidson was leading the game.

When I heard about Elsie's foot I decided that I wanted to write about her to explore how she coped with her disability. Her experience, I reasoned, would have been so different from mine. Whereas hostility was expressed towards me in the taunts and jeers of my classmates and even by physical assault, I reckoned that Elsie would have had to put up with prejudice of a different sort. To be patronised in a cloying, concerned manner, to be thought of as diseased or unclean, the result of some awful sin and therefore to be regarded as someone without hope – was her situation better than mine or worse?

What happened to me might have broken me – it nearly did break me – but I got through. There were people on my side and I made it. I thought that maybe Elsie went under finally sickened and stifled by the righteous attitudes that prevailed at the time. I arranged her suicide at the age of twenty-six and I felt that if this wasn't 'the' truth I had certainly approached 'a' truth. Poor old Elsie, I thought as I killed her off, but I felt fairly satisfied with my work. What did 'the' truth matter anyway since there was no one left to tell me more about Elsie except my mother, and her recollection of the events surrounding the disappearance were hazy at best? So, I felt justified in writing my life and death of Elsie in the way I did. I took her through school, I sent her to college, I married her off and then I made her take her own life.

And I got it all wrong.

In my own defence I can say that everyone else got it wrong too. This was revealed when the police made one rather important discovery about Elsie's body. I'm not going to tell you what that discovery was. Not yet. It will keep for a while, at least until I have recorded a little visit I made after I finished writing my life of Elsie and the episode concerning the Butcher.

THE F MAN

THE visit was a visit to the past. I wanted to take an event, an experience from my own past, and re-examine it through the recollection of someone else. I'm not sure what I hoped to achieve by this. It was something to do with homing in more precisely on what had really happened, seeing if it was ever possible to pin down the truth. I felt that I might be able to apply what I learned – if indeed I learned anything – to my attempts to reconstruct the life of Elsie.

Finding Alec Davidson was much easier than I thought although he surprised me by what he had become. But then, what could I have expected? The last time we had met, and that was fifteen or sixteen years before, we had been thirteen years old. How could I gauge his development on that hazy memory?

There were sixteen Davidsons in the book for Strondonald, four of them A. Davidson. However, it was a D. Davidson that I rang first as the address was familiar. Alec had lived on one of the three main streets north of the river and it had a name I remembered – Clashbea Road. Mr D. Davidson turned out to be Alec's father and after I had identified myself as an old school-friend of Alec's – I allowed myself a little poetic licence in this description – he confirmed that Alec still lived in Strondonald. In fact he had only been away from the town for one period of six years when he was at university in Aberdeen. The mention of six years suggested to me that Alec might be a doctor but I was wrong. Alec's father said that Alec was indeed one of the four A. Davidsons in the telephone directory – the Rev. A. W. Davidson. I thanked him and said goodbye.

My immediate reaction was to laugh. Alec had become a minister! I wondered at what point he had got religion. It must have been some time after we had last met. There had been one or two religious groups in school, I remembered, but I hadn't belonged to any of them and I was fairly sure Alec hadn't either. Anyway, I reckoned that this unexpected development might make my task a little easier. I was to phone him up and arrange to meet him. His profession would surely mean that he would listen to my request with a sympathetic ear.

And so it was. I did get the impression, though, that he wasn't really sure of who I was. I mentioned a boy who had only been at school for two terms, a boy who had had a limp, someone he had been friendly with for a time. As I was giving this description it came to me that I was talking about someone else. I could sense Alec's confusion, too. He wasn't sure who I was talking about and I had difficulty myself in recognising this creature of so many years before. Nevertheless I arranged to drive over to Strondonald the following Saturday afternoon and join him for tea.

The manse door opened before I reached it. I was greeted by a very attractive woman of about thirty. She had short blonde hair and was wearing a yellow blouse and a cotton wrap-around skirt also in yellow but blotched with large orange flowers. Her legs and feet were bare. She was carrying a young child who was slung in her arms and perched on her right hip. The child was perhaps a year old and was engaged in beating his – or it might have been her – mother about the shoulders with tiny chubby fists. Raising a hand to put an end to these blows the woman gave me a warm smile.

'You must be James Atherton,' she said.

'Yes, that's right.'

'Do come in, my husband is expecting you. I'm Jill.'

'Pleased to meet you,' I said.

'Do go in, won't you. Alec's through there.' She nodded towards a half-open door. 'I'll be along shortly with some tea.'

I muttered thanks and as she disappeared to the kitchen I stepped up to the sitting room door, knocked rather timidly and entered.

'James! How very good to see you.'

I did not expect the greeting to be quite so enthusiastic. More surprising by far, however, was what that tiny, snotty-nosed thirteen-year-old had become. The man who was now pumping my hand with just a little too much fervour was completely bald. I had no doubt he was the same age as me – his round face was not particularly lined – but he had the hairline of a ninety-year-old. There was not a single hair on top; he was reduced to a reddish fringe running round the back from ear to ear. He was also quite big. This surprised me too. He was at least as tall as me, perhaps an inch taller. That would make him about five feet ten. He was also broad and quite heavily built though not fat. The figure before me bore no relation whatever to the Alec I remembered.

'You've changed,' he said. He had stepped back and was looking me up and down.

'Beyond recognition, I imagine,' I said. 'I would never have recognised you.'

'No, no.' He grinned and passed a hand over his bare skull. 'Nature decided I was meant for hats very early on.'

'But you were . . . forgive the impertinence . . . you were rather small, if I remember correctly. You must have shot up from the age of fourteen or so.'

'Really?' He didn't look convinced. 'I can't remember. I suppose I was a bit on the short side early on in secondary school. Of course it's all such a long time ago.'

'Yes, quite.'

'But please, take a seat. Jill will be through directly with some goodies.'

I sat down in a very deep sofa. Alec perched himself opposite on the edge of an armchair. A coffee table lay between us. It was all tubular steel and smoked glass. I disliked it instantly. I had little time for more than a quick glance round the room. The place was clean and tidy but not regimented. The dining table was spread over with newspapers and books. A glass-fronted cabinet beyond housed more volumes arranged rather haphazardly, some on their edges but some stacked up lying flat one on top of the other.

'How long has it been, in fact?'

This question led us off into the usual calculations that take place on these occasions, sprinkled with the odd exclamation of 'No!', 'Really!' and 'Well I never!' All these were Alec's, I should add. I was as surprised as he was at what time had revealed but I did not join in when his boyish enthusiasm took hold. He displayed that strange other-worldliness that I have sometimes detected in other people who follow some strict religious code. I find it disconcerting. I decided to try to ignore it as I did not want anything to distract me from my purpose. My purpose?

'Was there a particular reason that caused you to look me up after all this time, James?'

This was my cue but Alec was looking across at me with a grin that was too eager and I faltered. It suddenly crossed my mind that perhaps he thought I had come to see him on a professional level, that I was in need of spiritual help or whatever. This idea was too awful to contemplate. I hoped that my relief wasn't too visible when Jill chose that moment to enter with the tea tray. A couple of minutes passed in setting out the tea things and exchanging minor pleasantries. Jill withdrew and after a sip or two of tea I began.

'Tell me about the Butcher.'

Alec looked confused. 'Who?'

'The Butcher. Surely you remember him.'

'Which . . . ? I'm sorry, I'm not quite sure . . .'

'The PE master, Mr Gillis. Don't you remember? We used to call him the Butcher.'

'Oh! I see! Of course!' Alec managed to slop tea into his saucer. Over-reaction again, I noted. He placed his cup and its flooded saucer separately on the coffee table and sat back in his chair. He gazed up in the air and appeared to be musing to the ceiling.

'Goodness me, yes. Well, well, that does take me back. The Butcher. Of course . . .' He sat up straight again. 'But the Butcher was Mr Campbell the maths teacher, not Mr Gillis,' he said, in a very matter-of-fact way.

'What . . . ?'

'Campbell. Maths. Remember, he always used to give us problems about cows and sheep, weights of different cuts of lamb and so on. He was the Butcher.'

I was unable to speak for about half a minute. He was right, of course. I'd been at that school for two terms, eight months at the most. Alec had been there . . . well . . .

'How long were you at the High School?' I asked.

'Oh, all my secondary career. Six years.'

'Yes. I see.' Six years. Of course he would know all the teachers and their nicknames better than I would. 'Then what the hell . . .' I looked up and saw the ghost of a frown. '. . . I'm sorry. What did we call Gillis?'

'Mr Gillis, the PE man. Let me see. He was . . . he was . . . Just "Gilly" if I remember correctly. Yes, it was Gilly. No more than that.' He leaned forward conspiratorially. 'I think, if truth be told, we were all a little afraid of him.' He actually winked.

'Afraid! Afraid!' I became aware that I was speaking too loudly. I sat back and placed my cup and saucer on the wide arm of the sofa. 'We weren't afraid of him,' I said evenly. 'We were terrified.'

'Oh come now, that's far too strong a word, surely. Would you care for a scone?' He raised a plate from the coffee table and held it towards me. At this point I began to have serious doubts about this man's hold on reality. I took a scone.

'The measuring rod. You remember that, don't you?' I said.

'Who could forget that! Yes, that was awful, wasn't it.' He was still smiling. 'But it was all rather good fun looking back on it.'

I very nearly choked. His comment had caught me in mid-swallow and I managed to spray little bits of scone onto the coffee table. I leaned forward and grabbed a serviette.

'My dear fellow . . .'

I waved away his solicitations and took a few mouthfuls of air followed by some tea. Composed again, if still a little red in the face, I sat back and muttered apologies. I decided to remain calm. I said, calmly, 'How can you call it fun? It was torture and you were one of those who suffered most. The man was an animal, a brute.'

'Now, James, I must take issue with you there.' He had the disconcerting habit of using my name as if he were addressing a butler or a chauffeur. However, perhaps this is my own prejudice. I dislike being called James; I am Jim. 'Mr Gillis,' he went on, 'is a well-respected member of the community . . .'

'You mean he's still alive?' I asked in surprise.

'Very much so. After all, he's only in his mid-sixties.'

I had never really considered this. When I was a kid all my teachers had been classified as old. Somehow this fuzzy logic had stayed on. I had expected Gillis to be long since dead or at best a doddering ninety-year-old. Alec was still talking. 'He is, moreover, an elder in the church.'

This sentence, delivered with just a hint of censure in its tone, convinced me that all further logical argument would be a waste of time. So Gilly was an elder of the church, an upstanding member of the community. Then I thought that maybe I was at fault, that I had borne a grudge too long. Maybe I had exaggerated things and Gilly wasn't such a bad old stick after all. In the silence that followed I reached for another scone. No, damn it, I was right. No matter how he had changed – if indeed he had changed – that man had once been a sadistic brute. The man sitting before me could not have forgotten that; he just chose to ignore it. I decided that I had not come all this way only to indulge in polite conversation. I began again, though quite calmly:

'No matter what he is now, Mr Gillis treated me badly at school and he treated you even worse. Don't tell me that you've forgotten that.'

'It was a long time ago . . .'

'That doesn't answer the question.' I was determined not to let Alec off the hook. He looked at me as if he was now wondering quite what it was he had invited into his home. His smile had gone. He took a sip of tea and set the cup aside. He sat back and folded his arms, giving me the impression that he was now ready to get down to some serious talking. I was wary lest this was just one more of his rehearsed poses.

'I have to admit,' he began, speaking quite slowly, 'that my early years at secondary school were not of the happiest. I was ribbed fairly mercilessly by the other boys, I remember, and picked on because I was, as you rightly said, the smallest boy in the class. But it changed, James. For one thing I learned to cope with it better and then, well, I started growing and nobody singled me out for ridicule any more. It was fine from then on.'

'Just like that,' I said.

'It was a long time ago, James, a long time ago. These things are best forgotten. Their effects weren't lasting, anyway.'

'Weren't they?'

'Not in my case, James. I would say that perhaps you still have some forgetting to do.'

'I think of all the boys that came after, all the ones that went before too and were subjected to Gilly's approach to education.'

'He mellowed, James, he mellowed considerably.'

He kept calling me James; somehow I could not call him Alec.

'I hope he did mellow. That would be something, at least,' I said.

'Perhaps you would like to meet him again!' His eyes lit up and I recognised with dismay the return of the interested, caring vicar.

'No thank you,' I said, a trifle too crisply.

There was another awkward little silence. I declined a third scone but accepted a ginger biscuit.

'I'm interested in the past,' I said, 'I'm fascinated by it.'

'So it would seem, James. But what is the past, anyway. It's only now a bit later on.'

I laughed out loud. It was partly the comment itself, partly the way it had been delivered, dead pan, a little gem just plucked unwittingly out of the air. He would have forgotten it already. He didn't understand what I was laughing at and I decided against an explanation. I merely apologised for my rudeness and accepted a second cup of tea.

From then on idle chit-chat returned and I made no attempt to direct things back to what I believed were more important matters. We took a stroll in the garden where we were joined by Jill. It was a bright warm day and the surroundings were pleasantly soft and quiet. You could lose yourself here, I thought, fall asleep for a hundred years. Alec and I parted on good terms. He asked me to call again and this invitation may well have been genuine; my acceptance was not.

As I drove the fifty or so miles back home I thought that I would rewrite the story, the history rather, of the Butcher. The white hat, I wondered, had that just been another trick of my imagination? I wasn't sure. Clearly I could not leave the story as it was, with the wrong nickname. That had been crucial, after all, hadn't it? Then, quite suddenly, it didn't really seem so important any more. Gilly, the Butcher, the grimy white hat . . . so what? I decided to leave it, to leave it just as it was, as I had remembered it. Anyway, if I changed it who could tell what other inaccuracies might creep in.

I realised I had not mentioned Elsie at all, and I was glad.

*

Now for what the police discovered about Elsie. As I said, I got it all wrong about Elsie in one important detail but then we all got it wrong. The error lay in a very simple but quite reasonable assumption which everyone made. We assumed that Elsie's death explained her disappearance, that the two events were one and the same thing. We never considered that they might be quite separate. It was quite a shock to learn that the Elsie found at the bottom of Loch Craig was not a twenty-six-year-old woman but a woman in her late fifties or early sixties. It was Elsie all right – the police seemed convinced of that – but she had died round about 1970, not 1934.

Suddenly the Elsie McAndrew affair was in the national news headlines. Who was Elsie and what had happened to her? I didn't know the answer and neither did anyone else. I found myself wandering round with a wry smile on my face and occasionally bursting into laughter at my own presumption. Oh yes, I knew the difference between reality and realism, I could argue about the truth of fiction and the value of creative reporting. I knew all about that. So what had I done? I had manufactured a woman called Elsie. I brought her up, gave her a few significant experiences, got her married, made her unhappy and killed her off. It was all carefully arranged and rather neat and I felt reasonably satisfied with myself.

Then, just when I had everything nicely rounded off what did this ungrateful creature of mine take it upon herself to do? Without giving me any warning at all she decided to bring herself back to life.

PART FOUR

1947

MEETING MRS WILSON

APART from the fact that he was wearing a suit of thick brown tweed on what was a warm day in early summer, the man walking along an elegant street in Kensington was unremarkable. He was in his mid-thirties, about five feet eight inches tall, thickset and, by his own standards, immaculately dressed. He had had his suit cleaned and pressed though the cost of this appalled him. He had bought a new white shirt and was wearing a regimental tie which had cost him tuppence in a jumble sale. His brown shoes which, like his suit, were a little too heavy for the warm weather, were nevertheless highly polished. His thick straight black hair was parted high on the left and plastered to his skull with hair oil. He was carrying what appeared to be a new hat. This was wide-brimmed, dark brown, with a beige hatband. The main reason that he was carrying it rather than wearing it was that it did not belong to him. He had borrowed it from a fellow inmate of the lodging house in Kennington where he had been staying for the last week.

He wondered if he would be able to stand the lodging house for much longer. He had been away from his wife and family for nearly two weeks now. If he were honest with himself, however, he would admit that he did not miss them; it was the comfort of his home that he missed. He thought about it a bit more and decided that home was the wrong word; it was just the place where he lived.

In the lodging house he had a tiny cubicle to himself but privacy was impossible. There were sixty such cubicles, two rows of thirty separated by a narrow corridor. The cubicles did not have doors, just curtains which barely covered the entrances, narrow though they were. Through these curtains came the sounds and smells of fifty-nine other men who ranged in age from seventeen to eighty-four. During the first few nights he had found sleep almost impossible. The other men snored, talked in their sleep – one or two shouted incomprehensible words – farted, belched, coughed, sneezed, swore, hawked and spat. Because some of the men were alcoholics there was often the sound of singing, or slurred attempts at it, and occasionally vomiting. For probably the same reason, he supposed, there was sometimes the sound of crying. That was the sound he found to be the worst, worse even than the cursing and swearing and threats he had witnessed last Friday night. He had never heard a grown man cry before.

He began to fiddle with the hat, made to put it on and then changed his mind. A few yards farther on he found the house he was looking for. It was hard to believe that the place he was now visiting was only a few miles from the squalor of the area round the lodging house. He felt intimidated by the high white building, the scrubbed step and polished doorplate. No, Kensington and Kennington might be separated only by a letter of the alphabet but the streets that came between them took you out of one world and into another.

He checked his watch. He was dead on time. He took out a handkerchief and mopped the slight perspiration from his face. He made sure his hands were dry too but while he wiped them he managed to drop the hat. He picked it up and brushed it off quickly. He mounted the five steps to the front door and rang the bell.

The door was opened almost immediately by a maid dressed in black with a white apron. Although quite young she was rather abrupt in her manner. 'Yes?' she asked.

She can see right through me, he thought. Even the bloody maid can see through me. All this damn preparation for nothing. 'I wish to see Mrs Wilson,' he said calmly. 'I'm expected.'

'I see. What name, sir?'

The 'sir' was just a little too grudging. Or was it? Perhaps he was imagining the whole thing. Maybe she treated everyone like this. 'Albert McKillop,' he said.

He was admitted to the most lavishly decorated and furnished room he had ever been in. At first he was shocked into admiration but as he waited he looked more carefully at the dark wood of the large, ugly pieces of furniture, the thick embossing on the pale yellow wallpaper and the heaviness of the dark brown velvet curtains. He began to find the room too oppressive. He sat down on a sofa which he realised was slightly longer than his cubicle in the lodging house.

Mrs Wilson entered and he rose. She was a woman in her mid-forties, he guessed. She was tall, a little on the stout side, and had long brown hair with one or two streaks of grey in it which was caught up in a bun perched on the top of her head. This made her look slightly ridiculous and McKillop had to fight back a smile. She was wearing a black, ankle-length skirt and a white blouse which was buttoned up to her throat. While not exactly threatening, her demeanor was hard and off-putting. She extended her hand.

'Mr McKillop.'

'Mrs Wilson, it was good of you to agree to see me.'

'Mrs Blackler of the agency advised me that you would be in touch.'

'That was very thoughtful of her,' he said. That bitch, he thought.

'Yes, it was. Do take a seat.'

He sat down again, his hat on the sofa beside him. Mrs Wilson sat in an armchair opposite. She seemed about to launch herself into a speech but then thought better of it. She took a look at this man before her and summed him up in five seconds flat: he was from the country; he was perspiring because he was wearing his one and only suit which was too heavy for the weather; his shoes were outrageous, huge, clod-hopping things, but at least they had been polished; his hands were heavy, his fingers thick as sausages so he was definitely a man of the land; despite all that, he was quite polite and well-spoken though with a strong accent that she could identify as being Scottish but from which part of Scotland she could not say; for some reason she was quite sure he was a liar.

'Will you join me for tea?'

'That would be grand,' he said.

Mrs Wilson rang the tiny bell on the table at her side. The maid who had admitted Albert McKillop appeared at the door almost immediately.

'Elsie,' Mrs Wilson said. 'Please bring tea for myself and our guest.'

The maid gave a brief curtsy and left.

'Elsie,' McKillop said. 'And not the first one.'

She looked at him. Again it seemed as if she was about to say something but changed her mind. Then she said: 'Mr McKillop, I'm not sure that I approve of your visit.'

'You mean you don't approve of someone wanting to find out where his only remaining relative is?'

'I didn't quite say that, no. It's just that . . . you say you are Elsie McKillop's brother . . .'

'That's correct, yes.'

'Well, Mr McKillop, I am bound to tell you that I find this most strange because the Elsie I knew assured me she had no brothers or sisters.'

He got to his feet. 'If you are inclined to disbelieve me, Mrs Wilson, I'd rather leave now. I'm not used to having my word doubted.' He spoke this in a forthright manner but without anger.

She was completely taken aback by the strength of his tone, its edge of moral indignation and the dignity with which it was delivered. She flushed with embarrassment and confusion. 'Mr McKillop, please! No, please, take a seat. I . . . I merely wish to point out that . . . well, the situation is at best confusing. You'll grant me that at least, won't you?'

He bowed his head slightly. 'Yes,' he said. 'Yes, I'm sorry. You're not to know the ins and outs of my family. No, I apologise if I was a bit hasty . . .' He sat down again. Christ, he thought, that was a close one.

'There are . . . well, several questions, yes, several questions I feel bound to ask you, Mr McKillop, before I can answer any of yours. In doing so I don't cast any doubt on your word. No, I assure you of that but, well, for one thing the Elsie I knew made it clear to me that she wished to make a new life for herself, start more or less from scratch. She trusted me to help her in this.'

'So you wouldn't wish to help even her own brother to get in touch with her again?'

'As I said before, Elsie told me she didn't . . .' Suddenly Mrs Wilson remembered the trouble this statement had already caused. She changed tack. '. . . I mean, I have no doubt that Elsie had one or two things to hide. She said as much . . . more or less . . .'

'And yet you still employed her to look after your children?'

'Yes, yes . . . I took a chance there but things . . . you might say things conspired in Elsie's favour. We were just about to go abroad when our usual nanny was taken ill and was advised not to travel. We had barely a week to find a replacement. Not the ideal circumstances in which to hire someone who is to look after your children for a couple of years or more . . .'

'No.'

'. . . But then our hands were tied.'

'I see.'

'Not that we didn't check on Elsie, as much as we could . . .'

'Mrs Blackler told me that she had worked somewhere else in London.'

'Only for a few months, yes. She looked after some children in their last year before they were packed off to boarding school. She was given an excellent testimonial.'

'I've no doubt. But did you ask her about her life before she came to London?'

'Yes, of course.'

'And what did she say about that?'

'Well, you must remember, Mr McKillop, that the information I got from Elsie on that topic wasn't given to me all at one time. I mean, I didn't sit her down and examine her on her own life-history. For one thing, I was in such a rush to get everything arranged for our move.'

'Your trip abroad.'

'Yes.'

'May I ask where you went?'

She thought about this for a moment or two and then said: 'I see no harm in that. We went to southern Italy, to Naples.'

'Naples.' He was surprised but nothing in his voice showed this.

'That's right. I'd been to Rome before, of course, but Naples . . . well, it's something altogether different. Have you travelled abroad much, Mr McKillop?'

Mrs Wilson looked intently at the figure before her and realised how ridiculous her question was. The man had plainly not left British shores and London itself was worlds apart from where he came from. She was surprised then to hear him say:

'I've spent some time in the Far East.' The words came slowly, quite softly.

'Why, how marvellous!' Mrs Wilson was suddenly bright and animated. 'I adore the Orient, particularly the Malay States. Have you been to Singapore?'

McKillop's face bore no expression. 'I have,' he said.

'Splendid. And what were you doing there?' She smiled.

I've got her, he thought. I've absolutely got her.

'I was in jail, Mrs Wilson.'

'In . . .' She stopped, finally aware of the terrible blunder she had made. 'Oh, Mr McKillop, I'm so sorry, I didn't realise . . . I . . . I spent most of the War in the United States though my husband, Robert, saw active service in North Africa. You . . . I take it you were captured at the fall of Singapore.'

'I was.'

'How utterly, utterly ghastly for you.' This was wrenched out with as much theatricality as good taste and decorum would allow.

My God, he thought, we're both frauds, both of us.

Mrs Wilson was particularly glad that the maid, Elsie, chose this moment to arrive with the tea tray. Any awkward silence that might have followed their last exchange was overtaken by the business-like rattle of cups and saucers as Elsie placed the tea things on the table nearest to Mrs Wilson. A side table was brought for McKillop and within a couple of minutes he had beside him a cup of tea and a plate with two small cakes upon it.

He decided to be humane and move away from uncomfortable subjects. 'Perhaps I should tell you a little about myself, Mrs Wilson,' he said when the maid had gone, '. . . a little about my family and Elsie's place in it and how I come to be looking for her after such a long time.'

'I confess it's this last point that interests me,' Mrs Wilson said. 'I can't help saying it strikes me as rather odd that you've left it till now to start looking for her.'

'I can understand that, Mrs Wilson. It has been a long time. When was it that you left for Naples?'

'Naples, let me see. It would have been 1935 or '36. Henry was only two, I remember. 1935. Yes, it must have been. Early summer. Frightfully hot when we arrived.'

'1935 . . . yes . . . ' McKillop seemed to be thinking hard as if struggling with some mathematical conundrum. 'Yes, '35. It fits in with what I know, certainly.'

'And what do you know, Mr McKillop?'

'Well, I know that my sister disappeared from home in March, 1934.'

'Disappeared?'

'Yes, without trace.' He paused. 'You see, Mrs Wilson, until recently we all thought she was dead.'

Mrs Wilson's eyes grew wide. 'My goodness,' she said quietly.

'She left no clues, you see, so no one really considered that she might just have run away.'

'No clues?'

'None at all. The police were convinced that either she'd had an accident or committed suicide.'

'Suicide?'

'Yes.'

'But then I feel sure we cannot be talking about the same woman, Mr McKillop. The Elsie I knew was a very bright girl, very self-assured, very confident, very capable, very . . .' She seemed to run out of words.

'I won't deny that, Mrs Wilson, but there was a period, just before she disappeared . . . well, I say just before she disappeared but it may have been going on for years, I don't know . . . there was a period when she was very unhappy, very unhappy indeed.'

'That's as may be, but I can't imagine Elsie committing suicide. It's impossible.'

'Perhaps this might help.' McKillop drew out an envelope from an inside pocket of his suit jacket. From this he took a photograph which he passed across to Mrs Wilson. She looked at it carefully.

'Well, I must admit it looks very like Elsie. The clothes are very different, of course. And who is the gentleman by her side? It isn't you, is it?'

'No, it certainly isn't me. It's a man by the name of Simon McAndrew, Elsie's husband.'

She looked across at him. He was turning the empty envelope over in his hands.

'Mr McKillop, I believe I've had my fill of surprises for one day.'

'There's liable to be a few more.'

'I'm not sure I feel inclined to hear them.'

'Well . . . ' He placed the envelope to one side, on the sofa, by his hat. 'There are aspects to this that are unpleasant – no, let's say unfortunate. The point is that if these things have to be revealed so that I can find my sister then I'm afraid that's the way it's going to be. I've come a long way – I may have to go much farther – and I'm not turning back now. Are you satisfied that that is Elsie?' He gestured towards the photograph.

'Yes . . . yes . . . I'm . . . well, it must be her. Yes, it is. I just find it all so difficult to believe, that's all.'

'There are more curious things in life.'

She looked from the photograph across to McKillop and he sensed that there was a hint of disapproval in her glance. No more homespun philosophy, he decided. He pressed on with the story:

'Elsie and Simon had been married for six years or so when she disappeared. I don't know how long it was that things had been going badly for them but I do know there were problems. I suppose it built up slowly over the years . . .'

'But why?'

'I don't know all the reasons, but I know one or two. Elsie couldn't have children, you see. I think that was important. Simon wanted children very much.'

'And Elsie?'

'Oh, I'm sure she would have wanted children too. She lost one, you know, and after that it just wasn't possible. I think Simon blamed her for this.'

'More than a trifle unreasonably, I would say.'

'Oh, certainly. I don't excuse him, I'm just trying to find reasons.'

'But there must have been more than that, surely?'

'It can mean a lot, Mrs Wilson, it can mean a lot.'

Instead of ringing for the maid she rose and poured more tea. McKillop declined another cake. When she had sat down again she said: 'So how is it that you're looking for Elsie now, so long after the event? What is it . . . thirteen years later?'

'Well, it's a long time, I admit. At first, you see, I felt that Elsie probably did die, though not by suicide.'

'By accident, you mean?'

'Most likely. She liked to go for walks and when things were going badly between herself and Simon she used to go out on her own a lot. You know about her foot, of course?'

'Yes, though it was hardly noticeable, to be fair.'

'Would you say that she limped?'

'I was seldom aware of it.'

'No. Well, the main theory was that she fell into the river on one of her walks. She was particularly fond of the river.'

'So you believed she died?'

'Yes.'

'And what changed your mind?'

'Well . . . ' He paused and took a sip of tea. 'First of all there was the fact that her body was never discovered. Now, they dragged one of the local lochs and they poked about in the river but they found nothing. The search didn't extend very far because Elsie never went more than two or three miles from home. I think one thing that blindfolded us a bit was the fact that the river was in spate at the time and if she had fallen in she'd have been washed out to sea. Of course no one pointed out then that in nine out of ten such cases the body would most likely be found on the beach sooner or later, maybe ten or twenty miles along the coast. Anyway, that was the theory about her disappearance and it changed from being a theory to being referred to as what had probably happened and then later still it was accepted. People just said that Elsie was the woman who fell into the river and drowned. In the village, mothers told their children this story to warn them to be careful when they went down to the river. So it goes . . . ' He drank the last of his tea and set the cup and saucer down carefully on the side table.

'So you began to doubt the story of her death?'

'Yes.'

'But why would she run away? I mean . . . were things so bad between her and . . . what was his name?'

'Simon.'

' . . . Yes, Simon. Were things so bad between them that she just had to disappear?'

'I think they must have been. You see, I think there was much more to it than just the fact that they were childless.'

'I should have thought so.'

'Yes, well, there were probably lots of things we don't know about. Certainly Simon treated her badly, latterly . . .'

'You mean he beat her?'

'No, no, nothing like that. I think he just ignored her.'

'Hmm.' Mrs Wilson finished her tea and placed her cup and saucer on the tea tray to her left. 'That's probably worse, if anything.'

'I agree.'

'But something else must have started you off on this search. I mean, there's not enough evidence there, surely?'

'No, no, there isn't. You're quite right. I was never really happy about the explanation but I had no proof of my own misgivings about it and anyway I wouldn't have known where to start looking even if I'd been convinced then that she was alive.'

'So, what happened? Did you get proof?'

'Well, no, not exactly, not what you'd call proof. But something did turn up.'

'Ah.'

'You see, Simon died last year.'

'I'm sorry.'

'Yes, he was quite a loss to the community, and still young too. I got involved because his family live some way away and they asked me if I could make the arrangements, sort things out until they got there. So I had to arrange the funeral and so on. Anyway, while I was organising Simon's papers I came across his diaries. He'd kept a diary for years. Obviously I was interested to find his entries for 1934.'

'And?'

McKillop gave a little laugh. 'Well, I suppose I'd expected expressions of grief, probably pages and pages of it. Instead I found no entries at all for the period from March to the end of that year. The first entry since Elsie's disappearance was on February the eleventh the next year, 1935. All he wrote was: "Elsie is twenty-seven today." I checked through the rest of his diaries and every year it was the same, an entry on February the eleventh saying: "Today Elsie is . . ." and then her age. I suppose it was the way he said "is" and not "would be". I suddenly started thinking that he knew, he knew all along that Elsie wasn't dead at all, that she was still alive. I became convinced of it and then . . . well, I was determined to find her.'

'There was nothing else in the diaries?'

'No, nothing at all, not a mention of Elsie at all except on her birthday. That was another thing which supported my argument. I thought it was so strange for him not to mention her anywhere else. It was as if he was dropping a hint or letting slip a little clue thinking that one day someone would read his diaries just as I was doing.'

'It wasn't much to go on, Mr McKillop.'

'No, but it worked, didn't it?'

'I suppose so, I'll give you that. But then how did you start looking? How did you come to be here?'

'Well . . .' He relaxed a little as he began his explanation. 'I decided that if she had run away she must have gone somewhere where it would be very difficult to find her. I excluded the whole of Scotland because she would have been a little too near home – even in Glasgow there was just the chance that someone might find her or she might bump into someone from home.'

'But surely London was a bit of a wild guess?'

'Not really. I felt it was the most likely place. She'd talked about London a lot when she was little and she used to get books out of the library with pictures of Westminster Abbey and all the sights. I thought she'd argue that she might as well go somewhere she'd always wanted to visit.'

'You couldn't possibly have realised how big a task you'd set yourself, trying to find someone in the whole of London.'

He gave another little laugh and then lowered his eyes. 'No, no, I'd no idea, really.'

'But you were lucky.'

'Oh yes. Now that I think about it, very, very lucky indeed. But I had a method. I mean, I came here with a plan. I had to decide what Elsie would have chosen to do. Now she'd done some training as a secretary – she'd been to secretarial college. That's where she met Simon, in fact. So I thought maybe that's what she was doing. I contacted all the secretarial agencies I could find . . .'

'You mean to tell me,' Mrs Wilson interrupted, 'that you went round every secretarial agency in London asking about someone they might have employed fourteen years before, someone who most likely had changed her name, and you expected to succeed?'

He smiled. 'Well, I did get a bit depressed at times . . . and I got through a few pairs of shoes.'

'I'm sure you did.'

'Then I moved on to hotels. You know, chambermaids, waitresses and so on.'

'How many hotels are there in London?'

'A lot. But I knew Elsie would start at the top and not go very far down. I started at the Grosvenor and visited about thirty-five before I stopped.'

'How long did that take you?'

He thought carefully. 'Let me see . . . about two or three weeks, I think. I've been in London now for two months. I spent most of my time – too much I would say now – on the secretarial agencies. I was convinced she'd be doing that. Anyway . . .' He shrugged.

'What happened after the hotels?'

'I moved on to agencies for domestic help, including nannies.'

'Ah.'

'Yes. That's where I struck gold. First time in fact. As I said, I was sure Elsie would have started at the top. Mrs Blackler's agency was number one so I went there.'

'Which brought you here.'

'Yes, although it wasn't quite as simple as that. I had to convince Mrs Blackler that I genuinely was Elsie's brother. She was highly suspicious at first, which is natural, I suppose.'

'Indeed it is.'

'And are you still uncertain, Mrs Wilson?'

She looked across at him as if giving him a final appraisal and checking for further clues in his face, in his clothes. 'Shall we say that I'm less uncertain than I was at the beginning.'

'And that's the best you can offer?'

'I'm afraid so, yes. You see, Mr McKillop, although I'm reasonably happy to accept you as Elsie's brother and I appreciate that you've put a great deal of work into tracking her down, I'm bound to say that I respect Elsie's wishes to start life afresh and leave her old life behind. No doubt she did some things that were . . . well, regrettable, I don't know, but she worked very hard while she was with my family and she was the best nanny we ever had. She never revealed her own secrets to me but then after a while I made no more enquiries – I didn't want to do anything to lose her.'

'But you say she did leave your employment.'

'Yes, she did.'

'And when was that?'

'Oh, years and years ago, after we'd been in Italy a matter of fifteen months or so.'

'As early as that?' He could not hide his disappointment.

'I'm afraid so.'

'And why did she leave?'

'Because we came home to England – the family, that is. Elsie decided that she wanted to stay in Naples.'

'She stayed in Naples?' This time not disappointment but surprise.

'Yes.'

'I see.' McKillop did see. He had recovered about two years of the thirteen since Elsie's disappearance. Although the main thing was that he now had clear proof that she was alive, he could see a lot more work ahead before he found her, if he ever found her.

'Mr McKillop, you've travelled a long way and you've worked hard but I think this is as far as you're likely to get.'

'Not a bit of it,' he said, brightening up. 'I know she's alive and I'll find her yet. Did you hear from her at all after you left Naples?'

'Just one letter in which she said, among other things, that she probably wouldn't be in touch again. I understood her reasons.'

'So you had no contact with her at all after that?'

'None.' This was delivered quite confidently. McKillop was nearly convinced.

'And no address for her at that time? It would be a starting point.'

'You mean you intend to continue this search?'

'Most definitely. I'll be leaving for Naples within the week.'

Fifteen minutes later McKillop was in the street waiting for a bus that would take him to Westminster where he could get a connection down to Kennington. He still kept his jacket on though the day seemed to have got warmer. He continued to carry the hat rather than wear it. However, his appearance had changed. He had loosened his tie and undone the top button of his shirt. His face was beaded with perspiration and as he wiped it with his handkerchief he dislodged a few locks of his heavily greased hair. He looked dishevelled and felt it. He wanted to get back to his lodging house as soon as he could and get out of his suit, these tight-fitting shoes and his new white shirt which was just a little too small and caught him under the arms.

On the bus he reflected that his interview with Mrs Wilson had gone well. He had not got very much information but he had got all that she could offer, he was sure of that. He was sure, too, that she had believed him and he knew that the reason for this was that the story he had concocted was so very unlikely that no liar could possibly have put his faith in it. Mrs Wilson had not thought him capable of either the guile or the imagination to make it up; it had to be true. He wondered if she would have believed him if he had told the truth. He was unsure about this but thought that the answer was probably no.

What was the truth, anyway? He smiled to himself as he thought about this question. It was easier for him to decide what was not true. His name was not Albert McKillop and he was not Elsie's brother. He had never been to the Far East – in fact he had not fought in the War at all. He had never read any of Simon McAndrew's diaries. (This would have been difficult as Simon was not dead.) These were the easy things to identify. To turn the question round and say what was true was more difficult. True, he was a reporter from a local Scottish newspaper. True, his editor had taken the surprising step of allowing him to pursue this story all the way to London. Because there was no doubt that he *had* come to London in search of a scoop. But these points did not fully answer the question of his motives. He knew, but rarely admitted to himself, that the search for Elsie was an excuse to get away. He had spent all his thirty-four years in and around one small town. He had followed the accepted paths – got a job, married, started a family – and now he was sick of it. Elsie offered him an escape and, more importantly, it was a legitimate escape. He knew, and again he had to force himself to face this point, that his escape itself was a dishonest one. He had left himself the option of return. He despised himself for this and consequently admired Elsie all the more. For her departure had been single-minded and irrevocable. It had a purity about it which he could not find in any part of himself. He wanted to find her, certainly, but not so much because of his job as a reporter, rather because of what he might learn from her.

If he had told Mrs Wilson this and even if she had believed him, she may not have wished to help him. No, he had approached the whole business in the best way, certainly. He wasn't as close to Elsie as he had hoped but he was about two years closer and that was something. There was one thing, of course, about which he had not lied. He gave a little sigh of resignation as he thought of it: to continue the search he would have to go to Italy.

The next day he made enquiries about the journey. He had never been abroad before and the whole thing scared him a little. He found that this feeling was not unpleasant. He needed a passport and when he got the correct form to fill in he wrote down his real name: Albert Sandison.

PAINT AND BLOOD

THE man in the white linen jacket and pale yellow straw hat left the church of Gesù Nuovo and made his way slowly towards Piazza della Carità. As it was a warm day with a bright sun overhead he walked in the shade wherever he could. At a corner he stopped to wait for a break in the traffic. In fact there were only a few cars but quite a number of pack mules, some horse-drawn carts and one or two *carozzelle*, fine horse-drawn carriages, most of which had seen better days. He found he was still standing there some minutes later, not because the traffic had been particularly heavy – there had been several opportunities to cross – but because he was lost in thought about what he had seen. It was not only the size of the church that had impressed him but the decoration, the overwhelming, almost suffocating richness of the baroque interior. Now, on the corner of Monteoliveto, and only a short walk from other similar churches, he felt once again that little nag of doubt: maybe all this was not as it should be after all.

This area was relatively well looked after. He would reach the Via Roma soon with its elegant shops many of which were already back in business after the War. But there were other aspects to the city. He had explored areas which ranged from the untidy and uncared for to the downright squalid. He found it difficult to reconcile the opulence he had just witnessed with the poverty of some of the surrounding districts. The situation was confused for him by the fact that many of the people he had seen in the church of Gesù Nuovo, the ones who had come to pray and adore, were dressed in rags. He pressed on to Piazza della Carità.

He sat down at a table of one of the outdoor cafés in the square and ordered a glass of wine.

'*Un bicchiere da vino, per favore.*'

'*Bianco o rosso, signore?*' The waiter was a portly middle-aged man, deferential but dignified.

'*Bianco.*'

'*Qualcos'altro?*'

'Ah . . .' He was stuck here. '*Qual* what? . . .' He fumbled for the little phrase book he carried with him but then suddenly remembered. 'Ah yes . . . *si, un cappucino.*'

'*Bene.*'

The waiter left and the man at the table felt satisfied that he had negotiated this basic exchange successfully. Then a doubt crept in. *Un bicchiere da vino bianco.* Was it *da* or *di*? He drew out the phrase book and flicked through the pages. *Un bicchiere* di *vino bianco.* Damn. The mistake irritated him. He practised the phrase a few times and then stuffed the book back in the outside pocket of his jacket.

He removed his straw hat and placed it on the empty chair beside him. He took a white handkerchief from the top pocket of his jacket and wiped his forehead. The square was bright, warm, dry and busy. The gentle breeze managed to cool down the heat of the sun a little but sustained the dust raised by the passing vehicles and deposited it in a thin film on the white tablecloths and the empty seats of the outdoor café. He looked down at his brown shoes. They were new shoes but already scuffed and dusty from the amount of walking he had done in the past few days.

The waiter arrived with the wine and the coffee. From the linen jacket the phrase book was removed again but the waiter had gone before the man could find an appropriate sentence. He placed the phrase book on the table beside the coffee. The pages of the book were dog-eared and the cover scored and discoloured. How long will it take me, he thought, how long will it take me to learn this language? Albert Sandison had been in Naples for three weeks and he was beginning to forget why he had come.

He took a sip of wine and then withdrew a small folded sheet of paper from inside the back cover of the phrase book. He opened it out and smoothed it flat on the table. On it was written a short list which he read through quickly. In the last week he had consulted it thirty or forty times:

ELSIE – still in Naples?
– new name? – remarried?
– if working, where? doing what?
– if not, still in Italy?
– if not Italy, where?

– consult other expats
– British library?
– any British associations, groups?
– passport control (what name?)

He took out a pen and added, at the bottom:

– where to start?

Then he crossed this out and replaced it with:

– how to start?

No, he knew where to start – he had to make contact with other British in the city. He had failed in this so far but then he had hardly tried very hard. No, that was untrue: he had not tried at all. Still, he reckoned this aspect would be easy to arrange. There was no embassy in Naples but there was probably some consular representation although the War had only finished a couple of years before and not just Italy but the whole of Europe was hopelessly disorganised. Nevertheless, 'where' was not a problem; it was 'how' that was the tricky one. He could not afford to make mistakes. First he would have to learn about this place, learn about how things worked here before he might start with a few tentative enquiries. He did not wish to upset people; he saw the need for discretion. He also realised that he had to learn more Italian than his little phrase book could teach him.

As he sipped his wine in the bright, busy square, he thought that although the language was certainly a problem and one that he would have to continue to struggle with, it only provided him with an excuse, really, an excuse for why he had not been able to get down to the job of looking for Elsie. He had been in the city for three weeks now and he had not even started to do what he had come here for.

Drinking off the last of the wine and moving on to the coffee he finally managed to confront himself with the question of why he had been so slow to begin. The fact was that he had been seduced. He gave a little laugh. Yes, he had been seduced by the city.

A couple of minutes later he rose. He placed a few coins by his empty coffee cup and waved at the waiter. He pointed at the table and the waiter nodded. He set off towards the bottom end of the square to walk down Via Roma in the direction of the sea. After fifty yards or so he sensed that something was wrong. He stopped. Above the noise and bustle of the street he was aware of a shouted '*Signore! Signore!*' He turned and saw the waiter bearing down on him with an anxious look on his face. He experienced a short moment of panic. Had he left enough money? Yes, he was sure of that. The waiter, flustered, arrived and said: '*Signore, il suo cappello.*'

'What? Oh . . .'

The waiter held out the straw hat which had been left behind on a chair.

'*Grazie, grazie.*' Sandison took the hat.

The waiter gave the slightest of bows, turned and set off back to the café.

Sandison drew out a handkerchief, mopped his brow and then positioned the hat carefully on his head, very slightly tilted over his right eye. He shook out the handkerchief and stuffed it back in the top pocket of his jacket. Yes, he thought. Must go there again. Certainly.

Half an hour later he was on Via Caracciolo near Piazza Vittoria. For a minute or two he walked along the seafront towards Mergellina in the west. Crowds of ragged children swarmed over the large boulders that fringed the bay. They sported in the water, laughing and shouting, and Sandison wondered how their tiny, bronzed bodies could hold so much energy. Several children did not join their friends in the water but watched them from the balustrade along the main road. They spotted Sandison's approach and raced towards him. Suddenly he was surrounded by ten or a dozen street urchins in rags, imploring him to be generous. Tiny hands stroked his arms and began to explore his outer pockets. Laughing, he shrugged them off. '*Signore! Signore! Fate la carità!*' He held his left arm tight against his chest to maintain the safety of his wallet and hurried on. The children skipped along with him for a few yards and he saw how beguiling their faces were, the large dark eyes, the straggle of thick black hair, the earnest looks of desperate innocence. He gave them nothing.

Suddenly, and all together, they gave up. He left them in his wake and when a little distance separated them from him, he heard one call out to him. He was unsure of the exact translation but he knew it to be very, very rude. So much for innocence, he thought.

A little farther on he cut across the strip of parched grass known as the Villa Comunale which separated Via Caracciolo from the long parallel sweep of the Riviera di Chiaia and made his way up the hill again, away from the bay. He passed along several narrow alleyways, the tight, over-crowded *vicoli* that led towards Via Crispi where his *pensione* was situated.

Within a couple of minutes of his destination he was approached by children again. This time hands reached out from a doorway and tugged at his trouser leg. He turned to see a little girl, who could have been no more than seven or eight, sitting on the doorstep. The colour of the filthy dress she was wearing was indistinguishable from the deep brown of her skin. One of her legs stuck out straight and was heavily bandaged around the knee by a strip of dirty blue material blotched with blood. Her feet were bare. Her hands were cupped before him in a stylised gesture which he recognised not as that of a beggar but of a supplicant, a penitent, someone reaching out for a blessing from God. He had seen the pose in several paintings in the churches and galleries he had visited in the past two weeks. He had seen it too in the mass he had witnessed in the church of Gesù Nuovo. He had sat far back and to one side but the congregation was small for the early morning service and he had seen everything clearly. It had been a strange experience and he had felt how different this magical rite seemed compared with the church services he remembered from home. He saw the members of the congregation approach the altar and kneel in a row. They waited for the priest to pass along with the thin wafer of bread and while they did so their hands were like this, cupped and raised in a gesture that might be offering or receiving.

He looked down at the girl and was moved. She was dry-eyed but her expression just faintly betrayed a struggle against the pain of her injury. For a moment he was swept by a desire to empty his pockets before her, give her everything of value that he was carrying with him. As he put his hand in his pocket to withdraw a few coins he knew that he was lost. But if he was lost, he was glad to be so. He knelt down to place a small pile of change in her hands. Although this probably represented ten times what she would normally expect she displayed no emotion as she accepted it. The *grazie* that escaped from her was barely audible and as she lowered her eyes in what appeared to be a motion of submission Sandison suddenly felt small and mean and condescending. He was about to fish out some more money when he realised this would make things worse – or at least his perception of things. Undecided and still bent over towards her he became aware of the patter of running feet, approaching fast. He turned and, in the act of rising, felt his hat being swept from his head. He nearly fell over. When he had recovered himself he looked up the narrow lane and saw a young boy racing into the distance, the white straw hat clutched in one hand and waving at his side as his arms pumped the air with the effort of running. Well, Sandison thought, it was maybe a bit big for me anyway. He turned back to the little beggar girl but she had disappeared.

'*Pittura,*' Franco said. '*Pittura.*' He was one of the regular barmen in a small bar in Piazza Amedeo. About thirty-five, he was tall and running to fat, his once handsome features now puffed out, his stance a round-shouldered slouch. The bar was quiet and he was taking the opportunity to do some washing up. '*Pittura,*' he repeated slowly.

Sandison was half way through his second glass of wine. He was in the middle of explaining to Franco the events of his day. He did not particularly like Franco whose view on life was rather cynical, redeemed only by the fact that he was quite willing to listen to Sandison's halting efforts to tell his tale in Italian. Since Franco spoke no English, Sandison had no choice in the matter. He convinced himself that speaking Italian to Franco presented a good opportunity to learn and therefore he should take up the challenge. Unfortunately this logic did not make his task any easier. And now there was this new word. '*Pittura?*'

'*Si.*' Franco pulled glasses two at a time from the sink and set them on the tiny draining board.

Sandison was flicking through a pocket dictionary. '*Pittura*. Paint. Paint?' He looked across at Franco. 'What the hell has paint got to do with it?' He said this in English. Franco gave him a wry grimace and shrugged his shoulders.

'No, no,' Sandison said and he turned the pages of the little book as fast as his fingers would allow. '. . . No, it was . . . it was . . . yes, here we are. *Sangue*. Blood.'

'*Che cosa?*'

'Blood. Blood. *Sangue*.'

'*Sangue, no. Pittura*.'

'You're a thrawn bastard, Franco. It was . . .' Sandison hesitated. '. . . Paint?'

'*Si*,' Franco said and he tried the English word: 'Pent.' He had begun to dry the glasses.

'Well bugger me.'

Franco put down the glass he had been drying and wrapped the towel round his bare arm. He turned on the tap, wet his fingers and said: '*Pittura*.' He sprinkled water over the towel and then went into a paroxysm of agony, nursing the injured arm against his chest and holding out his other hand for money.

'But it couldn't have been, surely,' Sandison said. 'My God, the child was in agony.'

The words meant nothing to Franco but the situation was all too familiar. He waved a hand in the air and then said: '*Un sacco di soldi?*'

Money. Sandison tried hard to remember how much he had given the girl. Far too much, probably. '*No, non molti*,' he said. Not very much. '*Il mio cappello*.' He pointed to his head and mimed the whisking away of his hat.

Franco burst into laughter. Recovering, he let out a stream of words of which Sandison understood almost nothing.

'Well, Franco, you've got me there, I think.' Sandison finished off his wine. Franco continued to jabber away, his words interspersed with little outbursts of laughter. Sandison placed his wine glass on the counter and Franco, unbidden, refilled it. 'This one's on you, anyway, Franco,' Sandison said. '*Sliante!*'

'Perhaps you would allow me to get this one.'

Sandison turned to find the only other customer in the bar now standing next to him. He had been sitting at a table in the corner reading an Italian newspaper and Sandison had hardly paid him any attention. Now this man had approached and addressed him in English and in an upper-class accent too. He was of medium height and was wearing a baggy and very creased cotton suit the colour of oatmeal. The outer pockets of the jacket were filled and sagging. A not very clean handkerchief trailed from the top pocket. The man was perhaps in his mid-fifties. He had a full head of jet-black hair – dyed, or so Sandison guessed – which was oiled and swept from his forehead straight back over his crown. He had a small black moustache which was neatly trimmed. His features were regular, rather ordinary, though some might well have thought him handsome. It was his posture, however, that was most striking. His stance was apologetic, almost cringing as if he expected to be dealt a blow. In fact he stood four or five feet away from Sandison, giving the impression he was still unsure of the reception he would get. He had a grey hat which he held tightly by the brim with both hands. It was pressed hard against his chest.

For a few moments Sandison allowed himself to take in the figure before him and he ignored what had been said.

'If you would permit me, that is,' the man said. 'I'm sure I could interest you in something better than Franco's usual offering.'

'Well,' Sandison said, 'that's kind of you . . . '

The man rattled off some instructions to Franco who retreated to the end of the bar and started hunting through the bottles on a particularly high shelf.

'Alfred Maidstone,' the man said. He extended a thin hand, very gingerly, as if afraid it might be bitten off.

'Sandison. Albert Sandison.' They shook hands. Sandison's grip was strong. Maidstone winced.

'I believe you had an unfortunate encounter with some of the scallywag population of this beautiful but decaying city.'

'You could say that, yes.'

'Your hat?'

'Yes, lost it, I'm afraid. There was little point giving chase. The boy was gone in a flash.'

'Sometimes they're so quick you don't even see them.'

'I can believe that.'

Franco returned and set two glasses before them. The liquid was dark brown. Maidstone had now stepped up to the bar beside Sandison but he still did not look to be at ease. He gestured to the glasses. 'Please . . .' he said.

Sandison raised his glass to the light. 'What exactly is this stuff?' he asked.

'It's a kind of liqueur, locally made. First rate. Well, your health.'

They touched glasses.

'Here's to lost hats,' Sandison said.

'Indeed, I've had several stolen myself.'

Is that why you're holding on so tightly to the one you've got? Sandison thought. Maidstone had not parted with it but held it firmly in his left fist. Sandison could see that the brim was crumpled and creased all round.

'You've been here a while, then?' Sandison asked.

'Oh years, dear fellow, years and years. Had to spend the War in England, of course – ghastly place, all wet and miserable and full of the bulldog spirit. Ugh! Got back here as fast as I could. Only place to be, dear fellow, only place to be.' He downed the dark, viscous liqueur in one go and motioned to Franco for more.

Maidstone explained that he had first come to Italy after the First World War. 'Paris was the place then,' he said, 'but I wanted to be different. Besides, ghastly people the French, so stiff and arrogant and vain with it.' He spent some time in Rome, later Florence and then, in 1923 or 1924 – he wasn't quite sure – he 'fetched up' in Naples. He was getting along quite nicely too, he said, until the War. The mention of this allowed him to express once more how 'utterly desperate' a place England was. And as for London: 'The end, my dear fellow, the absolute end.'

Sandison found it a little difficult to figure out exactly what Maidstone did. There was mention of some art history work, a few articles for various journals and a cataloguing job for one of the museums but it was clear that for Maidstone these were of little importance and did not really qualify for the title of job. Sandison suspected that he had some kind of private income but, judging by the state of his clothes, his means, from whatever source, were limited. Not that this affected his appetite for the bottles on Franco's highest shelf. During the course of an hour or so these were removed and replaced with remarkable regularity. Sandison, who had only had three or four glasses of wine, began to feel light-headed. Maidstone consumed at least double that amount and seemed perfectly sober.

'And you, dear fellow, what brings you to this city?'

Sandison was already getting tired of being addressed as 'dear fellow'. He realised that Maidstone was probably regarded as a local 'character', the kind of man who, met once, can be amusing and enjoyable company but thereafter can become a crashing bore. He might have an interesting tale to tell but it could probably be told in the space of thirty minutes and on later meetings hauled out and paraded again exactly as it was on the first occasion. Still, there was something about Maidstone that held Sandison's attention even after an hour. Also, he was the first English-speaker Sandison had met since his arrival in the city. He decided, however, that Maidstone should not be told of his reason for being in Naples – not yet, anyway. He might prove to be useful but would have to be handled carefully.

'I'm in Naples for a number of reasons . . .' Sandison began, though he could not imagine what these might be. His real reason for being there was odd enough without having to concoct others. He suddenly realised he had never thought of the possible need to tell lies about why he was there. There was an awkward silence which Maidstone might have broken with some amiable remark to save Sandison's face. Maidstone did nothing of the sort. He stood there waiting silently for Sandison to work his own way out of the difficulty and Sandison realised there was a calculating hardness to this man. He had better beware; Maidstone might be dangerous.

Then Sandison laughed quietly and Maidstone smiled. Sandison leaned forward and said: 'Suppose I were to tell you I was a detective, come to hunt someone down?' He winked at Maidstone and they both laughed out loud.

'My dear, dear fellow, if I had a lira for every time I've heard that story . . . well . . .'

'You'd almost have enough to buy some more drinks.'

'Absolutely! Yes!' He laughed again and waved at Franco who stepped forward to refill their glasses.

'Ah,' Sandison said. 'Joking aside, I've certainly had my fill. No more for me, thank you.' He put his hand over the top of his glass.

'A careful man, I see. Moderate. Temperate. I tried that once myself, you know. Devilish waste of time.' He motioned to Franco that his glass, at least, should be filled. 'Well,' he continued, 'you'll have one more, but perhaps a little later and I will insist upon it. Meanwhile, let's get back to the hat.'

'Ah, yes.' Sandison felt relieved that there was to be no pursuit of his reasons for coming to Naples. He retold the story of the little beggar girl with the bandaged leg and the theft of his hat. He enjoyed telling it because his first attempt, to Franco, had been made in a desperate sort of pidgin-Italian. However, he felt dismayed when Maidstone effortlessly translated the incident for Franco's benefit. Franco listened with no emotion showing on his face. He was polishing glasses and he held them up to the light to check them and thereby seemed to be ignoring Maidstone completely. When Maidstone had finished, Franco thought for a moment, shrugged and wandered off to the other end of the bar.

'Franco is not impressed by such events,' Maidstone said.

'Obviously not. Earlier on he was saying something about paint.'

'Oh yes. You see, some of the beggars feign injury. They're very good actors, know just exactly how much agony to put into it and so on. Then for props . . . well, a dirty old bandage and a spot of red paint. Works wonders.'

'It's hard to believe,' Sandison said.

'Oh, I know, I know. There's a lot of things like that in this city. Oh yes.'

'So it probably was paint?'

'It might have been blood but certainly not the little girl's. A little sheep's blood, perhaps . . . chicken, even fish would do. Who knows?'

'And the boy who ran off with my hat. Why the hat? Why didn't he try for my wallet?'

'Not sure, really, though the little ones tend to go for the easy stuff. I mean, the wallet might have meant a tussle. To be avoided at all costs.'

'Hmm. Well, it wasn't much of a hat.'

'Ah, but that's not the point. It was something rather than nothing. It had a resale value, even if it was no more than a few lire. Maybe it made the difference between having lunch or going hungry. This is a poor city, Mr Sandison.'

'Yes, I understand that a bit more each day.'

There was a rather sombre silence for a few seconds, broken eventually by Maidstone who said: 'Right! We'll have that last drink – you too, no argument! – and then we'll take a short walk up the side here to visit one of the oldest establishments in this area.'

'Oh, and what's that?'

'Hatshop. Who knows, you might even find your own hat there.'

Although Maidstone was now beginning to display the fact that he was far from sober – his walk was a little unsteady and one or two of his words did not come out exactly right – the visit to the hatshop passed off without any untoward incident. Sandison bought a very fine pale grey hat with a wide, flat brim and a white hatband. He would not have bought it had he been by himself but Maidstone assured him it was the right choice – 'Absolutely first rate, dear fellow.'

They parted at the hatshop and made an arrangement to meet at the same time the following day. Sandison watched, a little concerned, as Maidstone made his way, quite quickly but with a very uneven tread, towards the *funicolare* station above Piazza Amedeo. Sandison himself set off in the opposite direction, towards his *pensione*.

Back in his small room, Sandison lay down on the bed and slept for about an hour and a half. From the courtyard of the decaying five-storey building that housed the *pensione* came the shouts of children playing and the occasional revving of vehicles. But Sandison was dead tired. He felt as if he had walked for miles and knew that he had certainly had too much to drink. He slept deeply and when he awoke he was refreshed. He washed and went out to the nearest bar for a tall glass of water and a coffee. He returned to his room, sat down at the small table and wrote a letter:

Naples
June 5th, 1947

Dear Stewart,

My God, this is a rum place. You've been to Glasgow and seen the tenements there, the filth and the meanness of the streets but I tell you Glasgow is nothing compared with this place. There are areas where every child is in rags and learns to be a thief from the age of three. It's true! But in spite of all that, Naples contrives to be wonderful, in the real sense of that overworked word. You can't walk anywhere here without finding something to astound you, whether it be something sad or cruel on the one hand or quite beautiful on the other. Never have I been in a place of such contrasts.

As far as our Elsie is concerned, I confess I am no nearer finding her, not directly anyway. But I'm sure she's here. I can feel it. Today I met someone – an Englishman – who has lived here for ages (apart from the War years, of course) and he may be able to help me. I'll have to tread warily though, both with him and with the city in general. I may have to stay here a while yet. Of course, when I have firm news I'll be in touch immediately. Till then,

Yours,
Albert

Sandison folded the letter into a small rectangle and put it inside an envelope which he addressed. He went downstairs and asked the *portiere* where the nearest post office was. The *portiere*, an over-weight, ill-tempered man of sixty, shouted into the courtyard and a few seconds later his grandson Aldo arrived. Aldo was in his early teens. The *portiere* barked some instructions at the boy and made Sandison to understand that Aldo would see to it that the letter got posted. '*Inghilterra*,' Sandison said, and then, as this was not strictly accurate, he added: '*Gran Bretagna*.'

'*Si, si, si*,' Aldo nodded. He took the envelope from Sandison who also handed over what he believed to be enough money to cover the postage. Aldo gave a slovenly salute and left.

When he was a couple of streets away from the *pensione* Aldo tore up the letter into pieces as small as he could manage and dropped them in the gutter.

GOOD MEN AND ROGUES

THE next day Sandison followed almost exactly the same route through the town. He visited the church of Gesù Nuovo again and made his way to Piazza della Carità for coffee in the same restaurant. The waiter recognised him and Sandison spent five minutes explaining in his ragged Italian about his change of hats. The waiter found it all very amusing though Sandison was not quite sure if the laughter came from the story itself or his own clumsy attempts to tell it.

Again he left the waiter a generous tip and set off, with his hat this time, down Via Roma and along Via Chiaia towards the sea. He passed the same group of children playing on the rocks and was surrounded, as on the previous day, by a dozen or so pairs of inquisitive hands, young but not so innocent. He strode on.

He left the sea, crossed the Villa Comunale and headed off inland. He entered the maze of streets and alleyways below Piazza Amedeo, looking for the place where he had seen the little beggar girl with the bandaged leg. But all the doorways looked alike. He tried to remember if there had been a particular shop nearby but he failed. He walked along the same three or four streets twice until it seemed pointless to continue. He could not say what he intended to do if he found the girl. After all, conversation with her would be limited and he could hardly hope to find out if her injury was real or not, short of tearing the bandage from her leg.

Once, in the distance, he saw a girl who might have been the one. She was wearing a bandage, or seemed to be, but it was on her arm, not her leg. He quickened his pace to try and intercept her but the crowds on the pavement and the traffic on the street intervened. When he reached the spot where he thought he had seen her she had gone. He looked around and within a radius of twenty yards, both on his side of the street and over there on the far corner, he could see ten or a dozen little girls, each in a pale dirty dress and with hair in a dark, tangled mane. Any one of them could have been the girl he was looking for, with or without a bandage. Or none of them. He laughed at his own naïvety, his gullibility. Then, at his feet, almost indistinguishable from the other bits of litter and scraps of rubbish, he saw a long, dirty ribbon of material, covered along its full length with bright red blotches in awkward shapes. It was lying on the edge of the pavement, with one end trailing onto the cobbled street. Sandison laughed again.

A few minutes later he met Maidstone.

'It could have been her,' Maidstone said when Sandison recounted the incident. 'But unlikely, I think. There are hundreds, thousands of children on the streets here.'

'And the rag?'

'Oh, the *blood*-stained rag!' Maidstone laughed. 'My dear fellow, you could probably find one in every gutter in Naples.'

'Maybe I should have picked it up, found out if it really was blood or not . . .'

'And what would that prove? Eh?'

'Well . . .' Sandison gave a wry smile. 'Nothing, I suppose.'

'Precisely, precisely.' Maidstone turned and shouted towards the far end of the bar: 'Franco!'

The barman emerged, slowly, looking as morose as ever. He nodded to Sandison but this was the full extent of his greeting.

Maidstone ordered drinks. Sandison tried to gauge how many he had already had but was unsure. He seemed fairly sober. They took their drinks to a quiet corner table and sat down.

'This city is depraved, you see,' Maidstone began. 'Quite depraved. There's petty crime and crime on a grand scale, well organised. There's dealing in contraband; there's prostitution, racketeering, murder. The local government can't cope with the Camorra . . .'

'The what?'

'The Camorra, the local section of the Mafia.'

'Oh.'

'. . . And . . . well, central government has given up trying. They're not terribly interested in the depressed South so the depressed South gets more depressed. Public services break down . . . there are power cuts, water shortages . . . earthquakes knock down houses and disrupt power lines and drains and what have you. The streets aren't cleaned often enough or they aren't cleaned at all. There are more motor vehicles around than ever and you take your life in your hands just crossing the road . . . As for the War, well, that was a catastrophe, an absolute catastrophe. People in this town starved, several buildings were bombed and crime soared because you had to steal to eat. The Germans did some pretty horrible things here and then the Allies came and, well, they did some pretty horrible things too. This place has been occupied by just about everyone you could name over the centuries. It's a wonder it's still here but it's no wonder it's in such a God-forsaken state . . .' Maidstone paused. He raised his glass of wine and downed half the contents in one gulp.

'But you live here,' Sandison said.

'Ah yes, I do. I live here. I don't just exist, either. I live and I have a full life too.'

'And how do you manage that?'

'Because this place is magical, utterly magical. It never ceases to surprise me. Yesterday you had the strange experience of having someone bend over backwards to return your hat to you because you'd left it behind somewhere and then five minutes later someone stole it. I say typical. Absolutely typical of this place. They're all rogues here but for some reason I like them, I'm drawn to them. Bit of a rogue myself, I should say.' He laughed. 'And Franco's a rogue, too.' He turned to the bar where Franco was rearranging bottles on a shelf. 'Franco!' he shouted.

Franco turned.

'You're a rogue, aren't you, Franco?' This was also shouted. In English. Franco bowed slightly with great dignity.

'You see!' Maidstone found this very funny. 'Franco knows I'm making fun of him. Look at the malice in his eyes. I shall get short measure next time, but only for one drink. His annoyance won't last. He's a good man, Franco.'

'You just said he was a rogue,' Sandison said.

'And so he is. But look here . . .' At this point Maidstone leaned over the table in an earnest, confidential manner. Sandison found it difficult to take him seriously. '. . . Look here, I think you're making one basic mistake, dear fellow . . .'

'Oh? And what's that?'

'You don't seem to believe that it's possible to be a rogue and a good man at the same time.'

'I hadn't thought it was possible, no.'

'Ah. You live in a very black and white world. Dreadful mistake, dreadful.' Maidstone sat back in his chair again. He twirled his empty glass in his fingers. 'Take your waiter, for example . . .'

'My waiter?'

'The one who returned your hat to you.'

'Oh yes. What about him?'

'Well, what would you say . . . a good man?'

'Insofar as I could judge after only one small incident like that . . . yes, I suppose so.'

'And quite right too. Yes, obviously a good man, but a rogue as well.'

'Now you've lost me.'

'Well, let's see . . . how much was your hat worth?'

Sandison shrugged. 'I've no idea. Certainly not very much.'

'And did you tip him?'

'Yes, but . . .'

'Generously?'

'Well, reasonably so, I suppose, but after the meal, not after he gave me back the hat. I didn't give him anything then.'

'You didn't have to.'

'What do you mean?'

'Well, he knew, didn't he? I mean he knew you were good for a few lire more than usual.'

Sandison shook his head. 'I really don't . . .'

Maidstone pressed on with his argument. 'Did you go there today?'

'Yes, yes I did.'

'Same waiter?'

'Yes.'

'And did you leave a tip? A generous tip?' Maidstone's face displayed what could almost have been called a mischievous grin.

'Yes,' Sandison said, quietly and evenly. 'Yes, I did.'

'Aha!' Maidstone laughed. 'I rest my case. You see, he knew he would get more income in the long run from returning your hat than from keeping it and selling it.'

'Are you seriously suggesting that he worked things out so carefully?'

'Absolutely.'

'Oh, come on. I can't believe that. I can't believe that at all.'

'Ah, but you see, you're making the same mistake again!' Maidstone leaned forward once more, intent on proving his point. 'You think that such a calculating approach to life must be wrong. You condemn him for his self-interest. I applaud him for being able to marry self-interest with the needs of others. After all, you got your hat back and he got a nice tip. You both gained out of it so what's wrong with that?'

In spite of himself, Sandison smiled. 'Well, you've got me there, I suppose.'

'Oh I have, I have!' Maidstone was clearly enjoying himself. 'Yes, each Neapolitan is out for himself but he recognises the need to live as harmoniously as possible with everyone else.'

'All one big happy family,' Sandison said.

'Exactly, exactly. The family dominates Italian life and Naples is just one big family.'

'I find that hard to believe.'

'Believe it,' Maidstone said. 'Believe it now because you will in the end, anyway, if you stay here long enough.' He set his glass down on the table and looked across at the bar. 'Franco!'

Two or three drinks later Sandison felt relaxed enough to ask Maidstone about the other British in Naples.

'Oh, there are a few,' he said, 'but not so many in this area. The well-off ones live on the islands. Have you been to the islands?'

'No, I haven't.'

'Oh, do go, at least once. Then you can safely forget about them. Too crowded for my taste.'

'Worse than the city itself?'

'Much worse. I'm afraid space is at a premium in this part of the world. If you want more, go inland; if you can get by with less, stay in the city; if you don't need more than a square foot or so, go to the islands. Ugh! Frightful places.'

'Well,' Sandison said, 'if it affects you so much, why don't you go inland yourself?'

'But I do. Caserta, for example. Aversa, Capua . . .'

'But just to visit?'

'Oh yes, just to visit. I could never live there. Not enough magic. Too diluted by the fresh air. Here in Naples you've got a balance, if you like. Lots of bustle but just enough space to breathe. If it all gets too much for me, I go to church.'

Sandison laughed.

'No,' Maidstone said. 'I do, really. Not when there's a mass being said of course. No, nothing like that. I'm only interested in a bit of peace and quiet.'

'I see.'

'Yes. Lots of churches in Naples . . .'

'So I'd noticed.'

'And what's more to the point, lots of bars.'

Sandison laughed again.

'And I've been in every one of them,' Maidstone said.

'Which? The churches or the bars?'

'My dear fellow, the churches of course!' Maidstone laughed. It was a loud laugh which Sandison would have found embarrassing if there had been lots of people in the bar. At that time there was only one other customer, an old man standing quietly at the far end, near the door. He paid no attention whatsoever to the two men seated in the corner. Franco gave them a look which might have been faintly disapproving. Maidstone ordered more wine.

'As far as this part of the city is concerned,' Maidstone went on after the drinks had arrived, 'I think I'm the only resident Englishman.'

'Are there any Scots in Naples?' Sandison asked. He was aware of making an effort to pass this question off as casually as possible and thereby knew he had failed.

'One or two,' Maidstone said. 'One or two.'

After a few moments Sandison went on: 'Do you know them?'

'I know of them,' Maidstone said. 'I've never met them. Perhaps I've tended to avoid them but then I avoid the English as well, and the Irish . . . '

'And the Welsh?' Sandison asked, smiling.

'None here that I know of, thank God.'

'I see. So you stick with the local people, do you?'

'Absolutely.'

'So why do you manage to tolerate me?'

'My dear fellow, to meet in a bar two days running hardly constitutes a relationship of note. Still, I'll say this for you: you're the first Scotsman I've met who's prepared to put his hand in his pocket for a round of drinks.'

'Is that a hint?'

'Christ, no. Well, not quite yet, anyway.' He raised his glass to the light. It was still half full. He reduced this to a quarter and set the glass down on the wooden table with a clatter.

'Do you always drink so much?' Sandison asked.

'Now you're not going to lecture me, are you? I should be most upset if you were.'

'Not at all. It's just that while we've been together it's been the activity you've indulged in most. At home I drink a lot myself but I can't keep up with you.' Sandison was already beginning to feel the effects of the contents of Franco's special bottle, retrieved as on the day before from the most inaccessible shelf in the tiny, cluttered bar.

'Practice, m'boy, practice. I drink a lot at home too. This is my home.' He finished off his drink and set the empty glass down on the table with exaggerated care. 'Well,' he said, 'maybe it's time after all.'

Sandison called over to Franco but asked for only one glass of the special liqueur. Maidstone complimented him on his Italian. 'Coming on a treat,' he said.

'Practice,' Sandison said. 'Practice.'

Maidstone laughed.

They left the bar half an hour later. Maidstone expressed the wish to go for a walk – slowly – along the sea front. They wandered down the cobbled streets to the Riviera, across the Villa Comunale and then over Via Caracciolo to the balustrade that separated them from the boulders that sat on the edge of the sea. They were besieged by children who disappeared quickly when they recognised Maidstone. 'Never give 'em anything,' he said. Sandison was unsure whether this was an instruction or merely a statement referring to Maidstone's own approach. The children went back to the rocks and the two men never referred to them again.

They stood in silence for a while, leaning over the balustrade and looking out to sea. The air was bright and clear and the sea was almost completely flat. There were a few small fishing boats in the Bay each sitting in its place without moving. Apart from the children immediately below, the scene was almost devoid of movement. Sandison's idling thoughts were suddenly overtaken by his realisation that he was in a place far, far from home, a place so different and not exactly hostile but alien, perhaps unknowable. He smiled.

'It's a strange place, isn't it,' Maidstone said.

'Just exactly what I was thinking,' Sandison said. Then he added: 'What the hell am I doing here?'

'Ah well, well now, that's a tricky one, isn't it,' Maidstone said. 'I used to ask myself that one but I gave up trying to find an answer long ago.' He paused for a moment. 'What did you leave behind?'

'Oh, a wife and and one child.'

'And do you intend to go back?'

For one moment the question appalled Sandison. Of course, there was no doubt that he would go back. Wasn't there? Suddenly he was unsure and this made him feel afraid. It made him feel afraid but it excited him too. 'Do you know . . . I really can't be sure.'

'Ah,' was all that Maidstone said to this but it had a knowing sound to it.

Another group of children arrived but they joined their friends by the water without approaching the two men.

Sandison wondered if now he would be classified with Maidstone. Their clothes were remarkably similar. Both were wearing grey flannel trousers and pale beige or fawn linen jackets. Their hats were of different colours but almost the same shape. How long would it be, Sandison thought, before his hat resembled Maidstone's – old, stained with sweat and with a brim destroyed by the constant folding and rolling it received in Maidstone's small, tight, nervous hands. Already Sandison had too many things in the outer pockets of his jacket – dictionary in the left-hand one, notebook, pencil and map of the city in the other. The line of the jacket, its original tidy shape, was being worn down already. It was becoming battered and shapeless. He looked across at Maidstone. His clothes were in more of a mess but just because he had been in the city longer. Battered and shapeless. Maidstone's whole life seemed to be like that. What the hell did he do all the time, except drink? How did he live? Was he ever sober enough to write the articles he had mentioned the day before? Sandison reckoned that maybe there had been an article or two, perhaps three or four, but years ago. He had a feeling that Maidstone mentioned them to vindicate himself in the eyes of others. Perhaps he needed these faraway successes to convince himself that his life had once had value, might yet have value again.

'I know what you're thinking,' Maidstone said.

'Oh? What's that?'

'You're wondering how I get by, what the hell I do to get by. In this city. In this state.' He kept his gaze out to sea. 'Aren't you?'

Sandison felt uncomfortable for a moment or two but was then able to reply: 'Yes. Very perceptive. That's exactly what I was thinking.'

'And there's another thing too, isn't there?'

'Is there? I don't know.'

'Well, let's just say that it's crossed your mind that maybe, maybe if you stay long enough in this place it'll get to you in the same way as it got to me. Eh?'

After a few seconds Sandison said: 'Tell me about the Scots.'

'You are looking for someone, aren't you?'

'Tell me about them.'

'I don't think I should.'

'I've come a hell of a long way, you know. One hell of a long way.'

'If you came from just down the road it would make no difference. Distance and time, well . . . they're just excuses. We try to believe they've got power within themselves but it isn't like that, believe me. Just take my advice . . .'

'What's that?'

'Go home. Forget why you came. I don't know who you're looking for and I don't want to know but even I can see that whoever it is he won't be overjoyed to see you . . .'

'She.'

'She. That's worse. Much worse. Take my advice, please. Go home. Stay a few days and visit a few places, drink more wine, eat more pasta and then go. It's safer.'

Sandison said nothing. He took an envelope from his inside pocket. He drew from it the photograph of Elsie McAndrew that he had shown to Mrs Wilson in London. He handed it to Maidstone without comment. They were both still standing side by side at the balustrade, elbows leaning on the top rail. Maidstone accepted the photo with reluctance. He studied it for some time and then said: 'That's bad, I'm afraid. Very, very bad.'

'I want to see her,' Sandison said. 'I want to see her, at least.'

'Forget it. Please, take my advice and forget it before you get into something you can't control.'

'No,' Sandison said. 'It's too late to back out now. I've spent a lot of time and effort getting this far. I can't stop now.'

'Now look here,' Maidstone said, turning to face him. 'This lady . . .' He raised the photograph before Sandison's face. '. . . This lady is well-connected, well-respected . . . you don't make trouble for such people with impunity.'

'I'm not here to make trouble.'

'Your intentions have little to do with it, I can assure you of that.'

'I just need to see her, confirm that she's still alive.'

'Impossible.' Maidstone handed the photo back and turned to lean over the balustrade again. Apart from the frolics of the children on the boulders below them the scene was a quiet one. A light breeze came off the sea and provided a little relief from the afternoon heat. After a few moments Maidstone said: 'What's your interest in her, anyway?'

Sandison told him the whole story, the one he had told to Mrs Wilson: that he was Elsie's brother, that he was convinced she was still alive even though she had disappeared so many years before. He related how he had come down to London and systematically searched through the various agencies that might have employed Elsie, how he had tracked down Mrs Wilson and had gone to see her.

The tale took some ten minutes to tell, Sandison being careful to allow no inconsistencies to creep in. The one change to what he had recounted to Mrs Wilson lay in the time he had spent in London: he told Maidstone he'd spent six months there.

'I see,' Maidstone said when the story was complete. 'And you told all this to Mrs . . . the woman in London?'

'Mrs Wilson, yes.'

'And she believed you?'

'Yes.'

'Well I don't,' Maidstone said.

Sandison was not surprised by this but he was at a loss as to how to proceed. Maidstone offered a way:

'Look,' he said. 'I may not like London over much but I do know a bit about the place and one thing I know is that it's big, bloody big. Your chances of coming down to London and finding someone who may have been there over a decade ago are not just slim, they're non-existent. I mean, you weren't even sure she'd been there at all.'

He was right, of course, and Sandison knew it. He decided to risk a little bit of the truth:

'Well, let's say I reckoned Mrs Wilson needed to be told about struggle and hard work. I mean, I thought she'd be more inclined to help me if she had this image of me tramping the streets for weeks on end . . .'

'So what really happened, then? How did you really track this woman down?'

'Well . . . it was her feet that gave her away.'

'Her feet?'

'Yes. You know she's slightly disabled; she needs special shoes.'

'It's . . . well, it's hardly noticeable, really, but yes, her right foot . . .'

'Left . . .' Sandison interrupted, unsure whether this was a genuine mistake on Maidstone's part or a little test. 'It's her left foot that's misshapen.'

'Is it?' The look that passed between them showed a certain amount of respect but a little mistrust as well. They might have been playing chess.

'Yes, her left foot's the one. She used to get her special shoes from a little family firm in Glasgow.'

'So?'

'Well, I went down there, just on the off chance, really. I asked the old man about this client from the North and he remembered her.'

'Even after all those years?'

'Yes. He hadn't heard that she'd disappeared but he did wonder why all the orders had stopped. Still, he said, she probably got as good a service in London.'

'He mentioned London?'

'Yes. You see, the last order he'd had from her was made from London after she'd disappeared – although he didn't know that. He had the order books going back for years and years and he was able to show me. She disappeared in March 1934 but her last pair of shoes were sent for in 1935.'

'And he sent this pair of shoes to a London address?'

'That's right.'

'Mrs Wilson's address?'

'No, the agency which hired her out to Mrs Wilson.'

'Ah.' Maidstone thought about this. 'Doesn't seem very wise to me. I mean, If she'd covered her disappearance so well, why should she take a risk like that?'

'I don't know. Maybe she was just waiting for a chance to go abroad and wanted to be ready to leave at any time. Maybe she needed a pair in a hurry because the ones she had were worn out. There could be any number of reasons.'

'Quite a risk, though.'

'Oh yes. She had to give her real name when she ordered the new shoes. I suppose she just hoped that news of her disappearance hadn't made it as far as the Glasgow papers.'

'Hmmm.' Maidstone sounded as if he was not fully convinced. There was silence for a few seconds and then he said: 'And she's your sister, is she?'

Sandison looked him in the eye. 'That's right,' he said.

ELISA

THE following day, at ten thirty in the morning, Sandison was sitting nervously at a table outside a café near Piazza Vanvitelli in the Vomero district. This was high up above the Bay, on top of the hill. Earlier, he had visited the museum of San Martino, not to see any of the exhibits but just to take in the view, the huge curve of the Bay. But there was mist. The islands were not visible at all and only the lower slopes of Vesuvius could be seen. Sandison was not a superstitious man but he was disappointed. He felt that this little piece of bad luck might affect his whole day. He arrived at the café a full hour before he had intended.

He sat in the place that Maidstone had suggested, at a table at the end of the café's pavement area. This gave him a view up one of the sidestreets which led down to the corner of the square. He immediately started to watch the people arriving from that sidestreet. After a while he gave up. There were so many of them that the strain of trying to recognise each one started to give him a headache. He remembered Maidstone had said that ten thirty was the time, never before. He forced himself to be calm. He took out his Italian phrase book and studied it fiercely, learning nothing.

At twenty past ten Sandison put his book away and sat back to watch the people who were walking down to the square. He was glad that there were fewer than before. It was a bright day now but the café, tucked in at the foot of the buildings that hemmed in the square, was in the shade. It was cooler there and Sandison was glad of that too. The people heading for the square were mostly men although there were a few women, dressed in black. Sandison wondered what Elsie would be wearing, whether he would be able to recognise her at all. He remembered the built-up shoe.

He need not have worried. She was unmistakable. She was dressed in blue – a pale blue skirt which reached to mid-calf and a darker blue blouse buttoned to the throat. She had a light shawl wrapped round her shoulders. It was white with blue flowers on it. She stepped along quickly but quite gracefully. Sandison tried to catch a glimpse of her feet but found it difficult. He waited till she was closer.

For she passed by his table, within four or five feet of him. She paused too, just before she reached him, and he felt the whole thing could not have been stage-managed better. He watched her face as she scanned the street and the square ahead for a few seconds and then moved on. He remembered her as being pretty but this was quite the wrong word now. She was not beautiful either but the force of her attraction lay in her dignity, her confidence. This was a dimension he could not remember in the old Elsie. She was self-assured and unhesitating in her movements. Her head was held high, not out of arrogance, Sandison felt, but because she was interested if not engrossed in all there was before her. Her hair, which seemed much lighter than Sandison remembered, was gathered into a bun at the back. Her profile was strong but nevertheless pleasing.

He desperately wanted to get up and speak to her. She was here, the very person he had spent so much time and energy and money tracking down. She was only a few yards away. For a moment he felt that it did not matter what he had promised Maidstone. He failed to understand why that man was so adamant that he should not approach her. He half rose from his seat but at that point the waiter arrived with a coffee Sandison had forgotten he had ordered. The waiter obscured his view and distracted him. When he had gone, Sandison got to his feet but he had lost sight of Elsie. His attention had been drawn away for only five or six seconds and there were surely only half a dozen shops that she could have entered. If he were to run forward straight away he would almost certainly find her within a minute or two. As he debated this with himself, suddenly all urgency left him. He sat down. He would leave it. There was no point in taking risks at this stage. Besides, if Maidstone could predict so accurately when Elsie would appear then it would be a simple matter to find her again – perhaps at the same time tomorrow.

He took out the photograph which he always carried with him and compared it to the woman he had just seen. The physical likeness was inescapable but they looked totally different in character. The photo showed a young, happy woman smiling brightly towards the camera. The face had an openness and a gentleness that were not there to the same degree in this new Elsie who was more poised, a little more distant. The photograph had been taken in the late twenties, seventeen or eighteen years before. This shift of time was not apparent in the woman Sandison had just seen. She appeared more mature, bore herself in a different manner but did not look more than six or seven years older than her earlier self.

Sandison got up, put a few coins on the café table and set off to meet Maidstone. As he left the café he realised that he had forgotten to look at Elsie's feet.

At Franco's bar, Maidstone said no. 'No, absolutely no.' They were standing at the bar with their first glasses of wine in front of them. 'Completely, utterly, categorically no.'

'But why not?'

'You just don't realise what risks you run. You're interested in something that just isn't your business . . .'

'But it is my business.'

'No, it isn't. It doesn't matter what you think, it's what people round here think and I can tell you now that you could get yourself into serious trouble.'

'I'll take the risk.'

Maidstone laughed out loud. 'My God you're so naïve! You have no idea how things operate in this city. No earthly idea.'

'But I've come all the way from . . .'

'Irrelevant!' This was almost a shout. 'Who the hell cares how far you've come. You're a threat. You're a threat and nobody in this place tolerates that, least of all the Stasis . . .' He shook his head at his blunder. 'Oh shit!' he said loudly and then, quietly: 'Look what you've made me do.'

'Is that her name, then?'

Maidstone looked very put out but grudgingly replied: 'Yes.'

'What was it? Stazi?'

'Stasi. Her name is Elisa Stasi and that's the last bit of information you're getting out of me on the subject. Remember our agreement.'

Sandison remembered some vague promise he had made about leaving the city when he was satisfied that Elsie was indeed alive and well.

'You made a promise,' Maidstone said.

'So I did. Well, I never meant to keep it.'

'I realise that now. I should have realised it then too.'

'You were drunk,' Sandison said. 'You were drunk when you told me where to see her. Now you regret it and not because of the trouble I'll get into but the trouble *you'll* get into.'

'I . . .'

'Just be quiet and listen. You don't trust me and you never have. And I don't trust you. Unfortunately from your point of view we're both in this together now. We sink or swim together. Too many people have seen us over the past two or three days so anything I do will be linked to you. I understand just as much as you do what the dangers are. Give me credit for a little intelligence at least. You've got this superior idea that I'm some sort of half-wit from the back of beyond who hasn't the vaguest notion of what happens in the big, bad world. Well let me tell you that you're the one that's slipped up, not me. You know it too, and you're scared as hell. You've got a bigger problem than I have, though – you can't leave here but

I can. You can't leave here because no other place would tolerate you or be able to support you. You know that too and that's part of the reason why you befuddle yourself with drink. Don't get me wrong, I've done it myself in the past and seen just how far it got me. Absolutely nowhere, that's where it got me. And that's where you are now. This place is nowhere for you but it's the only place you can exist. So, if you want to stay here, you'll help me out and if you don't . . . well, we're both in trouble.'

Throughout this speech of Sandison's Maidstone stood motionless at the bar, unable to say a word. At the end he looked crushed and forlorn, crumpled like the brim of his dirty grey hat. For a moment Sandison almost felt sorry for him. Nothing was said for a while and then Maidstone straightened himself up.

'Right,' he said. 'Well . . .' Sandison could not be sure how much Maidstone had had to drink that day – it was still a few minutes before noon – but he knew that he was sober enough to understand fully what was going on.

'I suppose you want to meet her, then,' Maidstone said. There was no emotion in his voice and none showing in his face.

'Yes.'

'Right. I'll . . . I'll see what I can do.'

'I'll see you here tomorrow at ten o'clock,' Sandison said. His tone was sharp.

'I say, that's a bit early, old fellow.' Maidstone attempted a smile.

'No, it isn't, it's late,' Sandison said. 'Ten sharp.'

'Right . . . well . . .' Maidstone turned towards the door. 'I'll see you at ten then.' He walked slowly out into the hot street. Sandison waited for one minute and then also left, setting off in the opposite direction from Maidstone.

In the bar Franco collected the glasses. One of them still had two or three mouthfuls of wine in it. He was almost certain that it belonged to Maidstone but he would never leave half a glass of wine behind, surely. Very strange.

It took Maidstone four hours to decide what to do and during that time he drank only coffee. He managed to stay off alcohol because for the first time for a very long time he was truly afraid. He had been afraid before. The last time was during the War, while he was living in London. A German bomb had reduced the house next door to rubble and part of the ceiling of his own room had caved in on top of him. He had been scared then but it had been short-lived: terror lasting a matter of a few seconds, a minute at most. It was different now. There was a good chance that this Sandison fellow would cause trouble and he would be linked to it. And of course, it had to be the Stasis. My God, couldn't he have chosen another family. Maidstone craved a drink but he had to stay sober. He was going to visit someone and he had to be clean, bright, well-dressed, smart and quite definitely sober.

Maidstone rented a tiny apartment at the top of a very dilapidated building in the Vomero. When he got back there after leaving Sandison – after being dismissed by Sandison – he stood in the centre of his small untidy sitting room and removed every stitch of clothing he had on. He washed himself as best he could at the sink in the bathroom. He managed this with the help of a flannel, some scented soap from England which he kept for special occasions and a kettleful of hot water that took five minutes to boil on the single electric ring that served as a cooker and, in winter, as a heater. The bathroom had no shower and no hot water.

Maidstone was used to all this and he had got the procedures worked out so well that very little mess was involved. He placed an old towel on the bathroom floor so that it would not get wet and he ensured that everything he needed was within reach so that he did not have to move from the spot and so drip water everywhere. He hated everything to do with household chores and keeping the place clean so he concentrated hard on creating as little mess as possible. His apartment was certainly untidy but it was not dirty.

After washing himself down he shaved, trimmed his moustache, brushed his teeth, gargled and then greased and combed his hair. He scrubbed his hands until they were nearly raw. He spent five minutes cleaning his nails with a nailbrush. He inspected his face again and then his hands. He checked the state of his teeth. He seemed satisfied.

After making sure that his feet were dry, he left the bathroom, wrapped in a towel. From a chest of drawers in his bedroom he drew out a clean, well-ironed white shirt and a dark blue regimental tie. He had no right to wear the tie but he felt that it was rather distinguished and so far no one had caught him out. He took out fresh underwear and fresh socks. He laid all these items on the bed before searching in the small wardrobe for his only other suit. This search was not difficult as there were few other items in there – a couple of jackets, a greatcoat and five or six pairs of trousers. He wore the suit rarely and in one of the few points of discipline which he managed to impose on himself he always made sure that the suit, or the trousers at least, were pressed immediately after use. This not only kept the suit in good condition and therefore prolonged its life but also provided him with a smart outfit always ready at short notice, as now.

Maidstone dressed with care on this occasion and presented a very different figure from the usually dishevelled and always crumpled one who frequented Franco's bar. In fact, were Franco to see him now, he would very likely not recognise Maidstone who, sobered up, shaved, scrubbed and polished, in well-cut black suit and shining black shoes, looked quite the man about town. He also looked about ten years younger.

He made one last check – as best he could – in the tiny shaving mirror in the bathroom and then left his apartment. Once in the street he walked at a gentle pace. He had only a few hundred yards to go as the house he was planning to visit was also in the Vomero but he did not wish to arrive with perspiration on his forehead or dust on his shoes.

He reached the door, or rather the cast-iron gate as his destination was a villa, quite a large villa with a central courtyard. There was a bell-pull connected up to a small porter's lodge inside. Maidstone paused and took a deep breath. He desperately needed a drink but he knew he had to get through the next little while – ten minutes, half an hour, an hour – completely sober. After all, his life might depend on it. He rang the bell and when he was greeted by a rather surly butler he enquired, very politely, if it might be possible for him to speak with the Signora Calvino on a matter of the utmost urgency.

In his *pensione* Sandison slept for two hours in the afternoon. When he got up he sat on his bed and wrote a letter:

Naples
June 7th, 1947

Dear Stewart,

I've found her and I've actually seen her! She calls herself Elisa these days and she's married to someone called Stasi. It seems the Stasis are a well-known and influential family in this city, so she's done all right for herself. I've managed to arrange to meet her and talk to her and this should take place tomorrow (though it's being organised by a very unreliable man, one of the expatriate drunks that live here). So, I'll send you more information after I've talked to her. Anyway, run the story, Stewart, run it now. Can you think of a better way to boost circulation?

Yours,
Albert

As he was going to be passing the post office on his way to his favourite restaurant Sandison decided to post the letter himself. He put on his hat and went out.

A CHANGE OF HATS

WHEN Sandison arrived at Franco's bar the next morning at ten to ten, Maidstone was already there, sitting at a table, drinking coffee. 'I've fixed it,' he said straight away, without offering Sandison any greeting.

'Good.' Sandison sat down opposite him.

Maidstone mentioned an address in the Vomero and told Sandison to be there at nine o'clock.

'Nine? Tonight?'

'Yes.'

'It's a bit late, isn't it?'

'Take it or leave it.'

Maidstone was a different man. When Sandison had last seen him he had been a sad figure, a man approaching old age, tired, dishevelled and drunk. Now he was sharp and alert and as curt and direct as Sandison had been to him the day before.

'I think I prefer you drunk,' Sandison said.

'Do you now. Well, I think I do too but that's neither here nor there.'

'Are you coming?'

'What?'

'Are you coming to the Stasi place?'

'No, no I'm not.' He pulled out a folded sheet of paper from his inside pocket. 'I've drawn you a little map,' he said.

Sandison spread out the paper on the table and studied it.

'Start from Piazza Vanvitelli which is near the top of the *funicolare*, there.' Maidstone prodded the appropriate spot on the map.

'Right, yes. I've got you.'

'Then just . . . well, follow the arrows I've marked. You'll have no problem.'

'No, I think that'll be fine.'

Maidstone rose.

'Can I get you a drink?' Sandison asked, surprised to see Maidstone leaving so quickly.

'No thanks, no.'

'Another coffee?' Sandison had not intended this to sound like a jibe but it did.

'No, I'd better be off, I think.'

'Well, look, thanks for fixing things up for me. I'm grateful.'

'Yes, well, it wasn't too difficult after all.' He started for the door.

Sandison rose and shouted after him: 'Tomorrow. Will you be here tomorrow morning?'

Maidstone was at the door. He turned and after a few seconds said: 'Probably.' Then he added: 'Possibly.'

'I'll see you then,' Sandison said. Maidstone disappeared. Sandison looked over at Franco behind the bar. He was as bewildered by Maidstone's behaviour as Sandison was. '*Pazzo*,' he said. '*Pazzo*.' Crazy.

Getting through the day proved difficult for Sandison. He felt on edge about meeting Elsie or Elisa or whatever her name was now. Also, he realised that as he was reaching the end of his search he was reaching the end of his time in Naples as well. He had enjoyed the city and would have liked to stay longer. After he got home to Scotland he would write about Elsie, perhaps not just for the paper but for himself too. He thought he might write a book about it all. And then? He had no idea what he would do after that. Staying in a small town in the north of Scotland and working on the local newspaper for the rest of his life suddenly seemed a dismal prospect. He had never been out of Scotland before but he did not feel at all homesick. Quite the reverse; he was not looking forward to going back.

He thought of his wife and child whom he had not seen for over a month. He had not really missed them. He had written two letters, both to Stewart, nothing to his wife. He was intelligent enough to understand that his search for Elsie was, in part, an escape from his own family. If this Elisa woman really was Elsie – and he was convinced that she was – how he envied her. How he admired her ability just to walk out, disappear, leave everything and everyone. He wondered if he would ever be able to do such a thing himself.

He decided to fill in the day by making arrangements for his departure from the city. He told the owner of the *pensione* that he would probably be leaving in a few days and then he made his way to the station to ask about trains. He decided against buying a ticket there and then but satisfied himself with getting a list of trains to Rome. He made no enquiries about travelling any farther than that.

In the late afternoon he got back to his room, tired and unsettled. He managed to sleep for a couple of hours, then rose and wandered off to Franco's bar to see if Maidstone was there. He glanced round the bar from the door. No Maidstone. He was about to leave when he was spotted by Franco who called out to him. He went in and Franco, unbidden, poured him a whisky. Surprised at this, as whisky was in very short supply in the city, Sandison asked what was going on. '*Una brutta notizia*,' Franco said. Bad news. He set off on a long rambling account of something that had happened in the bar that afternoon. Sandison found it very difficult to understand him because he spoke very quickly and occasionally slipped into Neapolitan dialect. The whole thing had to be repeated three or four times before Sandison got the gist.

It seemed that Maidstone, who had been completely sober at ten o'clock when he left the bar, returned at about midday, still sober, but immediately started drinking heavily. By two o'clock he was very drunk indeed. Franco had never seen him so drunk and, although Maidstone's intake of alcohol had often been greater on past occasions, this time he just went to pieces. '*Non ce la fa piú*,' Franco explained. He just couldn't take it. At five past two Franco took the unprecedented step of refusing to serve him any more wine.

Maidstone had become quite abusive at this, swearing at Franco in English, Italian and Neapolitan dialect. He insisted that no one but he himself could decide whether he was going to drink or not and anyway, he had plenty of money, enough to buy all the drink in the bar if he wanted. He produced a wad of large denomination bills and waved them in Franco's face. Franco became very alarmed at this and told him to put his money away immediately. But by this time Maidstone was beyond all reason. He started to shout and scream, demanding that he be served with wine. Franco did not know what to do. If it had been one of the local men, he explained to Sandison, there would have been no problem, but Maidstone was another matter. He wasn't sure of Maidstone's connections, what friends he had. It was a tricky business.

Eventually Maidstone tried to scramble over the bar but he slipped and fell heavily onto the floor. His head collided with a table on the way down and he knocked himself out. For a few anxious moments Franco thought he was dead but he came round within a minute or so although he remained in a semi-conscious state. It was clear that he was in no condition to get himself home unaided.

It was Franco himself who took Maidstone home. He got his brother to look after the bar for an hour or so, bundled Maidstone into a taxi driven by a friend of his and set off for Maidstone's apartment in the Vomero. He managed to get Maidstone inside the building and upstairs without upsetting the *portiera* too much. Unfortunately the apartment was at the very top and it was quite a struggle to drag Maidstone up the eight or ten flights of stairs. There was no lift.

Franco put Maidstone to bed. He had taken Maidstone's money from him in the bar. He returned this now, putting the bundle of notes in the inside pocket of the creased, off-white linen jacket. When he left the apartment Maidstone was snoring.

It was hard work trying to understand Franco and by the end of the last telling of the story Sandison was happy to accept a second, though rather smaller, whisky. He also agreed to go round to Maidstone's apartment to see how he was. Franco repeated that Maidstone was crazy but he was a good man and a good customer too. He gave Sandison the address and asked him to do three things: check that Maidstone was all right, check that he still had his money and give him back his hat. From under the counter Franco produced the familiar battered grey hat which had been left behind in the confusion surrounding their departure for Maidstone's apartment.

Sandison took the hat and turned it over in his hands. He tried to straighten out the brim but it had been curled and folded so often it was beyond repair. The material sprang back into the uneven creases that had been shaped by Maidstone's nervous, insistent fingers. Sandison looked across at Franco and shrugged. He turned and headed for the door where he paused for a moment. It felt strange to be in possession of two hats. On an impulse he returned to the bar, took off his own hat, the one he had bought on Maidstone's advice, and handed it over to Franco for safe keeping. He left the bar with Maidstone's hat in his hand, gripping it firmly by the brim.

It was just after seven so he had two hours before his appointment with Elisa Stasi. He reckoned he had enough time to see Maidstone, then get down to the *pensione* and change before making his way back up to the Vomero again. However, it would not do to dawdle. He set off at a brisk pace for the lower station of the *funicolare* by Piazza Amedeo.

On the way there, Sandison saw how the pace of things had changed. For several weeks now he had been chipping away at this problem of finding Elsie, slowly nagging it into submission. The job had required perseverance and, above all, patience. Now, inexplicably, just as he was about to reach his goal, things had suddenly speeded up. Too many things demanded his attention at the same time. He wanted to arrive at the Stasis in a calm frame of mind; he wanted to settle himself and prepare for it. Instead of that, he had become involved in what was most likely a wild goose chase. Maidstone was almost certainly all right, just sleeping off the effects of too much drink. Sandison could imagine the reception: 'Worried about me? My dear fellow!' For a moment he wondered if he should leave his visit to Maidstone till later, till after he had met Elsie. He actually paused in front of the *funicolare* station and considered this.

He found that he was rolling and unrolling the brim of Maidstone's hat in his fingers. He glanced at his watch and decided there was still time. He went into the station.

The building that housed Maidstone's apartment was in poor shape. Half of the stucco work had crumbled away and some of the shutters on the windows had broken free of their hinges to dangle precariously over the street. There were cracks in the walls and the steps up to the entrance had been reduced to an uneven and rocky slope. It was the last block in the street and the side wall was supported by a network of wooden scaffolding that stretched all the way up to the fifth floor. The building had survived the earthquake of two years before, but only just. Sandison was amazed that it was still standing.

The *portiera* was an old deaf lady and it took Sandison five minutes to explain who he was and who he wanted to visit. He made his way up to the top floor, found Maidstone's apartment and knocked on the door. There was no reply. He began hammering on the door and calling out Maidstone's name. Still no reply. He went back down and confronted the *portiera* again. He explained that Maidstone was ill and that it was essential to get inside the apartment to see how he was. It took him another five minutes to get across the fact that no, he was not a doctor but yes, he was a friend, a very good friend. The *portiera* was clearly unimpressed by anything Sandison said. Finally, exasperated, he produced ten lire. The effect was immediate.

The old lady was quite sprightly for her age but it took a long time for them both to reach the top floor. She obviously trusted no one else with the keys to the apartments. The selection of the correct key added on another minute or so and Sandison could only look on feeling helpless and frustrated.

He burst into the apartment. Maidstone was still in bed, lying on his back with his mouth open. His face was grotesquely puffed and had taken on the colour of dark purple. Sandison did not even bother to check his pulse or try to revive him. Maidstone was dead. The old lady, following Sandison into the tiny bedroom, dropped to her knees, crossed herself and started up a high-pitched wailing, interspersed with fragments of speech which Sandison found completely incomprehensible. He decided that the best thing for him to do was to leave as soon as possible, before other people arrived and the situation became very complicated. After all, there was nothing he could do to help Maidstone now. He backed out of the bedroom, leaving the old lady still on her knees before the bed. He glanced round the small untidy sitting room and saw Maidstone's jacket on the back of a chair, presumably placed there by Franco. He quickly searched through the pockets.

There was no wad of money. For some reason this did not surprise him at all.

He got out of the building and into the street as quickly as he could. He hurried away until he had managed to put half a mile between himself and the body of Maidstone and then he slowed down. He flicked back the cuff of his jacket to glance at his watch and as he did so he saw that he was still carrying Maidstone's hat. His first impulse was to throw it away, to rid himself of anything that might link him with Maidstone and Maidstone's death. Then he thought better of it. What did it matter, really? He held onto the hat and hurried on.

He was running short of time. He might have to abandon his return to the *pensione* to change and go straight to the Stasi address. That depended, of course, on whether he decided to go through with it or not. The whole thing was getting out of control. Without doubt there was a sinister side to events now. Maidstone's peculiar behaviour earlier that day, Franco's strange tale about the pile of money Maidstone had showed him in the bar and now Maidstone's death itself. It was just possible, Sandison thought, that Maidstone had died naturally – if choking to death in your sleep after a huge binge could be called natural – but that would not explain the disappearance of the money. If there had been any money in the first place.

No, Maidstone had been right all along: Sandison knew nothing about what went on in the city. He had naïvely stumbled into the middle of a very complicated and dangerous situation.

Sandison desperately wanted to meet Elisa Stasi but he was not prepared to risk his life doing it. He paused at a street corner and tried to come to a decision. He looked round and realised that he was not quite sure where he was. He had intended to head back to the *funicolare* station but perhaps he had taken a wrong turning somewhere in his hurry to get away from Maidstone's apartment. It would not be too difficult for him to find his way again, however. He was fairly sure that the edge of the Vomero, the slope of the hill, the Bay and the sea lay to his right. He imagined himself to be in the centre of the city now, surrounded by its magnificent old crumbling buildings, its churches and palaces, villas and castles filled with the rich trappings of the centuries and set about by the bustle, the noise, the filth, squalor and abject poverty of the streets. No, it was too much for him to understand; he could stay here for years and never understand it.

Yet here he was, so very very near to his goal. If he gave up now it would be like walking a hundred miles and then refusing to take the very last single step that would complete the journey. He was holding Maidstone's hat in both hands, turning it, feeding the brim inch by inch through his fingers. Abruptly he stopped doing this, took hold of the brim on either side of the crown, raised the hat and placed it firmly on his head.

Suddenly he had the strangest feeling. He felt that the forces that had brought him to this narrow corner of a Neapolitan street – the wish, on the one hand, to track down Elsie and now the fear, on the other, that this search would lead him to harm – these forces might hold him there, his foot on the edge of the pavement overhanging the choked and filthy gutter, in a kind of uneasy equilibrium and he might stay there for a long, long time.

PART FIVE
1936

THE BEAUTIFUL CITY

FROM the broad and busy thoroughfare of the Riviera di Chiaia which is separated from the sea by the Villa Nazionale, a narrow strip of untidy parkland, the little street called Santa Maria in Portico leads inland and uphill over uneven cobbles to the church which bears the same name. In a city of splendid ecclesiastical architecture ranging from the mediaeval to the baroque the Church of Santa Maria in Portico is unremarkable. Several other churches have green domes topped with cupolas; there are many buildings with a more impressive sweep of steps from street level up to the main door; larger and better-kept churches abound. Throughout its three-hundred-year history the Church of Santa Maria has frequently been clothed in the wooden scaffolding that has allowed builders to attempt repairs after recent earthquakes. The church has been jarred and cracked, shaken and split more times than historians have been able to count. With every tremor a stone falls, a joint is widened or a lintel is dislodged. The massive front door once refused to open when the alignment of the doorposts was shifted. The local people took this as a sign of displeasure from the Almighty who was shutting the doors of his house against his sinning congregation.

That the church still stands is itself remarkable. Because it is not one of the more imposing buildings for which public funds are more readily available, it has had to rely on the care and attention of those who live around it and they are among the poorer people of the city. Their houses, the tall, crumbling tenements with their cracked roof tiles and their creaking balconies huddle together round the church as if they want to shoulder it out of the way. Some local people also work close to the church, daily setting out their stalls of fruit, vegetables or fish in the narrow alleyways, the *vicoli*, which spread out from the tiny square, no more than a broadening of the road really, before the church. Some of these people have never left this area of town, have never passed a day of their lives without seeing, if not entering, the Church of Santa Maria. After mid-morning Sunday mass many come from the church, walk down the short steep hill of Santa Maria in Portico, cross the Riviera di Chiaia and stroll along the Villa Nazionale for a sight of the sea and the majestic sweep of the rocky shore of the Bay of Naples.

One very warm morning in June 1936 a young woman left her room on the fourth floor of a *pensione* at the west end of the Riviera di Chiaia and descended to street level. As she was about to leave the building she exchanged greetings with the *portiera* who handed her a letter which had arrived earlier the same day. The young woman glanced at the letter, whose envelope was quite dog-eared, and put it, unopened, inside her brown leather handbag. With a murmur of thanks to the *portiera* she stepped out into the street.

She was a slim, attractive woman in her late twenties and had long fair hair which was tightly piled up under a straw boater. She was wearing a white blouse, frilled with lace at collar and cuffs, and a long, mid-grey cotton skirt. From the front door of the rambling *palazzo* which housed the *pensione* she turned left and walked along the Riviera. She very much wanted to read the letter she had received and she thought of crossing over to the Villa Nazionale. There she could sit at one of the outdoor cafés and read her letter undisturbed while sipping a cool drink of lemon or perhaps iced tea. She decided to delay the moment, however, and increase her expectation by leaving the letter until later on. She would complete her morning's business first and then retire to one of the cafés in the park.

Glad to leave the bright sunlight of the Riviera and the noise of the traffic she turned from the main street into Santa Maria in Portico. Although her quest was not one of religious devotion her destination was the Church of Santa Maria. She walked slowly up the street on the shaded side, stepping carefully round the stalls set up on the pavement and the goods displayed by some vendors which were spread out on cloths on the pavement itself. Every two or three yards she was accosted, '*Signora! Signora!*' as a ripe fruit or some trinket or other was thrust before her for her inspection. She was used to this by now and dealt with every approach quietly and without fuss. She was careful to show no interest whatever in anything that was shown to her.

Halfway up the street she paused to look above the church to the hill beyond. A few villas, white or pale yellow buildings, could be seen dotted haphazardly across the face of the hill, separated by small groves of olive trees and the occasional stand of poplars. Near the top of the hill stood the large white building which was the San Martino Museum and above it, and in contrast to the museum's firm elegant lines, could be seen the solid brown ramparts of St Elmo's Castle. Beyond the castle there was nothing but deep blue sky.

The young woman had visited both the museum and the castle before and had looked down from their heights onto the epidemic of streets below, between the top of the hill and the broad curve of the Bay. She had been impressed by the view, the quite breath-taking view, from the headland of Posillipo round to the curiously named Egg Castle, a box of brown stone on its rocky promontory in the Bay and on farther to the Sorrento Peninsula beyond. The islands had been pointed out to her, Capri and Procida and the ghost of an outline of Ischia. She had seen the boats in the Bay, pleasure boats to the islands and the bigger commercial vessels entering and leaving the port area. From her vantage point in the museum and later in St Elmo's Castle she had spent several minutes in wonder at the view. On both occasions she had been struck by the contrast between on the one hand the beauty of the Bay itself, the islands, the fine buildings towards Posillipo and on the other the cramped and jumbled desperation of the mean and bustly streets immediately below her.

During the few moments in which she paused in her ascent to the church she reflected that now she was looking at the view the other way round; now she was in one of the overcrowded little alleys visible from San Martino as merely a crack in a vast expanse of roof tiles and crumbling masonry and noticeable from that lofty vantage point because of the fluttering of the washing hung out on poles over the street to dry. Perhaps there were more of these poles in Santa Maria in Portico than in other *vicoli* because there were two laundries in the street. The buildings above these laundries displayed the densest clustering of washing poles. The young woman smiled as she imagined a broad rectangular ship with scores of short stubby masts and multi-coloured, ragged sails cruising up the face of the building.

She had visited many such *vicoli* before, but rarely unaccompanied. Her present situation was the result of her growing confidence in her own ability to cope with events and her increased understanding of the language. She felt herself to be reasonably proficient in Italian and she had begun, rather to the disapproval of her employers, to learn a few words of the Neapolitan dialect. The dangers of the Naples street-life did not bother her; she believed that no one would mistreat her. So far, no one had.

The two laundries were towards the top of the street, near the church. This was just as well because the washing was not only hung up on poles above but spread out upon drying racks in the street itself. Had the laundries been at the Riviera end all the detritus from the other businesses, the discarded vegetables and smashed fruit of the greengrocers, the scales and fish heads and guts deposited on the street by the two fishmongers, would have passed by and probably soiled some of the clothes as the intermittent hosing down of the street caused all this muck and filth to edge its way slowly down towards the Bay. As she crossed the street towards the far corner by the church entrance, the young woman was careful to step over the littering of prawn shells and orange peel, fish tails and broken heads of artichoke that had accumulated in the numerous depressions afforded by the badly laid cobbles. The smell was unpleasant too but she resisted the temptation to remove her scented handkerchief from the cuff of her blouse. She did not wish to display any gesture that could be interpreted as precious or affected.

She must have been noticed as being very different from the local ladies who were either young girls dressed tidily but poorly, or older women in black. There seemed to be few females outwith these two categories. Consequently, this young woman would have aroused curiosity because she was well dressed and, though no longer a girl, she was not wearing black. There was also the fact that she had fair hair only partly hidden under her straw boater, a most peculiar hat in these parts.

She was not unapproachable, however. Cries of '*Signora! Signora!*' continued as she made her way to the top of the street. Determined but polite efforts were made to interest her in the purchase of tomatoes, plums, oranges, artichokes, mussels, scallops, chickens and even a swordfish steak. The fishmonger at the top, opposite the church, was selling this last item. Half of an enormous fish – the head end with its sword broken off but still nearly two feet long – was laid out on a trestle table and the fishmonger was slicing inch-thick steaks from it. She made the mistake of pausing here and inspecting the fish. It was an error because the fishmonger immediately started to cut a steak for her. She remonstrated with him and explained that she had stopped because she had never seen such a fish before. It was so big. Oh, very very big, he explained and stepped away from the end of the table to indicate with his hand where the tail would have been on this particular specimen. She expressed her wonder at this and asked for the name in Italian. *Pesce spada*, he told her. He performed a brief mime of someone fencing. This drew a little laughter from one or two shoppers who had gathered to listen to the exchange between the fishmonger and this well dressed and clearly foreign lady.

Spada. Of course. A sword. She explained that it was a sword too in English. Ah, said the fishmonger, so you are English. Scottish, the young woman corrected him. Ah, *Scozzese!* Of course. He complimented her on her Italian which was very good, he said, very, very good. The group round about murmured their agreement. And was she a visitor in Naples? No, she lived there. Wonderful! Wonderful! And what did she think of the city? This city, she said clearly and confidently, is the most beautiful city in the world. This brought out a few gasps of admiration from the onlookers. *Bella!* said the fishmonger. So beautiful! He raised his hands to the sky.

But so many problems, so many, many problems! He shook his head as he registered this fact. All cities, the young woman said, all cities have their problems. So true, he agreed, so very, very true. She smiled and took her leave. The fishmonger blessed her for calling and wished her a continued pleasant time in their beautiful city.

The interest that the young woman had engendered had spread beyond the fishmonger's stall. The women by the next couple of street sellers paused in their shopping to watch her pass and two or three men who had heard her conversation raised their hats to her. Two others had noticed her as well. They were boys of fifteen or sixteen and they were watching her keenly from a position by the railings at the far corner of the church.

As she made her way across to the church steps she found herself suddenly in bright sunlight and away from the crowds. She paused at the bottom of the wide stone staircase and looked up at the heavy doors of the church which had been drawn back and allowed a partial view of the dark interior of the building. The doorway itself was framed by the network of wooden scaffolding which covered most of the front of the church. There had been a severe tremor a couple of years before and repair work was still going on.

Lowering her gaze from the intense sunlight reflected on the upper walls to the leaded doors, she placed a foot on the first stone step. She was only dimly aware of the approach of the two boys who were walking swiftly from the street corner. One skipped up the steps and passed directly in front of her, brushing against her. Her surprise at this and her immediate step backwards allowed the other one, now passing behind her, the opportunity to wrench her handbag from her grasp. Somehow she managed to grab hold of his shirt and she shouted out her resistance. The first boy, still above her, turned and pushed her violently to the ground. They both then sprinted off and were out of sight before the group of concerned shoppers could reach her as she lay in a faint on the bottom step below the church.

When she regained consciousness she found herself lying on a large settee in a dimly lit room. There were several female faces above her and the sounds of the street still reached her though they seemed distant and somewhat muffled. Someone asked if she was all right and she found this such a strange question. Why on earth would someone ask her that? She was unsure how to reply. The question was repeated. Something cool and damp was pressed to her forehead. She began to remember what had happened. She tried to raise herself from the settee but gentle hands restrained her. I am all right, she said, I am fine, but she made no further attempt to rise. She felt very tired and as she shifted position she detected an ache in her left hip. Her left elbow was tingling too and as she felt for it with her right hand she found that the sleeve of her blouse had been torn. Her forearm below the elbow was bruised.

Her head was clearing and she wondered how long she had been unconscious. She was about to ask the nearest of the women when she suddenly realised fully what had happened. 'My bag!' she said out loud and then, more softly but with more than a touch of anguish, 'Oh no, the letter!'

Despite the protests she sat up now and swung her feet from the settee. Her hat lay beside her and she found that her piled-up fair hair had been released and had fallen about her face. She accepted a glass of water and for the first time looked round in order to take in the room and the people before her. She felt herself to be still very slightly dazed, disorientated enough to give the impression that she was a disinterested observer of the scene and not quite able to realise that these things were in fact happening to her. She was in a large room which was well furnished. It seemed to be a parlour or sitting room. The marble floor was scattered about with individual rugs. The large settee, upholstered in dark blue material, was one of a suite with three matching armchairs. She noticed an open fireplace with an ornate mantelshelf in black marble. Above this was a large rectangular mirror in a gilt frame. The walls of the room were pale green. There was an upright piano in the far corner with a row of framed photographs on top. A glass-fronted cabinet displayed a collection of crib figures. She could see French windows at the far end of the room. Heavy dark green velvet curtains were partly drawn across these and allowed only a single column of light to enter the room. There were three women before her, none of whom was dressed in black.

So much detail was not available to her then but she would have agreed to it all and later she would be able to describe more of the room, the contents of the cabinets, even the names of the people represented in the photographs on top of the piano; she did not know then that this was the first of many visits to this room.

Of the three ladies who were attending to her, two were in middle age and the third in her early thirties. This younger woman was very attractive with a dark complexion and thick black hair tied in a pony tail. Her face was made up, though not too obviously so, and she wore lipstick. This in itself seemed unusual. The lipstick was dark red and matched the colour of her carefully manicured nails. It was the shiny red of these nails that the woman on the settee noticed with surprise as another glass of water was offered to her. She accepted the glass and muttered a word of thanks. The woman before her introduced herself as Antonietta Calvino.

Antonietta sat beside her on the settee and explained that a doctor would be along soon. A doctor? the visitor asked. But of course a doctor as she had injuries to be seen to. At that moment one of the other two women who had left the room for a couple of minutes returned with a bowl of water and began to bathe the injured arm.

Also, I will get for you another blouse, Antonietta said. And then, striking a dramatic pose she announced that she was terribly ashamed. Ashamed? Why yes, ashamed that the people of my city have done this terrible thing to you. But of course these boys, these disgusting creatures, these street urchins unworthy of being called Neapolitan, they were not from this area at all, no, not at all.

There was a commotion at the door and a tall elderly man entered. He had a grey walrus moustache and was wearing a collarless shirt with the sleeves rolled up. He carried a leather bag which he placed on the floor by the settee. Antonietta greeted him and introduced him as Dr Silvino. As she did so she realised she did not yet know the name of their unexpected guest. She asked the woman on the settee to reveal her identity. You may call me Elisa, she said.

Twenty minutes later Elisa was fully recovered from the incident although her arm still ached slightly under Dr Silvino's expert bandaging. Antonietta had given her a blouse which, she noticed with interest, was of superior quality to her own. She had arranged her hair again and reinstated her hat though as she performed this operation at the dressing table in Antonietta's elegant bedroom she thought how ridiculous the hat looked. She would buy another soon, an altogether different one.

Back in the main sitting room where she had been at first she was introduced to Antonietta's husband Gennaro who was the head of the household. He was about thirty-five and of medium build but beginning to fill out. In spite of the heat he was very smartly dressed in a dark three-piece suit. He had returned for lunch from his office in the city centre. After the introduction had been made Antonietta left the room.

'I am most upset that you have been treated so badly by my countrymen,' Gennaro said in a quiet steady voice. 'I can only apologise for them.'

Elisa was surprised to be addressed in English and remarked upon this.

'I have spent some time in the United States,' he explained. 'Many of my family are there.'

'I see.'

'And you, *signora*, you are from England, no?'

'In fact no, I'm Scottish, from Scotland.'

'Ah, *Scozzese*!' he said, smiling. 'Of course I know that I must not make this mistake. It is very serious, no?'

'Not at all,' Elisa replied. 'But I cannot say what I am not.'

'Ah, to be so honest, it is a great virtue, a great virtue.' He had seated himself in an armchair adjacent to the settee to which Elisa had naturally returned although now she was sitting rather prim and upright on the edge. Gennaro seemed quite relaxed. He had a pleasant face whose lines were more likely the result of his generally cheerful disposition rather than worry or the onset of middle age. A full and very black moustache covered his upper lip and during conversation he frequently smoothed it down in a rather absent-minded fashion with the forefinger of his right hand. He turned and said something that Elisa could not quite catch to a young girl, unnoticed before, who had stationed herself by the door. She muttered a brief reply and left.

'My wife has informed me that the two boys who attacked you stole your handbag.'

'That's correct, yes.'

'Terrible! Terrible! To bring such shame upon the area . . .' He shook his head. 'But tell me, was there much of value in the handbag? My wife has informed me . . .'

'Nothing of great value,' Elisa cut in, 'except a letter.'

'A letter?'

'Yes, a letter I received this morning from a dear friend of mine . . .'

'A letter . . .' Gennaro seemed unsure how to react to this. '. . . From a dear friend, you say . . .'

'Yes, but unopened . . .'

'Oh . . .'

'I received it as I came out this morning and I didn't have time to open it.'

'Ah . . .'

'There was nothing else in the bag . . . a little money . . . a few other things of no importance.'

'And your papers?'

'I wasn't carrying them.'

'No?'

'No, I left them in my *pensione*.'

'Forgive me . . . *signora* . . .'

'. . . *Signorina*.'

'Ah, excuse me, *signorina*. Yes. Forgive me but it seems to me strange that a lady such as you . . . how shall I say . . . should stay in a *pensione*. You are . . . you are comfortable there?'

'For the moment, yes.'

'I see.'

Her confident reply dissuaded him from further questions along this line. He decided to return to the question of the letter.

'This letter,' he began, 'this letter is very important for you?'

'Yes, it is. It's very important. It will take some weeks now before I can contact my friend and ask him . . . ask for the information to be repeated.'

'Yes, I see. So, a letter from home, no?'

'Yes.'

'I see.' Gennaro saw quite a lot. He had noticed the slight hesitation over the gender of the letter writer. He was still intrigued by the sudden arrival of this most attractive English . . . no, Scottish . . . lady in Naples, living in a *pensione*, receiving letters from a male friend from her home. Some of the pieces began to fit but there was a great deal more that he wished to find out. Suddenly he rose. 'You must excuse me, *signorina* but I will make now some telephone calls. You will stay to lunch of course.'

'Well, *signore* . . .' Elisa rose in some confusion, wishing to remonstrate with her host about the abundance of his generosity. She was too late however, as he was already at the door and a moment later, without a further word, he was gone.

Lunch was a grand if rather noisy affair. The twelve at the table included Antonietta's three children and her mother. There were also two of Antonietta's brothers, a brother and sister-in-law of Gennaro's and one of Gennaro's uncles. The food was served by three maids and a man who gave the impression he was the major-domo of the house. He was particularly smartly dressed in black trousers and waistcoat, white shirt and red bow-tie. Elisa realised that she had stumbled, almost literally, into a very well-to-do household.

During the meal Elisa was able to find out what had happened to her immediately after the attack on the steps of the church. A small crowd had gathered and she had been carried across the street and inside the nearest shop in order to get her out of the sun. Efforts were made to revive her there but these efforts failed. Antonietta, who was in the shop at the time, then took charge. She had Elisa taken to her car to be driven to the house a few streets away. Meanwhile she despatched the fishmonger to fetch Dr Silvino as she feared that Elisa might be seriously hurt. Within a few minutes Elisa was on the settee in the sitting room where, at last, she regained consciousness.

Elisa made a mental note to return soon and thank the fishmonger for his care and attention. At the moment, enjoying a piece of swordfish which

Antonietta had bought from that same man, she wondered how she would be able to repay the kindness and generosity of this family.

Antonietta asked what Elisa was doing in Naples. It was a question often put to her; she was careful not to let the answer sound too glib.

She said she had been hired as a nanny by an English couple called Wilson who lived in the city. She had met them in London the previous summer during their annual holiday and had agreed to travel out to Naples with them and look after their two young children. After a few months however, Mr Wilson had been recalled to London as the head of his company had been tragically killed in an automobile accident. Promotion for Mr Wilson followed and after a brief visit to Naples to tie up affairs he returned to London. It seemed clear that his new duties would keep him in London for some time – certainly his stay in Italy was at an end. Consequently, when he had found suitable accommodation, his wife and children had also gone back to England. Elisa had been expected to return too and continue her duties but she had decided to stay in Naples. She now made a living giving private lessons in English. She lived in a very comfortable *pensione* near the Piazza Sannazzaro.

Once again the information that Elisa was living in a *pensione* provoked murmurs of surprise. She repeated that she was very comfortable there and lived there by choice. She realised from the quizzical looks that met this further information that she had made matters worse rather than better. It was difficult to know what to say next. After half a minute's silence she added that her life in the *pensione* was nevertheless temporary as she hoped to gain a full-time position in a private school shortly and accommodation was provided with this particular job. This news was greeted with smiles and exclamations of approval. Clearly living in a *pensione* for a short time was acceptable but only until something better came along. It was unthinkable that one would actually choose to stay there when other possibilities arose.

In fact Elisa was not being entirely honest about her situation. The story about the Wilsons was true enough and she herself had chosen to stay in Naples although the motivation for this, initially at least, was mainly a wish not to return to Britain. It was true also that she gave English lessons and that she had applied for a full-time job as an English teacher in a small private school. However, the *pensione* was not particularly comfortable and she preferred to spend more time away from it than in it. Fortunately she had become interested in the art and history of the city and spent most of her free time visiting galleries, museums and churches.

Twice during the meal Gennaro was called away to the phone. The little maid whom Elisa had seen earlier standing by the door in the sitting room came into the dining room on both occasions and whispered something into his ear. Gennaro rose, excused himself politely and disappeared. He returned shortly afterwards but gave no indication to anyone of who had phoned. In his absences the meal progressed as normal. Antonietta still had some questions for Elisa. The conversation continued in Italian.

And why had Elisa chosen to visit the Church of Santa Maria in Portico? Because of Luca Giordano came the reply. Silence followed. Luca Giordano, Elisa went on, thinking that she had placed her hosts at a disadvantage, was a particular favourite of hers and she could easily see why he was regarded as one of Naples' finest painters. Yes, of course, Antonietta agreed. And such wonderful, wonderful paintings, influenced by . . . by . . . who was it? Caravaggio, Elisa said. Of course, Caravaggio. Marvellous, marvellous artist. But was there a painting by Giordano in the Church of Santa Maria? Antonietta asked. Two. Two! Yes, two. Well, well, who would have believed. Did anyone else know this? Antonietta looked round the table. How ironic, Antonietta's mother remarked, that it took a young lady from a foreign country to educate them about one of their own artists! Laughter greeted this. The uncle however had something to add. He said he commended their guest for her knowledge of Neapolitan art which no doubt surpassed that of most Neapolitans. However, he had to point out that there were no paintings by Luca Giordano in the Church of Santa Maria in Portico. Perhaps the young lady was confusing this church with another a little further up the hill, the Church of Ascensione a Chiara. Ah, Elisa said, yes, of course, she had made a mistake. It was about this time that the meal ended.

Elisa thanked Antonietta profusely for her hospitality. She would never be able to repay her kindness. Now she would have to take her leave. Gennaro asked Elisa if she would please just wait a little longer. Perhaps she would care for a coffee? It would have been impolite to refuse so Elisa found herself back in the sitting room. None of the family joined her, however, except Antonietta and Gennaro. Even then Gennaro was called away to the phone once more. As he left the room he urged Elisa not to go away before he got back. When he returned, after a slightly longer period than on the two previous occasions, Elisa had been persuaded to have a second cup of coffee. After a few minutes more the conversation was beginning to flag. Elisa was about to make her second attempt to leave when a bell was heard – the front-door bell. Without waiting to be summoned Gennaro rose and excused himself again. 'Just one minute,' he said. 'I will be back.' Elisa continued to sip from her now empty cup. She did not want to accept a third coffee. She and Antonietta had begun to talk about fashion and materials and had moved on to curtains when Gennaro returned. He came over to Elisa. 'Forgive me, *signorina,*' he said. 'The bag is gone forever but I have been able at least to recover this.' To her astonishment he placed the stolen letter in her trembling hands.

TWO LETTERS

My Dearest Elsie,

It is now over a year since I last saw you and believe me Elsie it seems like an awful lot more time than that. The time is so long and the miles too. I cannot for the life of me imagine a place as distant as Italy. I went to the library the other day and had a look in the atlas to see where Naples is. It took me a devil of a time to find it I can tell you.

But it does not matter Elsie how far away you are because I will always love you. I cannot change this and I do not wish to. I may never see you again Elsie but even if I never do I cannot change the way I feel. It is something that I know is fixed. I do not know any other way to express it. I am not very good with words I am sorry to say, so that is how my imagination allows me to tell you what you mean to me. It would be so much easier Elsie if there was not this huge amount of land separating us and if I could just talk to you for a little while face to face.

I do not know if you want news of the village or not. I will not go into detail but your disappearance has been more or less accepted now. There was a period when the police were very busy looking for you. They questioned a lot of folk though not me I am glad to say. Anyway when they had done the rounds of your local relatives they contacted your father. He came up for a few days and stayed in Mackay's Hotel in Ardallt. He has done well for himself Elsie and it seems he does not drink any more. At least he had nothing while he was up here. I believe the police spent some time asking him questions but he had obviously not seen you so that was that. He left after a few days as I said.

Then they got to thinking that maybe you were dead. Someone mentioned your foot. I thought that was unkind really since it was never very noticeable and most of us had forgotten all about it. It was noted however and then the theory was that perhaps you had stumbled when you were out walking and fallen in the river. They had a look in the river and on the banks but found nothing of course. There was a heavy spate a week or two later and the river rose a good five feet higher than normal. The water was thick and brown and went down through the top end of Spaladale at a fearful rate. They reckoned then that anything in the river would have been sent half way across to Norway so that put paid to that search.

After that they dragged Loch Craig with a net. I was hoping they would find my curling stone, the one that I lost that night that Stewart Candless's Metalurjic or whatever it was went into the loch. Do you remember that Elsie? What a night that was. I will never forget it. I cannot believe that that man Candless stayed on top of his car all that time. It must have been an hour and a half at least before we managed to get the thing out of the water. He never forgave us you know. The car never ran again and Stewart himself was in bed with a bad dose of the cold for a week. Well he was a bit mad Elsie you know that and I am afraid he has got worse now. Did he not go and shoot someone at the clay-pigeon shooting in Ardallt two months ago! It was an accident of course but old Colonel Saunchie got a few pellets in him. I will not tell you where Elsie! Anyway no more clay pigeons for Candless. He has decided now that horses are the thing. He has bought himself a couple of Hunters and he plans to do some show jumping of all things. Well Elsie he has been seen out on Kilmont Farm dismounting without orders quite a few times. More money than sense he has that one.

No Elsie they found nothing in Loch Craig but a huge pike. Nobody knew there were any in the loch but then we only got the one and it would not surprise me if he had not eaten all the others if there had been any others that is. I was there Elsie when they pulled in the net. I watched the whole thing. I do not know for certain why I went up there to watch them doing it. Somewhere in the back of my mind I think maybe I was afraid that they would find you although I had heard from you by that time and knew you could not possibly be there at the bottom of Loch Craig. It was as if I needed proof that your first letter was not some kind of trick and you were dead after all. No Elsie I did not really believe that but my heart was pounding I can tell you when they pulled that net in. There was quite a crowd at the bank of the loch and I wondered why they were all there, whether they were genuinely concerned about you or perhaps that death had some awful attraction for them. I could swear that some of them actually wanted the police to find a body. You know how it is Elsie when you go to the show in August and they have those horses jumping and you are waiting for one of the riders to fall off. It does not seem right if all of them succeed. Do you know what I mean? I felt that some of those on the bank waiting for the net to come in were wanting a body and wishing hard for a corpse. It is awful to think so Elsie I know but I am sure some of them felt cheated when nothing was found.

There was a moment of drama though when this big pike started thrashing about in the net. At first someone thought it might be a salmon but how could a salmon get into Loch Craig? Anyway when they pulled it out of the net it was plainly a pike and somewhere between fifteen and twenty pounds I am sure. Murchison the Slinnart bobby was all for killing it and he had a stone raised to despatch it when I said no. I am not usually a forward sort of person as you know Elsie but I thought there had been enough talk about death enough of wanting bad bad things so I said why kill it it is not a fish for the pot. Aye you could be right Murchison said and he slipped it back into the water. It stayed there in the shallow water for a while. It was stunned I suppose from its ordeal. Then it gave a flick of its tail and it was gone.

I got a good look at it though while Murchison had it in his hands and then when it was lying there in the water just looking up at us all. I can tell you Elsie I have never seen a fish like it. I have seen a few salmon in my time and caught a few too but this thing was not like a salmon at all. A huge head it had on it with rows of teeth and this long sleek green body with all the fins sort of pushed down towards the tail to give it speed in the water I suppose. It was a fearsome beast in a way although I felt sorry for it when Murchison was going to kill it. No I thought to myself you do not deserve this death and the you I was thinking of was not the fish itself but all those people standing on the bank. You have seen your monster I thought and this time the you did mean the fish. And that is enough I said.

But here I am Elsie spending more time writing about a fish than about people. Perhaps you do not want to hear too much about people anyway. But I can tell you that Simon is well. He became a bit morose for a while a bit inside himself which is fairly natural under the circumstances I suppose. After a few months though he seemed to accept the situation. He got out and about more and began to enjoy life again. On the few occasions I have met him it has been very difficult for me not to let slip something about you. Your name has never been mentioned. Whether he suspects anything or not I do not know. Certainly he has never given a hint that he knows anything. I think that the clever way that you worked out your own disappearance has managed to convince not only the police but Simon too. I could not swear to it though.

Heather is well too. I do not love her Elsie. Perhaps yes I did love her once but not any more. Our situation is not very happy but I can tolerate it. I cannot leave her Elsie. Even if you were only a few hundred miles away instead of a few thousand I could not leave her. She has been good to me and although she knows there is something wrong and maybe suspects there is something I have not told her about she gives nothing away. I am only guessing because we do not talk about things like that. She mentions you a lot however. She misses you Elsie and sometimes I want to say to her she cannot miss you more than I do. I say nothing of course.

Because I do miss you Elsie I miss you more than I can say. I want to be with you and still hope this will be possible one day. Write to me at the post office in Slinnart. I can pick up a letter there without any bother. I cannot wait to hear from you again to know you are well and happy. Perhaps I am in your thoughts as often as you are in mine dearest Elsie.

With all my love,
Donald

My dear Donald,

It was wonderful to hear from you, really wonderful. I'm sure it's difficult for you to imagine what my life is like out here but one thing is certain and that is that there are very few people I can talk to. I don't mean that the language is a problem. It is, in fact, but I'm getting better and better at it. I mean the English people I've met here (and one or two Scots). I haven't got any really close friends. Of course it's early days yet, I suppose, but I do so wish there was someone I could tell the whole story to. It's impossible, of course, and I realise that. Still, it would be nice to get some of it off my mind.

In fact I have made one very important friend in the past week or so and it's ironic that your last letter is responsible for this friendship! Let me tell you briefly what happened.

Your letter arrived early last week – Tuesday – and I picked it up as I was on my way out of the guest house where I'm staying at the moment. Although I wanted to rush back upstairs and read the letter straight away I decided to hold onto it and read it later. Near the sea there is a little park which has open-air cafés in it and I decided that I would go along there and read your letter while I relaxed with a cup of coffee. Before I could do this someone snatched my handbag and made off with it. The letter was inside, unopened.

I can tell you, Donald, it was a very unpleasant experience, particularly as I fainted in the street just as the thief disappeared. I suppose this was partly to do with the heat – it is very hot here at present – but to tell you the truth I don't remember very much about it. The next thing I do remember is waking up in a very grand house a few streets away from where the robbery took place. The couple who own the house, Gennaro and Antonietta Calvino, are obviously well off. It seems that Antonietta was nearby when I fainted and arranged for me to be taken back to her house. She also had a doctor brought in who examined me and said that I was fine. I recovered quickly, I'm glad to say, but I couldn't leave because they insisted that I stayed to lunch. I suppose I was a bit of a novelty for them, in a way. I met the rest of the family, had a fine meal and then at the end Gennaro, who is the head of the whole household, gave me your letter!

I'm learning new things every day here, Donald, and I can tell you it's an extraordinary place. Everybody seems to know everybody else and nobody can do anything without someone knowing what is going on. This man Gennaro obviously has a lot of influence even among the less desirable characters in this city, or at least in this part of it. He made a few enquiries and was able to track down the thieves. He couldn't get my bag back for me, or the other contents, because they had some value

– although very little I'm sure – whereas the letter, having no value at all (except for me of course!) was thrown away. I asked Gennaro how he came by the letter and he merely said that he knew the right people to approach. I also asked whether he would be giving his information to the police so that they could catch the criminals. He said that this would be unnecessary and I got the distinct impression that I should not ask any more questions about it but be content that I had got my letter back.

And I was, Donald, I was so happy to get it back and read it and learn that you are missing me as much as I am missing you. In one way life for me is difficult under these circumstances because, as I said, there's no one really that I can talk to. In another way, however, I'm finding it easier to cope with because there is so much to see and do here. There are lots of galleries and museums and marvellous churches and castles. I can't really describe what sort of place this is. The old part of town is just full of magnificent old buildings. How I wish I could draw, Donald! I would spend all my time trying to capture this place on paper.

But there is so much poverty! I never knew people could live in such dreadful conditions. There are whole areas here, Donald, where basic facilities such as water, for example, are in very poor supply or simply don't exist at all. Such areas are filthy too. The rubbish just gets put outside in the street. There is no official collection because it is immediately picked over by a series of scavengers – first adults, then children, then dogs and cats. Consequently the streets of these poorer areas are strewn with rubbish and in hot weather there is frequently a most unpleasant smell.

Despite all of these bad aspccts to life here I love this place, Donald. I thought it would take me time to adjust and it has. I'm not saying it has been easy. No, at first it was difficult but then I had the Wilsons to help me. I enjoyed my life with them and I don't think I could have coped in the beginning without them. When they left, however, and I made the decision to stay, I knew it might be hard for me but I knew also that I was doing the right thing. Antonietta, my new friend, finds it difficult to understand that I enjoy living alone as I do, in a strange city. She can't know how I value my freedom, Donald, the freedom to do what I like and take advantage of the opportunity to explore a new city, learn a new language, try my hand at a way of life I didn't know existed. Of course she doesn't know what my life was like for six years or so, although I may get round to telling her, in time. I am a bit of an oddity here and this has opened a few doors for me. Maybe Antonietta herself will tire of me when the novelty wears off. Only time will tell but I don't think so. We'll see.

So, I am determined to stay here, Donald. It's not expensive to live here and I earn enough from my lessons to keep me going. There are some bad things, as I have said, and it can be dangerous at times too as I discovered only recently. However, out of that unpleasant experience something good was generated and that is how it will go on, I'm sure. Some of the surprises in store may not be very nice but most of them will be. That's how I've decided to approach my life here. I know I can't come back to Scotland, Donald, and I have no wish to live in England. I am determined to stay here, for some time at least. I know too that you can never be with me here and for that reason I have taken a decision. It was not easy but I think it is for the best, in the long run. We must stop writing to each other, Donald. I know it's hard, believe me, but continuing will only make life harder and harder if we are never able to meet. I left Simon but I had very good reason to, as you know. You cannot leave Heather, despite what you feel for me, because she has been so good to you. I know you couldn't hurt her for the world. You couldn't hurt her for me and I wouldn't wish you to.

I'm sure it's better, then, for us to stop writing. It will be difficult at first but going on would only lead to more sorrow. It would, Donald, I feel sure. I will never forget you and I will think of you often and I will always love you. I will.

Elsie

THE ISLAND

THE drum must have been made of very robust material as the drummer was not beating it so much as savaging it. It was quite a large drum, perhaps of the size of an orchestral kettle drum and with a similar bowl-shaped underside. A loop of stout tape allowed it to be carried, very awkwardly, while slung round the drummer's shoulders.

The procession, the long and noisy column winding its way down to the sea from the Abbey of San Michele Arcangelo, halted for the second or third time as the narrow street became clogged with people once more. The drummer took the opportunity to unhook the drum and set it down on the cobbles in front of him. A dark wide stain of sweat discoloured his blue jacket where the tape of the drum had pressed down hard on his shoulder and across his back. Six men, also wearing short blue jackets over their long white robes surrounded the drummer and one of them stepped forward to steady the drum and keep it from rolling over. The drummer threw back his white hood to reveal a tangle of black hair, a forehead sheened with sweat and a neatly trimmed black beard with one fleck of grey. He placed his hands on his hips, arched his back and tried to stretch the tiredness out of his body. The drumstick which resembled a white-headed mallet was still clutched in his right hand. He now raised this high in the air and allowed his wide blue sleeve to fall to his shoulder revealing a pale but muscular arm. Holding the folds of the sleeve with his left hand he brought the stick down hard on the drum's taut surface to release a report more like a cannon blast than a drumbeat.

The sound of the drum, struck at irregular intervals before the procession began to move off slowly once again, drew cries of complaint from the crowd crushed into the tiny space between the members of the procession itself and the crumbling plaster fronts of the houses which also seemed to be jammed in, shoulder to shoulder, along each side of the narrow defile which led up the steep uneven hill to the Abbey. In fact it was difficult to tell who were in the procession and who were merely spectators. Many of those standing by wore the blue and white costume prevalent among those who marched or rather shuffled along slowly in the procession itself. Most of the children, in or out of the column, were dressed in black outfits embroidered heavily in gold. The most striking thing about their caps – also black and gold – was that each one had a huge black ostrich plume stuck into a band at the front. The street was full of these tiny people who would have looked like Indian princes except for the fact that they pushed and shoved their way through the crowds, danced and played tag in among the floats that began to appear once the drummer and his group of attendants had passed.

Antonietta and Elisa had positioned themselves at the bottom of the hill, on the corner where the street gave on to the wider dock area. A pavement began at this point and they stood on the very edge of this, allowing the extra few inches gained to give them a slightly better view of proceedings. Antonietta pointed to the floats as they were manoeuvred past and tried to explain to Elisa which saint was being commemorated on each one. However it was difficult for her to make her voice heard above the general din which was a mixture of singing, religious chanting and the shouts and salutations of the bystanders when they recognised a friend or relative in the procession. The drummer was some way ahead now but his drum could still be heard.

The floats were mostly wheeled platforms with shafts to front and rear. Several men or young boys clung on to each shaft and guided the vehicles as they clattered over the cobbles. Two of the floats took the lamb of God as their theme. Elisa saw the first one approach with its abundance of flowers. In a small space at the foot of a cross stood a lamb. It was wearing a collar and a small boy sat on the very edge of the float holding on to a piece of twine which was knotted onto this collar. He leaned over occasionally and stroked the bewildered and frightened animal whose persistent bleating could hardly be heard above the noise. Elisa was particularly taken with this float, with the gentleness displayed by the child looking after his pet lamb. After three or four other floats had passed the second lamb of God arrived. This time pictures of Jesus in gilt frames and statuettes of the Holy Family had been fixed in position on a carpet of flowers. In front of these a lamb was curled up, motionless. No boy attended this one. Elisa moved forward to get a closer look. The lamb had been killed and allowed to stiffen in its apparently peaceful pose.

Not long after this the crowd became silent. It was a sudden and eerie silence. Elisa turned to Antonietta and found that the merest whisper was all that was now necessary. She asked what was going on. Antonietta nodded up the hill to indicate that something or someone special was about to arrive.

The festive outfits of the float attendants gave way to the no less gaudy official robes of the priests and acolytes of the church. Several of these walked slowly behind a young man wearing a white surplice who swung a censer on a long golden chain. The air was being purified for the Mother of God. She was a tall wooden figure clothed in long robes similar in style to the outfits of the children – black with embroidery in gold. She had a rather far-away look upon her face and seemed to be gesturing towards an uncertain future. Elisa felt that any chance of being moved by this figure was destroyed by the ridiculous crown she had on her head. It was very large indeed and above its dome of silver a golden ball was fixed out of which sprouted a jewelled cross.

Four men in ordinary clothes carried her platform at shoulder height. They stepped carefully on the treacherous cobbles and concentrated totally on their task. As they and their precious cargo passed everyone in the crowd fell to their knees. Within a few moments Elisa was the only onlooker still standing. She turned and saw to her surprise that Antonietta too was kneeling in an attitude of prayer. Not knowing why she should allow herself to be so pressured and angry with herself for giving in to such nonsense Elisa also dropped to her knees on the pavement.

One or two saints followed, plaster or wooden Elisa could not say. A few of the onlookers knelt for them, but not all did so. Some stepped forward and touched a foot or the gold-trimmed hem of a robe.

Finally the dead Christ arrived. The sight of this stretched out figure in polished wood brought silence once more. Elisa expected everyone to kneel again but was surprised when there was instead a push forward towards the recumbent figure. Elisa found herself caught up in the press of people and there was a moment of near panic when the crush suddenly threatened to sweep her off her feet. She twisted round to look for Antonietta but they had become separated in the crowd. Unable to do anything else, she moved along with the tightly packed knot of people for thirty or forty yards. At one point she was pushed hard against the litter on which the wooden Christ lay. She caught a glimpse of a leg with whorls of dark polished wood and her eye fixed for a moment on a split, a fraction of an inch wide, which stretched along the calf. At one or two points on the jagged edge of the exposed grain had been caught fibres from the cloth or duster used to polish the statue. Elisa reflected that, well, it was just like any other piece of furniture. The Christ was old and not in very good shape.

Farther along the seafront Elisa was released by the crowd and managed to rejoin Antonietta. They decided to move away from the procession and find a quieter spot. Antonietta led the way to a house several streets away. From the hot dusty street they were suddenly in an area of coolness and quietness. A man appeared. He was unshaven and slightly dishevelled and was drying his hands on a white tea towel.

Antonietta was rather curt with him, issuing a series of instructions so quickly that Elisa could not quite follow what she had said. She led Elisa through to the back of the building where they entered a small but bright sitting room. They sat down in armchairs opposite one another, both tired from their walk.

'We will have lunch shortly and then perhaps visit more of the island.'

'It's a beautiful place,' Elisa said.

'Everyone wants Capri,' Antonietta said, raising her eyes to the ceiling. 'Capri, Capri, they all say. But people from round here know that there are other islands and they are as beautiful. One day I will take you to Lipari, much farther away but very, very beautiful.'

'That would be wonderful.'

Silence followed. Elisa felt awkward. She was bored by pleasantries but unable to speak as openly as she wished. She felt close to Antonietta but today she was very much a guest and it would not do to say anything that might offend.

'Tell me,' Antonietta said, 'are you happy in Naples?'

'Yes. Very.' The answer was so immediate and decisive that Antonietta was taken aback.

'So you intend to stay.'

'Yes, I do.'

'Ah. In spite of the problems?'

'Problems?'

'Naples has more than most.'

'I know that but I have a job, a place to stay and good friends.' She found herself forced into a blush.

'There are difficult times ahead, Elisa. You may find that these things you have mentioned are not enough.'

'No?'

'No. This country is wonderful and you are enjoying it now, seeing new things, learning new things, but it will not always be like this. You must make plans for the future.'

'That is one thing I do not want to do.'

'No? Why not?'

'I've done it before and things went wrong. When you've planned things carefully and then they go wrong it's very hard to take. Now I prefer not to plan any more.'

'This is a luxury, Elisa.'

'Is it?'

'Yes, and you may not have it for much longer.'

'I'll continue in this way for as long as I can and if it becomes impossible one day then so be it. I'll worry about that when the time comes.'

'Ah.'

The untidy servant appeared once again. Atonietta listed the dishes that she wanted fcr lunch. There was no discussion of this menu. The servant withdrew with a bow.

'You are not a religious person, are you Elisa?'

This was much more direct than Elisa had expected. 'It depends what you mean,' she said.

'I mean what the words say.' Antonietta shrugged. 'You are either a religious person or you are not. With you, I think not.'

'Religious belief is a strange thing. I don't really understand it and sometimes I despise it but it fascinates me.'

'You visit churches and you watch processions but you do not bow down.'

Elisa paused for a moment. She smiled, realising that unwittingly or not Antonietta had expressed the situation very well. 'No,' she said at last. 'That is the difficult part.'

After lunch they walked slowly up the hill to the Abbey. The procession had broken up but groups of robed figures were still making their way homeward. A little boy passed them pedalling hard on his bicycle whose path was erratic because cradled in one arm he held the lamb from one of the floats they had seen earlier. The lamb, still nervous, bleated out its complaint which was audible now that the street was nearly empty of people. Antonietta pointed to the boy as he disappeared round a bend up ahead of them. 'They will have lamb for dinner,' she said.

Elisa thought of the other one, the lamb already dead and shaped into something beautiful for the procession. 'There was another one . . .' she said. 'Another one . . . already killed.'

'Ah yes. Probably cooking at this very minute.'

Elisa said: 'Bowing down gets more and more difficult.'

Antonietta said: 'Don't confuse what other people do with what is right. After all, most people get it all wrong.'

When they reached the Abbey they found that the wooden statues of the saints and Christ had been returned. They had been set up in the courtyard outside, all except the dying Christ which had been taken inside the Abbey. A queue had formed in front of this figure. Elisa noted with some distaste that as each person reached the Christ he or she kissed the gnarled wooden feet. She suddenly realised that she was in the queue herself with Antonietta guiding her forward. Reaching the reclining Christ she remembered that a couple of hours before, while watching the procession, she had dropped to her knees before Mary, the Mother of God, and she had done so because everyone else had done so.

This time she steeled herself and stepped past the Christ without touching it. Antonietta leaned forward, crossed herself and planted a light kiss on the Christ's big toe. Watching from a distance of only a few feet, Elisa found this action at once grotesque and ludicrous. As the two women stepped out of the Abbey and back into the bright sunlight Antonietta said, 'One day you will learn to kiss his feet, Elisa, I am sure.'

Elisa said nothing, as if she hadn't heard.

Elisa and Antonietta followed the priest down a steep flight of stone steps. The only light available to them was that emitted by the single candle in an ornate silver candlestick which the priest carried. The poor light, the steepness of the steps and the age of the priest – he was a wizened old man in his seventies – meant that progress was slow.

The floor at the bottom of the steps was uneven; sharp edges of rock poked through beaten earth. In the gloom a huge sideboard became visible along the right-hand wall of what appeared to be a large room although its full extent could not be gauged. The priest placed the candlestick on top of this weighty piece of furniture. He then opened a door below and withdrew two further candlesticks. As he lit these more of the room became visible. It was revealed to be a cavern rather than a room and quite narrow too. Ahead of them a door stood ajar. The priest gave a candlestick to each woman. He said something to Antonietta who stepped past him and headed for the door. She turned and motioned for Elisa to follow.

'The priest is a superstitious old man,' Antonietta said when they had passed through the door and had advanced some way down a narrow corridor. 'He doesn't believe it is good to visit this place too often.'

'I can understand why,' Elisa said. 'It's rather an evil place.'

'Evil? You mustn't say that, Elisa. No, no. It's a bit dark and maybe a bit frightening but you have to see these things. It's necessary.'

'Is it?'

'I believe so.'

The corridor became wider. On their right there was a rectangular hole in the wall. The bottom edge of the hole was about four feet up from the floor of the corridor. A rudely constructed wooden ladder led up to it.

'There,' Antonietta said. 'Go up there and look in. Take care though because the ladder is unsteady.'

'Tell me,' Elisa asked, 'do you bring all your friends here?' She managed a wry smile.

'No, only the special ones. I mean that truly too.'

Elisa turned to the ladder. She was unsure about this whole adventure. Barely five minutes ago she had been inside the Abbey watching Antonietta and others kissing a slab of wood made to represent Christ.

Then she had been out in the bright sunlight again where she had seen some of the last few members of the procession making their way home. The drummer was there, struggling with the huge kettle drum, his hood down and his shoulders damp with sweat. Suddenly she had found herself being drawn towards a door at the side of the Abbey. Antonietta had clearly arranged all this because the old priest had been there waiting for them. Now she was deep underneath the Abbey inside something that resembled a cave. Her foot was on the first rung of a rickety old ladder that led up to something she was sure would be disturbing at the very least. But she would see it through if only because she found the whole thing quite bizarre. She found that more and more she was able to accept situations which would have shocked her several months ago. Things happened to her these days that she would not have believed possible then. Here she was on the bottom rung of a ladder, in a cavern, with a candlestick in her hand and something quite awful ahead of her. Yet this was not all that unusual, she felt, not very out of the ordinary.

'Let me take the candle,' Antonietta said. 'I'll pass it up to you when you are a little higher.'

Elisa passed the candlestick down. Holding on tightly to the ladder with her left hand she drew her long skirt away from the lower rungs with her right and stepped carefully up. As she approached the top of the short ladder she transferred her left hand to the side of the aperture in the wall. She could not yet make out what lay inside but she positioned herself on the lip of what seemed to be another small chamber. When Antonietta passed up the candlestick she found she was right; she was on the very edge of the floor of a small room barely ten feet square. The floor was covered with human bones.

Elisa steadied herself. Her first impulse had been to step back but she grasped the inner edge of the wall to prevent herself from falling backwards. Recovering from the initial shock she raised the candlestick above her head. No part of the tiny floor space was visible; the entire area was covered with bones and most of these were skulls. They extended from wall to wall and right up to Elisa's feet. She looked down and saw that she had already dislodged one skull with her left foot. Carefully she moved an inch or two backwards. She could see that her heels were now flush with the edge of the opening. Antonietta was talking to her but she could not hear. She turned her attention back to the bones in front of her.

Although only a thin coating of dust covered all the skulls she could see, the room had clearly been undisturbed for years. In the centre there was an open coffin whose wood seemed to be in a state of gentle decay. The figure that lay inside it was no longer a body but not quite a skeleton. The only thing in the room that was almost entirely dust free, it looked as if it was made of old brown paper stretched over a tangle of thick wires. Flesh resembling delicate parchment was visible along a shrunken thigh. Although the head was definitely a skull as no features remained and eyes and nose had gone, the cheeks also retained this fine paper-thin covering of what had once been skin. Elisa noticed that the skull was not quite in the correct position; it was drawn over to the right shoulder and then turned back slightly towards the left shoulder. She realised the head had been severed and placed in the coffin separately.

The room was cool and very still. Elisa remained where she was for two or three minutes. She began to count the skulls but gave up and merely guessed that there were more than a hundred. She began to wonder who they all were and how long they had been there. There were lots of questions to be answered, especially about the open coffin before her. After a while she thought that perhaps these questions were not very important after all, that it didn't really matter if she could put a name to one of these skulls. To know a name or a date would add or subtract nothing to the contents of the room but merely give her the satisfaction of pinning something down and categorising it. She realised such knowledge was designed to give her the illusion of understanding and, more importantly, control. But she knew that all this experience was beyond her control, far beyond her ability to classify and thereby tame. What was important was to understand her reaction to it, why she did not feel in the least bit afraid.

Elisa and Antonietta said nothing until they had left the catacombs and were above ground again. When Antonietta finally spoke it was on another subject. The Abbey, the catacombs and the bodies were never mentioned.

'I want you to stay in Naples too,' she said. 'But, contrary to what you think, plans are necessary.'

'Are they?'

'Certainly. I hope that you will trust me. You will probably not approve of what I am going to say, not at first anyway, but I want you to understand that I have only your welfare in mind. Shall I go on?'

'Yes, go on.'

'So . . . first of all you must marry.'

'I felt sure you were going to say that.'

'And how do you feel about it?'

'I'm already married.'

To Elisa's surprise this statement did not disconcert Antonietta at all. 'How many people know?' she asked. 'In Naples, I mean.'

'Only you.'

'Are you quite sure about that? This is very important.'

'Yes, I'm sure.'

'What about your passport?'

'I was able to get it made out in my maiden name.'

'Good.'

The late afternoon streets were deserted. The sun continued to shine and it was very warm. As she was wearing her usual long skirt Elisa began to feel uncomfortable.

'It is a little unusual, I agree, but you can marry, I'm sure of that. First you must come and live with Gennaro and me and you will be a teacher for the children. You may spend a little time with them if you wish but that is not important. What is important is that you must move out of the *pensione* and move in with us.'

Elisa mulled this over for a short time. 'And then?' she asked.

'And then you will marry Giorgio.'

'Giorgio?' She stopped walking and turned to face Antonietta. She pronounced the name not with distaste but in complete surprise. 'Giorgio?'

'You had expected someone else?'

'I didn't know who to expect.'

'Giorgio is most suitable. First of all he is my brother . . .' Antonietta allowed herself a smile. '. . . And although he is not very rich he is comfortable. His wife died two years ago; his two children are nearly grown up; he needs someone; he has a beautiful house . . . and he is very fond of you.'

'But he has hardly ever spoken to me.'

'He admires you.'

'Does he indeed.'

'He admires your independent spirit.'

'. . . Which would have to disappear if I married him, I suppose.'

'Not necessarily.'

'Ha!' Elisa shook her head.

The two women reached the seafront and stood watching the few people who were moving about on the pier. The boat that would take them back to the mainland would not arrive for another half an hour or so. After the bustle and commotion of two or three hours before, the place was abandoned. There was no clue left to indicate that anything out of the ordinary had happened. Elisa thought of how quickly situations could change, how easy it was to move, how difficult to stay still.

'Think about it for a few days,' Antonietta said. 'Join us for lunch on Thursday. Giorgio will be with us and we can take things from there.'

'You've got it all arranged, haven't you?' Elisa said.

Antonietta paused for a moment. She seemed to be searching for some word of explanation but finally she just said 'Yes.'

'Why are you so convinced that I will agree to your plans?'

'Because you want to stay here. I don't necessarily understand why but this is what you want to do. You must know that this will be impossible if you try to continue living as you do. Up to now you have been a novelty and your style of life eccentric but acceptable. Any longer, though, and you will be regarded as strange. Also there is the difficulty of the political situation, so Gennaro tells me. Anyway, if you really want to stay here I can offer you a way to do it. Think carefully before you turn it down.'

'I see.' Elisa leaned against the railing and looked out over the sea in the direction of Naples. 'I suppose I would have to join the church too,' she said.

'Yes.'

Once again Elisa was amazed at Antonietta's forcefulness. She had never seen her in quite this kind of mood before. It was as if she, Elisa, had no influence over what was going to happen. Everything had been arranged and all she could do now was play her part like some sort of mechanical device.

'I don't think I will be able to join the church,' Elisa said at last.

'Don't worry, that is the easiest part.' Antonietta turned and placed a hand on Elisa's arm. 'Trust me,' she said.

LAST LETTERS

My dear Elsie,

Although your last letter came as a shock I suppose I should have expected it really. You see Elsie I was always hoping that you would come back that I could see you again even though I did not know how or where that would happen. You make a decision at some time in your life Elsie and you find later on that you are strangled by it that it fixes you in a course of action which cannot be changed. That is what I do not like. When I was a young man, too young and with no sense I did something that decided the way my life would go for years and years and for as far as I could see. But you managed to do it Elsie. You managed to free yourself and I admire you for it. I am jealous too because I know I do not have the strength to do it myself. I just do not have the strength.

Which is why it will be all the more difficult to accept your silence and why I must ask you please to reconsider. I know it is dangerous Elsie and that all it needs is for one of these letters to be discovered for us both to be in trouble. I think it might destroy Heather such a discovery but I am willing to take the risk because that is all I live for any more. All I want is to be with you and failing that to keep in contact with you and receive your letters. Do not deny me this Elsie I beg you.

With all my love,
Donald

Dear Donald,

I received your letter nearly two weeks ago now and I've been unable to reply to it not because I haven't known what to say, no, it's the manner of saying it that's the problem. You see, Donald, I've decided to stick to my original decision. I think it's for the best if we stop writing to one another. It was your love that gave me the strength to break away from Simon and when I did so I thought there might be some way we could be together. Even when I got here to Italy I thought maybe there was still hope but I know that it's gone now. I've known this for some time.

Maybe it sounds harsh, Donald, but love by letter is just no use at all, not for long periods of time anyway. How long could we expect to go on like this? No, it has to end and ironically it's through you that I have found the strength to make another major change in my life. If that sounds as if I've used you, Donald, then I apologise because that is not what has happened. But I've gained a lot in the last year or so and the force that helped me with one big decision has enabled me to alter my life again. If I hadn't been helped towards that first change by you, Donald, I couldn't even have contemplated the second.

Things are difficult here at the moment. I'm fine but it's the political situation that I'm talking about. They tell me that foreigners are maybe going to have a rough time soon, especially the British. They tell me too that there is only one way I can stay in this country – and I do so much want to stay in this country – and that this one way is marriage.

I have decided to marry. It will not be for love – that has been denied me – it will be because at last I have found a place where I think I can be happy. The man I am to marry is kind and gentle and, yes, I will say it, he's quite rich. I have the promise of a comfortable life, Donald, and that prospect is a very attractive one. There have been times in the past when life has been a struggle for me – you have witnessed some of them yourself – and now I'm looking forward to a bit of ease, a bit of comfort, just a little bit of luxury. Maybe I have become selfish but I can't apologise, Donald, that's the way it is.

I know I'm taking a risk writing this down and I must ask you to destroy this letter as well as the others I have sent you. I have no right to insist on your silence, Donald, now that I have told you that it is over between us but I know you are not a vindictive man and I pray that you will understand me when I ask you to let me be and, if you can find it in your heart, forgive me for the hurt I've caused you.

Elsie

PART SIX

1938

AN ANGEL IN FLIGHT FROM THE NAME OF GOD

LIVING in beautiful places dulls the mind. It's true. We have a house in Posillipo, down by the sea. You reach the house by descending from Via Posillipo. There are several flights of stone steps and then a long narrow tunnel cut through the rock. When the lights fail, as they do frequently, the tunnel scares me but I have to take it; the only other way to reach the house is by sea.

I call it a house; some of the family call it a cave. If it is a cave then it is the most beautiful I know. It is built into the rock and the main room has a huge plate-glass window from which you can see rocky outcrops to either side and before you the sea. On the calm hot days of summer you can sit outside this window on a narrow balcony and take the sun. The sea is only a matter of a few feet below. Giorgio said that he used to fish from the balcony when he was a child. He would fall asleep on a couch with the fishing line tied to his big toe. I don't believe him of course – he always has a glint in his eye when he mentions this. It's what he would like to have done. He wanted to go fishing, climb trees, go swimming and do so many other physical things like that but he didn't. It seems he was a delicate child. When I ask him if he was ever bored here in this house by the sea he says no but he hesitates and I wonder. It's difficult to know what the truth is. Maybe he doesn't really know himself. Maybe already he has willed away the boredom and convinced himself that this place was always good, always absorbing.

Because for me it is not like that. I stay here four or five months of the year and when I arrive here it is marvellous. I decide that all I want to do is sit and watch the sea. Let the sea get on with it; it has all the energy and drive. Every day it's different; it can be calm and quiet, petulant and moody, gay and flighty, sombre, angry and, once or twice a year, enraged. So I place my chair in the correct position and settle myself to study the water, the sky, the small tree that clings to a nearby outcrop and then I find that five days have passed, days which were not unenjoyable but I am tired of them. Watching the sea is not enough. I know then that it is time to visit Spaccanapoli or take a trip out to Nola. I could sit and watch the sea for years and remain quiet and undisturbed but I would wake up then and ask myself what have I done? I am afraid that the answer would be nothing. I would have achieved nothing, changed nothing, given nothing, taken everything. My life would be valueless. This is not the way it should be.

So I take myself off, away from the beauty here to the squalor, poverty and drudgery of the centre of town. I have spent some time examining my motives for doing this and tried to convince myself that I haven't just been salving my conscience or doing a little penance by spending an afternoon away from the comfort and beauty of my own home. Of late I've decided that too close a scrutiny of your motives is not necessarily a good thing; you can worry yourself into inaction and end up just feeling sorry for yourself. When I go to the poorer parts of the city it is not to do good works or save souls or anything like that. It's rather that I need to gain a little perspective on life because after a few days in Posillipo the world is very beautiful, very quiet and calm and very flat.

Spaccanapoli is not flat. This thoroughfare that cuts the old city in two rages with life. I am always amazed that such a narrow street can contain so much noise and colour, so many jostling bodies each one intent on its own purpose. In fact there are points where the street fails to accommodate all the people who set up their stalls on its margins or struggle to travel along it. There are a few small squares just off to one side and these try to cope with the overspill of fruit and vegetable stalls, fish-sellers and vendors of books and stationery – the university is close by. People on bicycles and, increasingly now, people on motorcycles as well as drivers of cars, trucks and lorries try to make their way down this street which was never designed to cope with motorised transport. Donkeys can still be seen and horse-drawn carts. It's difficult to believe that all these people and animals and vehicles can exist together but they do.

I usually escape to the Church of Santa Chiara. There is a cloister there, a beautiful one with tiled walls and pergolas. There are benches where it is possible to sit and take the sun. I have been there on a few occasions when no one else was present, not one soul. At such times the cloister is a magic place simply because it is completely quiet. I don't really know how it is possible but the sounds from the street only a few yards away cannot be heard. In the middle of all that noise and chaotic bustle there is one place that does not allow sound to enter. I go to Santa Chiara quite often.

Sometimes on these visits I take a book with me. I am reading the history of the city at present. As my Italian improves I can see how many more interesting books there are for me to read. So I might sit in the Santa Chiara cloister in a silence that is at first relaxing, a blessing. After a while it becomes oppressive, or I find it so, perhaps because I know that it is not the natural condition of the area. Besides, I will usually get to thinking that here I am, reading a history of the people when the people are only a few steps away, separated from me by the massive cloister wall. On which side of the wall should I be? Then I realise that such introspection will get me nowhere in the end. There is a time to be in the street and there is a time to be away from it. It is merely a question of working out how they should be apportioned.

I go to Nola once a year to watch the dance of the lilies. The festival began many many years ago as a kind of thanksgiving. Lilies were displayed. Someone must have decided that a bigger display of these flowers was necessary. Towers were built and the lilies fixed to them. The towers were carried round by teams of villagers. Now every year there are seven or eight towers made of wood and canvas. Each one is about fifty feet high and secured to a wide base. A score of men is needed to lift each one. The towers are carried forward very slowly and made to dance when each side of the base is raised and lowered in turn. The first time I saw these huge constructions waving about in the air I was terrified. I was sure they would fall over and crush the crowds of people who were pressed in around them. As far as I know none of them has ever toppled over.

I wonder if that person who first thought of the idea of a tower covered in lilies could have guessed at how things would develop, how over the years the towers would grow and grow. I wonder if he realised that the stage would be reached when the most important thing would not be the flowers but the towers themselves. The towers aren't built to display the lilies now; there are no lilies any more. I suppose that this is the way things change; the emphasis shifts and after a while the original idea, the original reason for the event, is lost.

Each year, when the dance of the lilies is over, the towers themselves are forgotten. I have seen the village square in the evening after the festival. The square was almost empty apart from two of the towers which had been positioned in a corner and left. Maybe the men who carried them were too tired to move them on any farther. Whatever the reason for their abandonment they looked forlorn and dismal, already beginning to decay. A few strips of canvas had worked loose and flapped in the early evening breeze. A group of young boys, barely more than children, were using the lower part of one of the towers for target practice with their bows and arrows. I thought then how the cycle seems to go with these things. A great deal of time and effort and skill is invested in the creation of something which is the centrepiece of the festival and is applauded, wondered at, perhaps even revered for a few hours. Later, as its significance wanes the only interest left is in its destruction. Finally all that remains from this wonderful thing is a bundle of broken spars and strips of torn canvas. Everything has been reduced to the status of waste. The only thing that endures is the knowledge that the following year the whole procedure will begin all over again.

San Gennaro bothers me too. Twice a year there is a festival which concerns two little bottles of his blood. The blood is solid and brown but after a great deal of prayer by the huge congregation in the Cathedral it becomes liquid and some say it appears to boil. Who can deny it? Hundreds of people witness this strange event every time it happens. No one can explain it in scientific terms. Not many of the congregation want to explain it in any way other than the miraculous. It is a gift of God, a manifestation of his power and love. I am not convinced. I have been there and seen what the priests do. There is no trickery, I am almost sure of that, but it is difficult to see. The Cathedral is packed. There is a press of people eager to witness the twice yearly miracle. Who can tell what really happens? Is it really necessary to find an explanation? I leave these festivals, the liquefaction of the blood of San Gennaro and the dance of the lilies at Nola, thinking that perhaps all the people involved are missing the point.

I found something that might be called hope in the cribs, the *presepi*, that appear at Christmas time. In fact it wasn't the cribs themselves but certain of the crib figures. You can buy these in San Gregorio Armeno near Spaccanapoli throughout December. Then the usually busy streets and alleys are even more crammed because there are extra stalls set up for the sale of all the crib figures. You can buy a thousand different Marys if you have a mind to, just as many Josephs and of course double or treble that number of the infant Jesus. You can get them made of various types and qualities of clay and porcelain, carved from a dozen varieties of wood or moulded in metals both base and precious. They come in a multitude of sizes and dispositions, with or without haloes. On some the haloes are detachable. Mary's oufits range from first century biblical simplicity to the ornate gaudiness of the baroque.

And the animals. The collective imagination of centuries is on display in the countless variations on scores of species many of which would be unable to survive in the climate of the Holy Land. Asses, sheep, goats, horses and even camels are expected and I suppose there is nothing extraordinary about dogs and cats. The cattle bring with them the first suspicions as there are some very unusual strains on offer: those with big horns, short horns or no horns at all; cows with humps on their necks or bells hung round them; bulls with rings in their noses. There are black cows, white cows, brown cows and red cows. I have even found one that is all of these colours, a sort of patchwork quilt of the cow family.

There are stalls where zebras can be bought, giraffes, elephants and lions. After the first shock I came to thinking well, why not, they are all God's creatures. Then the birds are admitted, not just the hens, ducks, geese and the common wild birds such as sparrows and crows but over there, on that stall tucked away at the back almost in apology, you can find eagles, ostriches, pheasants, birds of paradise. The sellers of crib figures in Spaccanapoli cater for all tastes; they reflect the great variety of life that is found on this earth.

But there is one group of figures that I have never been able to find on the stalls. As far as I know the only examples are to be found in the San Martino Museum. There is a whole display case devoted to them there but few people seem drawn to it. Those who do stop and stand before it appear fascinated. They are repelled but unable to break the hold that the figures have over them. We are often enthralled by the grotesque.

Here you can see the human monstrosities that nature brings forth. There are men with no legs and men with no arms, men with huge heads and empty expressions on their faces. There are some with limbs of uneven length and one or two with humps on their backs. There are women too – one with three breasts and a smile of broken teeth, another with a goitre like a big balloon fixed to her neck, a third with elephantiasis, one leg thin and fragile while the other is as wide and solid as a tree trunk. All of these look towards you with their afflictions on display, scarcely hidden by the clothes they wear. Nearly all are dressed in rags. Nearly all are smiling.

These are *gli storpi*, the lost ones, the afflicted ones, the mistakes and misfortunes and accidents of human generation. They are all here because it is believed that they have a place, that all the manifestations of mankind are in some way blessed. I believe it too. I strive to believe it. I hope it is so.

For I have decided that there is only one way to approach this place and that is to embrace it totally. In the streets here you can find every type of person you could think of and each one has his place; in the Christmas cribs everyone is represented, no one is rejected. In the same way, I am accepted here and, in turn, my response must be to accept the city. There can be no half measures in this; this is not a half-hearted place. If I want to stay, to take it on, then I must go at it with a will, deny the city and myself nothing. It is not easy; at times it seems impossible but I am lucky enough to have people around me to help me. I have Antonietta and I have Giorgio.

Antonietta led me to Giorgio and I am ever thankful for that because he is a good man. To marry him I had to join the church and I did so because it meant nothing to me whereas Giorgio meant a great deal. I told him that what I was doing I was doing for him, that joining the church was an act of pretence on my part. This did not surprise him. He said it didn't matter, he knew I would come round eventually, that I would accept the church along with all the other aspects of the city because they all interlock and it is impossible to separate them without separating yourself from the very heart of the place. I remember smiling when he told me this. I smiled because I did not believe I could change that much. I did not believe I could ever accept any religion. Now I think I was wrong. I accepted the city and I accepted Giorgio. Accepting the church will be harder and I am not there yet. But I am not far from it either. Already it seems to have accepted me.

PART SEVEN

1969

THE LOCH

WHEN the train was an hour out of Euston the heating failed and by the time it pulled into Crewe all the carriages were cold. In a first-class compartment at the head of the train a lady sat alone. She was about sixty years old and was very smartly dressed in a grey coat and pale blue cloche hat. She was cold. She felt that she had not been so cold for many years. Outside, as the morning began and light filtered through from the east, a winter landscape was revealed; grey smoking towns and in the distances between them white fields and white trees. A hard frost had settled on old snow; the houses sparkled as if they had been dipped in sugar.

The woman shivered. She had put on her extra jumper and her coat on top of that. The guard had brought her a blanket to wrap round her knees. She wondered where he had got it from. As this was a day train surely there was no sleeping carriage. Perhaps the heating failed so regularly that blankets were laid on as a matter of course. She wondered if only first-class passengers got blankets or second-class travellers too. Maybe they were left to shiver. Whatever the reason for their appearance and however unfair their distribution might be she was glad the blankets had been issued. She thought that if the guard passed again she might catch his attention and ask whether or not a second blanket was available. She was very, very cold.

At Crewe the train was supplied with a new locomotive and within fifteen minutes the compartment began to heat up. When half an hour had passed it was possible for the lady to take off her coat and her outer jumper. The cloche hat was placed carefully on the rack. The guard visited her and said that all was well but he would not collect the blankets yet in case they hit a spot of bother later on. It was cold, after all, he said, very, very cold. She agreed.

The train was not crowded. The lady was able to enjoy a table to herself in the dining car for lunch. She noticed only five other diners and wondered if each of these had a compartment all to himself. All were seated separately. She thought how typically British it was for each one of them to seek such privacy. She found it strange but reflected that she was herself British. However she qualified this by reminding herself that she was by no means typical. No, it was not a question of perverse pride or gloating eccentricity, she just could not possibly describe herself as typically British. That would not do at all.

After lunch she returned to her compartment and began to search through her handbag for her documents. She possessed a British passport and some extra identity papers issued by the British Embassy in Rome. She also had a couple of letters which bore her name. From a small suitcase she extracted a toilet bag. She put the passport and the other papers inside this and then left the compartment. When she reached the toilet she took these papers from the bag and placed them in the sink. She also took out a pair of scissors. With these she cut up all her identity documents, including the stiff covers of the passport, into small pieces and flushed them all down the toilet.

Back in the compartment she knew that it was not only the warmth that comforted her. She began to feel relaxed. As the miles passed and the train crossed the border and headed deeper into Scotland she felt more and more at ease as if something had been arranged and was nearing completion.

She arrived in Glasgow in mid-afternoon and took a taxi to a hotel five minutes away from the station. She booked in as Mrs A. Jenner, went to her room and took a nap which lasted about an hour. She rose, washed her face and, despite the cold, put on her grey coat and left the hotel. She walked for over an hour, looking in shop windows and watching people in pursuit of their lives. She knew that many in her situation would shake their heads and express their wonderment in terms of things lost, bemoaning the departure of old buildings, old ideas and old values. She did not feel this. She was like a child in some sort of magic land. 'And why not,' she thought. 'Why not.'

She dined at six thirty and afterwards went straight to her room. So far she had managed to avoid contact with anyone except on the superficial level required by her dealings with railway guards, porters and hotel maids. She was glad of this. So far, things were going to plan. She paused to think of this business of a plan. Yes, perhaps she did have one. From her small suitcase she extracted everything and laid the articles out on the bed. She was amazed by how little there was. The clothes she had brought were sufficient for only three or four days and occupied quite a small pile. It was a pity about the mohair jumper, she thought. Perhaps she could leave it in a drawer here in her room so that the maid would find it. There was no guarantee of course that the maid would eventually get it. No doubt attempts would be made to trace the owner, this Mrs A. Jenner, and return the jumper. No, that would not do. It would have to travel on with her.

She repacked the clothes, including the mohair jumper, and turned her attention to the other things that still lay on the bed.

Beside her toilet bag lay two photographs. Both in monochrome, one was a portrait of a man; the other showed a close-up of two people, a man and a woman. The man in the second was the same as in the first and the woman was a somewhat younger version of the woman who now picked up the photos and took them through to the bathroom. She had been silly, she realised, to bring the photos with her but she had needed something to help her. She felt that she would not have been able to get this far without them. It hurt but she tore the photos into small pieces and dropped them into the toilet bowl.

That left just her toilet things, a small bag of sweets, a paperback novel she had hardly opened, an apple and a Bible. This small black book was in Italian and had been given to her by her husband some years before. An inscription on the flyleaf indicated this. As she flicked through the pages this inscription caught her eye and she realised with a start that it would have to go too. She tore out the thin sheet of paper, careful not to damage the rest of the book. She returned to the bathroom and tore this last item of identification into tiny pieces before flushing it away to follow the fragmented photographs.

The day before, when she had destroyed her passport and other papers, she had felt a kind of release, an inkling of freedom. A similar feeling overcame her now but it was tinged with excitement, the excitement that came from knowing that now there was really no way back, she was at last completely without identity and completely alone. This last thought also filled her with sadness.

The next morning she rose early and went to mass in a nearby church. She was one of a congregation of seven. As she made the responses she felt how strange they sounded in English. She also wondered why she was there at all in this huge gloomy church so early in the morning talking to a faraway God in what was for her a foreign language. It was a struggle to find the relevance of the ceremony to her present experience. In Italy it had been different. It was as if the brightness of the climate had made things a little easier to see. Here she found herself in a cold draughty church with a tiny group of tired people. No, perhaps that was harsh; she should not speak for the others, sleepy though most of them looked. However, the priest gave her no confidence, repeating the words of the service in a bored, mechanical way. She wondered if she should take the Eucharist and then did so for no other reason than force of habit. Not a sound basis for her action, she knew, but she covered this lapse by assuring herself that it was so important not to stand out from the others. She did not want to be noticed. When the other six members of the congregation stepped forward she fell in quietly behind them.

She wished that the service offered more time for private prayer. When the opportunity came she prayed hard, as if to turn this spiritual moment into a solid, physical event. She prayed for forgiveness for the terrible thing she had been responsible for and she prayed for understanding because she was about to do something equally terrible.

As she made her way back to the hotel for breakfast, along cold, icy streets swept by a bitter wind, she reflected that even when logic and reason overturn a fondly held belief it is possible that some kind of dull mechanical necessity will come into play and maintain the status quo.

After breakfast she took a taxi to the station. As she boarded the Strathinver train a breathless taxi driver caught up with her; she had left her suitcase in the back of his cab. She tipped him generously and then made her way to the first-class carriage. She had not deliberately tried to leave her suitcase behind, or had she? She really was unsure about the whole thing. A porter placed the suitcase on the rack in an empty compartment. She would have to get rid of the case at some stage but it would have to be done in such a way that no one would be chasing after her or trying to find her. No matter, she would think of something. So far all was well. She was alone in a first-class compartment and the heating was on. She settled back in comfort and began to think once more of the strange visit she had received only a few days before in Naples, the visit that had led her to make this journey.

She had first noticed the young man as she made her way back from the shops one morning. She noticed him because he was obviously not a Neapolitan – and probably not Italian – but he did not seem to be a tourist. He was about twenty, she guessed, and was wearing a pale beige jacket and blue slacks. He had sandy coloured hair, cut quite short. He had a book or a wad of papers in his hand but carried no bag and no camera. She passed quite near him at one point and overheard his attempts in faltering Italian to gain information from one of the market stall-holders. She could not be sure what the enquiry was about and was soon out of earshot. That same evening, on the way home from visiting a friend, she had seen him again. This time he was sitting in Piazza Sannazzaro at a table belonging to one of the restaurants. It was unusual for the tables to be outside so late in the year but the weather was still mild if not exactly warm. There were few diners however. The young man was waiting for his order to arrive and was studying a book intently. She guessed that he was probably a student and she thought no more about him.

A few days later, however, he was at her door. Lucia, the maid, indicated that there was a young gentleman to see her, a foreign young gentleman. This was most unusual. She asked Lucia to find out what he wanted. She thought he might be an art student trying to sell some pictures. This had happened before. But no, this was not the case. Lucia returned with the information that he wanted to speak to the *signora* on a most important matter. This news was insufficient. Lucia was obliged to return to the front door and ask him to be a little more specific about his business. A couple of minutes later she reported that he had asked her to tell the *signora* that he came from the north of Scotland. This was another matter altogether. With her heart beating hard inside her chest she told Lucia to show him in.

She kept him waiting. She decided that she was mad to agree to see him but she felt the decision was made and it would be impossible for her to go back on it. He was now in the house, waiting; she would have to see him. But why had she agreed in the first place? In fact it was not difficult for her to answer this. Although only in her early sixties, she felt herself to be old. Her husband was now dead and with his death many things in her life had become less important, certain major questions did not matter any more. She was almost relieved that after all these years she would make contact again with her distant past. She was also curious.

She composed herself and then went into the kitchen to ask Lucia to bring tea. When she entered the sitting room fully five minutes after the young man had been shown in she expected him to be on edge or at the very least impatient. Not a bit of it. He rose and greeted her formally in Italian. She was momentarily taken aback when she recognised the young man from the Piazza Sannazzaro. He was wearing the same jacket and possibly the same slacks. He was a little taller than she remembered but she was almost certain she had got the age right. He was twenty, perhaps twenty-one. But there was something she noticed now that had not been apparent when she had seen him before: he looked tired. It wasn't just lack of sleep, she thought, it was a tiredness that came from inside.

'We can speak in English if you prefer,' she said.

'I'd like that better, I must admit,' he said. She felt he was relieved but she saw no trace of a smile. She got the impression that he was caught in the effort of forcing himself to relax.

'You have a good accent,' she said. And then realising this comment could be misconstrued, she added, 'Your Italian – have you been studying it for long?'

'About two weeks.'

'Two weeks! But that's quite remarkable. You sound so . . . confident.'

'It's bluff mostly,' he said. 'You learn a few key phrases, practise them to get the sound right and then you trot them out as appropriate. In fact my vocabulary is pretty limited. It's all a bit of a con, really.'

'I see.' She paused for a moment, still attempting to get the measure of the man. She realised that the seriousness in his face was the product of the tiredness she had noticed right from the start. There was something else, too, in his face, that was reminiscent of someone. But she could not remember who. If only he would smile, however faintly.

'Sit down won't you,' she said. 'I've asked Lucia to prepare some tea. Or would you prefer coffee?'

'I don't mind,' he said 'Whatever. Tea is fine.'

'Good,' she said, though his response had hardly satisfied her. She sat down opposite him. He was perched, elbows on knees, on the edge of the sofa. She settled into her deep armchair although she did not feel relaxed. 'Perhaps you'd better tell me your name,' she said. 'That would be a start, wouldn't it.'

'Yes, of course. It's George Candless.'

'I see. And you say that you come from the north of Scotland.'

'That's right.'

'Where, exactly?'

'I'm from Ardallt.'

'Oh.'

A short silence followed.

'You know where that is, don't you,' he said.

'Yes,' she said. 'I do.'

'But I think it's some time since you were last there.'

'It certainly is. A very long time.' She rose rather abruptly. 'Excuse me, won't you. I'll just check on the tea.' In some confusion she stepped towards the door but before she reached it Lucia entered bearing a tray. Instead of allowing the maid to arrange things she took the tray from her and brought it to the centre of the room herself. Lucia left, looking rather bewildered.

Elisa Stasi transferred all the items from the tray to the table. She did so slowly and deliberately, forcing herself to be calm. She poured the tea. About three minutes passed in silence before George Candless said, 'I know who you are, you know.'

'Do you indeed.'

'Yes.'

She handed him his cup and saucer. 'I could have refused to see you. Maybe I should have refused.' She gestured to the sugar bowl. He declined.

'I would have waited outside and approached you in the street.'

For the first time she looked directly at his face.

'I think you would have, too,' she said. 'You seem a determined young man.'

'I am.'

'And what is it that makes you so determined?'

He sipped his tea and then placed his cup and saucer on the table between them. 'I want to find out the truth about something, or rather about someone.'

'Not about me, surely?' She was able to give the flicker of a smile.

'No, not about you. I know about you already. Most of it, anyway.'

'Oh do you now. Do you.' She found herself at last out of patience with this softly spoken, humourless man who was blunt to the extent of being rude. 'So you know all about me, do you?'

'Not all, no, just the important bits.'

'And are there many of those "important bits", as you call them?'

He took another sip of tea. 'Not really, no.' She stood up, stung not only by this rudeness but by the fact that she had unwittingly presented the opportunity to him. 'Whatever you want from me, young man, you're going the wrong way about it. You'll either mend your manners or leave.'

She paused, aware that her face was red and her hands trembling. She looked down at him as he calmly replaced his cup on the table, sat back and, for the first time, smiled.

Momentarily disabled by this effrontery she sat down again though she positioned herself on the very edge of the armchair. 'You . . . you . . .' she began, but he started talking now, talking across her and she was forced to stop and listen.

'I'm always amazed,' he said, 'and amused too, I suppose, when people rate good manners so high on their list, higher than . . . well . . . telling the truth, for example.'

'So now you're accusing me of lying, I suppose.'

'I don't know yet. Perhaps. Then again you may only be guilty of lying to yourself.'

She shook her head. 'I just don't know what you're talking about,' she said. 'And I think you should leave. Now.'

His reply was to pick up his teacup. He drank off the remainder of the tea but instead of rising he sat back again. 'You'll give me five minutes of your time, *signora*. At the end of that, if I haven't convinced you that I have a valid reason for being here, well, then I'll go.' He replaced the cup on the table. 'How does that sound?'

He seemed tired again and his face reverted to its former look. She remembered then who it was that this look reminded her of. It was the look that belonged to a thousand beggars, the ones who receive cash or curses with equal indifference, who are so inured to their work that they are almost unable to distinguish the responses they receive.

'Why are you so tired?' she asked and there was more than a trace of concern in her voice.

'I've travelled a long way,' he said. 'I had very little money so I hitched my way here from Scotland.'

'Hitched?'

He had to explain the term to her. Then he said, 'France wasn't so bad but hitching in Italy is a waste of time. It took me five days to get to Rome from the French border and then another five from Rome to here. I walked most of the way. Now I'm staying in a hotel that is little better than a slum and this morning I had my passport stolen. I've spent several hours talking to the police about it. They seem singularly unimpressed.'

'Oh,' she said. And then, 'Where was it your passport was stolen?'

'Near the Piazza Sannazzaro, I think.'

'I'm sorry about that.'

'No,' he said, 'don't be. I don't want pity.'

She decided there was no venom in his voice. 'So,' she said, 'what is it that you do want?'

'I want you to tell me about my father.'

'Your father?'

'Albert Sandison.'

'Sandison?' She looked confused. 'But you said . . .'

'I know,' he interrupted her. 'That wasn't the name I gave you before. I said I was George Candless and it's true in a way. It's the name I was brought up with and it's the name on my passport' – he shook his head – 'my stolen passport.'

'But not your father's name?'

'No.'

She began pouring more tea, without asking if he wanted any.

'Does the name Candless mean anything to you?' he asked.

She put down the teapot. 'I'm not sure . . .'

'Stewart Candless?'

'Stewart? . . . Was he? . . . Ah, yes. I think I remember now. He was quite well off. He used to join every club, every group there was and then leave. He was . . . well, I didn't really know him. I probably only spoke to him a couple of times. So he . . . brought you up?'

'That's right. He and my mother married when I was about three or four. It seems my father disappeared when I was about one.'

'Disappeared?' She felt that he was studying her face intently.

'Yes. He ran off; he abandoned the family. Well, so I was told. And that's what I believed up until about three weeks ago. Imagine, all that time . . . ' He picked up his fresh cup of tea and drank.

'So what happened three weeks ago?' Elisa Stasi asked.

'Stewart Candless died.' The words came straight out with no show of emotion. He took another sip of tea.

'I'm sorry.'

'Don't be. Stewart treated me like a son in every way. He took care of my education, made sure I always had money – well, until two years ago or so, when the money began to run out. But then, about four weeks ago, just before he died, he told me that he had lied to me all along about my father.'

'Lied to you?'

'Yes. For the best part of twenty years. Well, you can imagine how I felt.' He paused. 'I don't know, maybe you can't. I don't think you can imagine how I felt. Anyway, he told me what really happened to my father, or at least as much as he knew.'

'What about your mother, did she know?'

'Oh yes, some of it, I'm sure, but not all. But then she died two years ago so it was too late to ask her.'

'I'm sorry,' she said. She was aware that it was an automatic response she had made three or four times now but on this occasion he made no comment on it. 'So what did happen to your father?' she asked.

He leaned back in the sofa. 'My father and mother didn't get on all that well. That was in 1947, when I was only a year old. He was working for Stewart at that time, as a reporter . . . '

'A reporter?'

'Yes. Stewart was the editor of the *Ardallt Journal.*'

'That is a surprise, from what I remember of Stewart.'

'Yes, well, he took it over just after the War and he was editor until about six months ago when he became ill. It seems that my father was not bad at his job but he kept going off after marvellous scoops which never materialised. I think he felt a bit of a failure. He'd been working on the *Journal* for several years and he wasn't getting anywhere. Then he remembered you.'

'Me?' She seemed genuinely surprised. 'He remembered me? But I can't remember him. What was his name again?'

'Albert. Albert Sandison. It doesn't mean anything to you?'

She appeared to think hard for a few moments. 'No,' she said at last. 'No, it doesn't mean anything.' She shook her head.

'Maybe it wasn't you in person that he remembered, but your situation, what happened to you. You see he knew about your disappearance. He knew that everyone thought you were dead although they'd never found your body. They poked around in the river, you know, and they dragged a loch or two . . .'

'Yes,' she said, 'I know.'

'So . . .' he went on, but then paused. 'You know? How do you know?'

She realised she had been caught out but she was not sure how much it mattered. Surely none of it mattered any more. 'Tell me,' she said, 'is Simon still alive?'

'Simon McAndrew?'

'Yes.'

'No,' he said. 'He died about two years ago.' Then he added, surprising her, 'I'm sorry.'

'It's all right,' she said. 'It's all right.'

'Did you communicate with him after you left?'

'Not with him, no. Not with Simon.'

'But you were in touch with someone?'

'Yes, I was, but I don't think I can tell you who. No, I can't do that.' She seemed quite firm on this point.

'Well,' George Candless went on, 'maybe it doesn't really matter now. Did you stay in contact for long?'

'About a year, perhaps a little more. I can't remember exactly. But you were talking about your father.'

'Yes, my father. Well, he managed to convince himself that you were still alive. How he managed this I don't know and neither did Stewart. Anyway, he reckoned you were out there somewhere and finding you would be the scoop of the century – well, for the *Ardallt Journal*, at any rate.'

'But it was so long after I left,' she said. 'How could he really have had any hope of finding me?'

'I know, I know. It seems so unlikely. But I think a great part of it was down to his wanting to get away for a while, to get away from my mother.'

'And Stewart Candless encouraged him in this?'

'Ah!' George Candless smiled for only the second time since the visit began. 'This is where things get complicated. Not only did Stewart encourage him, he gave him money to go down to London for a while to continue his search. And he did that because by this time he was having an affair with my mother and he wanted my father out of the way.'

'Ah.' It was Elisa Stasi's turn to sit back. She relaxed against the armchair cushions and balanced her second cup of tea on the wide arm of the chair. 'So your father's interest in me was quite convenient.'

'That's right.'

'So what happened after that?'

'He came to Naples.'

'What!'

'He came here. He uncovered something in London that pointed to Naples. He contacted Stewart. Stewart sent him some more money and he came here.'

'But how did he track me to Naples?' She was concerned now, less relaxed. The tea sat neglected on the arm of the chair.

'I don't know and Stewart didn't know either. At least that's what he told me. He just got a phone call from London: "She's in Naples." That's all my father would say. Maybe he didn't want to give too much away until he was able to write it all up himself. Anyway, he asked Stewart for more money and Stewart sent him some.'

'And what happened then?'

George Candless finished his second cup of tea. 'I was hoping you could tell me that,' he said.

'Me?' She looked puzzled. 'How should I know anything about it?'

'Because he came out to Naples and he found you.'

'Found me? Found me?' She was aware that her voice was rising. She forced herself to say, calmly, 'No, you're certainly mistaken there. He never found me.'

'No?'

'No.'

'I have a letter,' George Candless said and he drew out of an inside pocket a very faded and dog-eared envelope. 'It's a letter from my father to Stewart Candless and it was sent from Naples. Would you like to read it?' He held it out towards her.

For a moment she looked at it as if examining something rather unsavoury. 'No,' she said. 'You can read it, if you must.'

'I will then,' he said. He opened the envelope and extracted the letter which he unfolded very carefully. 'It's dated the seventh of June, 1947, but Stewart said he didn't actually receive it till August or September.' Then he read:

'"Dear Stewart, I've found her and I've actually seen her! She calls herself Elisa these days and she's married to someone called Stasi. It seems the Stasis are a well-known and influential family in this city, so she's done all right for herself. I've managed to arrange to meet her and talk to her and this should take place tomorrow (though it's being organised by a very unreliable man, one of the expatriate drunks that lives here). So, I'll send you some more information after I've talked to her. Anyway, run the story, Stewart, run it now. Can you think of a better way to boost circulation? Yours, Albert."'

*

She watched him fold the letter, put it back inside the envelope and then the envelope back in his jacket pocket.

'So,' he said, 'what do you make of that?'

'I don't know,' she said. 'I don't know what to think.'

'So you never met him?'

'Met him?' Her tone suggested the idea was not only impossible but absurd. 'No, of course I never met him. I wasn't even aware he existed.'

'You're sure?'

There was silence for a few seconds. 'You don't believe me, do you?' she said. It was a statement rather than a question.

He leaned forward, picked up his empty cup and set it down again. 'I don't know what to believe,' he said. For the first time she thought him to be sincere. The bitterness had left him and he just sounded tired.

'What about your father?' she asked. 'What happened after Naples?'

'I think I told you already. He disappeared.'

'What do you mean, "disappeared"?'

'Simple: he never came back.'

Elisa Stasi began fussing with the tea things. She moved the sugar bowl from the table onto the tray and then back again.

George Candless continued: 'He came out here looking for you, he found you, he arranged to meet you and then he just disappeared. He never came back to Ardallt and no one ever heard from him again.' He paused for a moment and then he went on: 'So what do you think?'

'Me?' She set down the silver milk jug which she had raised from the tray. 'I've told you, I don't know anything about your father. If he arranged to see me then it was without my knowledge. I didn't even know he was here.'

'If that's the case then someone near to you knew about him.'

'Oh? What do you mean by that?'

He pulled himself more upright on the sofa, an action completed with some effort. 'I think you've lived here long enough to know what I mean.'

'I'm afraid . . .' she began but she stopped. After a few seconds thought she said, 'If you're suggesting that someone close to me intercepted your father and . . . and then . . .'

'Yes?'

'Well the idea is preposterous, quite preposterous.'

'Why?'

'Because it is.' She appeared to be quite agitated now. She stood up and walked the few paces over to the window. She turned to face him. 'These things don't happen . . .'

He laughed.

'. . . In this family, I mean. I'm not so important . . .'

'Ah, you mean if you *were* important, it might happen?' He smiled at her and at that moment she disliked him intensely. 'Look,' he said, and the smile disappeared, 'you had a past, you were settled in with a well-to-do family and any raking up of your past, particularly the fact that you were already married, would have been . . . well . . . at very best embarrassing.'

'I see. So you think my family arranged for him . . . to be "got rid of"?'

'Exactly.'

'No,' she said firmly. She made her way back to the armchair. 'Absolutely not. It's quite out of the question. I mean, any number of other things could have happened . . .'

'For example?'

'Well . . . Naples is . . . it's true, it's a dangerous place, or it can be. I mean, after the War, if he got into the wrong company . . .'

'Well,' he smiled, 'it's possible, I suppose. But only because just about anything is possible. We could even say that perhaps nothing nasty happpened to him at all. Perhaps he came out here, fell in love with a Neapolitan and decided to stay. That's not entirely out of the question, is it?'

She knew she was being mocked but she had her answer ready. 'That's precisely what happened to me,' she said.

She could see this took him by surprise. He thought about it for a few moments, then he got to his feet. '*Signora*, I'm tired,' he said. 'I need to go to my *pensione* and sleep. But I want to come back here. I want to come back after you've done some investigation . . .'

'Investigation?'

'That's right. You'll know who to ask. Just ask them. That's all I want. I think you'll tell me the truth. I don't know why I believe that but I do. I also believe that you might be interested in finding out . . .'

'Why?'

'Because . . . because you might be implicated in a murder. You'd want to know about that, wouldn't you.'

She felt her cheeks reddening. She seemed about to cry out but she thought better of it. 'What you are suggesting is evil,' she said, 'but I'll look into it for your sake, though I don't really know why I should. Then when I've told you that your understanding of the situation is completely false you'll go away and not bother me again?'

He shrugged. 'Possibly. But I can't guarantee it.'

'I see. And that's the best you can offer.'

'Yes.'

They made their way to the door. He turned to her and said, 'I think you're an honest person . . .' – she had the rather uneasy feeling that this was almost a blessing he was conferring on her – '. . . but just make sure that other people don't lie to you.'

'Have you lied to me?' she asked.

'No,' he said, quite firmly.

She opened the door. 'Oh, tell me one more thing,' she said as they passed into the corridor. 'In the letter you read your father suggested to Stewart Candless that he should print the story, I mean about finding me.'

'That's right.'

'Did he do it?'

'No, he didn't.'

'Why not?'

'Well, for one thing, my father had conveniently disappeared and Stewart didn't really want to revive interest in him – I mean I'm not sure how much my mother knew at that stage, but probably nothing. Anyway, there was another problem, another reason why Stewart didn't print the story.'

'Oh? You mean he didn't believe it?'

'Oh no. No, no. He believed it, or so he told me, anyway. No, he believed it but the thing was, he didn't think anyone else would. Don't you think that's amazing?' He smiled and shook his head. 'Here we have a newspaperman who didn't want to print a story that he knew to be true because he felt that no one would believe it. I mean, it's turning the whole thing on its head, isn't it? "How could I answer the questions?" he said to me. "A reporter somewhere in Italy, maybe not coming back at all, how could I prove it?" You see, he was actually worried about the credibility of his paper. Amazing, don't you think?'

'I don't know what to think, frankly. The whole thing is most strange.'

'Oh, it certainly is, and it will probably get stranger. But I remember him saying to me . . .'

'Who?'

'Stewart Candless. He said something like . . . just remember that because something actually happened that doesn't in itself make it credible. Often it's much easier to get people to believe something that isn't true rather than something that is.'

They were at the front door.

'Come back here tomorrow evening,' she said, 'at this time.'

'I will,' he said. He stepped out into the sunshine.

'Can I . . .' She knew she was laying herself open to his anger, possibly contempt, but she went on anyway, 'Can I give you some money?'

He looked at her. 'I need it, *signora*, and thank you for the offer, but I can't take it.' He turned and descended the short flight of steps to the pavement.

Within an hour Elisa was at the house of her friend Antonietta.

'Who?' Antonietta asked. Now in her late sixties she was a tall, white-haired lady, very elegantly dressed. She wore gold rings on six of her long, rather claw-like fingers and several gold chains round her neck. Like Elisa Stasi she was a widow.

'A man called Sandison,' Elisa said, 'Albert Sandison.'

'But such a long time ago. When did you say?'

'1947.'

'Oh, impossible, impossible.' She threw her hands in the air, 'What are we now? '69? But that is twenty . . . twenty-two years. You want me to remember something so long ago?'

'It's important,' Elisa said.

'I don't doubt it. Otherwise you wouldn't be here so late in the evening. So why is this man important?'

'He came here looking for me.'

'Ah.' It was a staccato sound indicating understanding, a sound that perhaps Antonietta regretted immediately she had uttered it.

Elisa said, 'You do know something, don't you?'

Antonietta looked to be deep in thought. 'The name . . .' she said, '. . .the name means nothing.'

'But you do remember, don't you? I can see that you remember something.'

'Perhaps. I'm not sure. Such a long time ago.'

'Please Antonietta. Please try to help.'

'But why is it so important?'

'His son is here.' Elisa said.

'Son? Whose son?'

'The son of the man who came here to find me.'

'The son of that man?'

'So there was someone?'

'No . . . I mean, this is what you are saying.'

'But there was someone? Was there?'

There was a long silence before Antonietta said, 'There may have been someone.'

'May have been? May have been? What does that mean? Either there was someone or there wasn't. Was there someone?'

After a few more seconds Antonietta said, 'Yes, there was someone.'

'But, but why didn't you tell me? At the time, I mean?'

'It didn't concern you.'

'How can you say that? Of course it concerned me . . .'

'I felt not.'

'You . . . you . . . you felt not? You decided?' Elisa Stasi was beginning to realise that there was much more to this business than she had originally supposed. 'Someone came here looking for me, and nobody thought to tell me about it?'

'It was for the best . . .'

'For the best?'

'Of course it was. I mean consider your situation, Elisa. You were married to Giorgio, you had a place, a situation . . . it was . . . it was possible that all this could be destroyed because someone came poking his nose into things that did not concern him.'

'So what happened?'

'What happened?' Antonietta looked as if this question was a most unusual one. 'Well, you were protected. There was no cause for any difficulty, any embarrassment . . .'

'No, no,' Elisa said, 'I mean what happened to the man. To Albert Sandison?'

'Oh, him . . .' She gave the impression that he was an item of very little importance. 'I've no idea.'

'But what did you do? Did you meet him?'

'Me? No, certainly not. No, someone told me that there was a man asking questions about you so I mentioned this to Gennaro and he said he would handle it.'

'Handle it? What does that mean?'

'I don't know and I don't wish to know. These are things that I left to Gennaro; I had no place in them. He said he would handle it and a few days later he said to me that the whole thing had been taken care of. After that there was no problem.'

'But what did he do?' Elisa said, aware that her voice was rising. 'What exactly did he do?'

'I told you; it was not my concern.'

'But it is mine.'

'Why? Why is it?' Antonietta too found her voice to be louder, sharper. 'It was a long time ago and it is over. Such things are better left now . . .'

Elisa grabbed at this last comment. 'What things?' she asked, or rather demanded. 'What kind of things?'

Antonietta was losing patience now with her old friend. 'Oh you are impossible, Elisa! Leave it alone now. It was a question of your safety and your security. I do not understand you. You are like a child sometimes, you know . . .' At this point her voice grew calmer and it began to sound as if she were talking to a child. 'You have lived here for so many years and you don't seem to know how things are here, or you don't admit it to yourself.'

'I don't approve of hurting people,' Elisa said.

'You will not say this,' Antonietta said and there was no doubt she was angry. 'You will not say such things because you do not know. You have no proof.'

'Antonietta, the man disappeared. He never returned to Britain. You know what happened to him and I now know what happened to him. We don't need proof.'

'So you know what happened to him. Then why ask me? As far as I know he might have been given money and told to leave. What's wrong with that?'

'He wouldn't have done it.'

'So? If he didn't know what was good for him he deserved what was coming.'

'But Antonietta,' she said, her voice rising, 'if he died . . .'

'Elisa!' This was almost a shout. 'If he died then he is to blame as much as the man who . . . helped him die. Yes, if you like, Gennaro is to blame and I am to blame and you are to blame too . . .'

'Me?'

'We all take a share, yes, you as well. Because when I first met you I liked you and then later I loved you and I decided that I would protect you.' Her voice lost its anger and became quieter. 'I wanted to save you from people who would hurt you. I could see you had suffered. I could see that, right from the start.'

A terrible thought came to Elisa. 'Have there been others?' she asked.

'Others?'

'Others like this man Sandison, asking questions about me?'

Antonietta paused. 'I don't know,' she said. 'Perhaps. After that first time, well, things might have been arranged without my knowing. I don't think anyone else came but I can't be sure. Maybe.'

'I can't believe all this,' Elisa said.

'Then don't. What does it matter anyway. It's too late.'

When she left Antonietta, Elisa Stasi was in a state of shock. She knew that in Naples crime was never very far away, but that her family might involve itself in this most violent of crimes was unimaginable. And because of her. From Antonietta's house to her own was no more than a five minute stroll but she set off in the opposite direction, determined to walk the streets of the city until she was tired out. Pushing her forward was the idea that George Candless had given to her, the fact that she was now an accessory to murder.

She walked for an hour. She chose the most unfamiliar of the *vicoli*, the network of narrow alleys in the area of Spaccanapoli. She had never explored them all and now, late at night, was not the best time to do so.

But she was not interested in exploration. What she wanted was distance passing beneath her feet, a journey with no real direction or end, just tiredness to be measured in cobblestones and cracked paving stones.

There was danger here, too, and she welcomed it. She could remember the first and only time her bag had been snatched from her, more than thirty years before. She had been scared then and after that she had always taken care about where she walked and what she carried with her. Now, on this late evening walk it did not seem to matter. In fact she wanted hurt, she wanted to be robbed, perhaps even injured, as if this would in some way absolve her of the guilt she felt. After an hour she arrived at her door tired but unmolested. She had met several people during her walk, all of them strangers to her, and they had been polite and courteous. She wanted to weep but could not.

The following morning, after a restless night, she rose early. She felt worn out but she was determined to organise herself as there were several things that had to be done. First she made some phone calls. Then she took a taxi to the station where she bought a ticket to Rome. She returned to her house and found that it was only eleven o'clock. George Candless was due to arrive at seven. The eight hours which stretched in front of her seemed like something physical and solid that she had to clamber over, painfully. She made some more phone calls. She decided that at least part of the time till seven would have to be filled by the composition of an appropriate response to George Candless. But what could she possibly tell him?

She decided on the truth.

In fact there had been little question that she would tell him the truth. She could not have done otherwise. Even if she had wanted to lie she knew she was not very good at it. And, in a way, the truth was easy. It was the manner of telling it that presented problems.

She tried to rest in the afternoon. In fact she managed to sleep for an hour or so and rose a little refreshed. At five thirty she had a visitor. He was a man of about forty, casually dressed and with a dab of perspiration on his lip. He did not come into the house but spoke to her on the doorstep for less than a minute. He gave her a small package and she handed him an envelope. Back inside she checked the contents of the package and added to it the train ticket she had bought earlier in the day. She asked Lucia to bring tea and she settled down to wait for George Candless.

By six thirty-five she was no nearer to a decision on how to tell George her news than she had been at eleven in the morning. She felt that it would probably all come tumbling out. It struck her then that she could offer no details about Albert Sandison's death. She hadn't even considered that such details would be available. How could she explain this?

So here was another problem which occupied the remaining minutes to seven o'clock. Then, exactly at seven, she decided she needed to freshen up. She was annoyed with herself for not doing so earlier as she was sure that George would be punctual. She dabbed at her forehead with a cold cloth and applied some face powder. She checked her appearance and decided she was being silly. She returned to the sitting room and sat down to wait again. It was four minutes past seven.

By twenty past she was beginning to grow concerned. At twenty-five minutes past seven she realised in a moment of acute horror why George Candless had not turned up. In frustration she beat the arm of the sofa with her fist. For a few moments she was unable to rise. She wept at her own naïvety, her stupidity. She wanted to throw something or stamp something into the ground. After a minute or so she wiped her eyes and rose uncertainly to her feet. She asked Lucia to go out into the street and hail a taxi.

She was fairly sure that George Candless had told her he was staying in a *pensione* near Piazza Sannazzaro. There were four or five overlooking the Piazza and she started with these. In the first two, she was told there were no foreigners staying. In the third, the *portiera* said yes, there was one foreigner who had booked in three days before. Elisa fumbled with the package she had received that afternoon. She drew out George Candless's passport and showed the *portiera* the photograph. She squinted at it for a few seconds and then announced that yes, this was the man. No, he was not in. He had gone out in the morning and had not returned. Yes, he was expected back as he had left a jacket and one or two other things in his room.

Elisa Stasi left instructions with the *portiera* that he was to make contact immediately he returned. Then she went back to her house. It was now nearly nine o'clock. She rang Antonietta. The maid answered and explained that the *signora* had left earlier in the day to spend a few days at her cousin's house near Caserta. Elisa put the phone down. She now had confirmation of what had happened to George Candless. Antonietta had gone to a place where she could not be contacted as her cousin had no phone.

Elisa spent the rest of the evening trying to convince herself that something else had happened to George Candless. He had gone out for the day and had been delayed. This was rather weak but not if he had gone some distance – to Positano, for example, or one of the islands – as public transport was at best unreliable. Yes, for a few minutes she managed the trick, George was alive and well and struggling to get back to his *pensione*. He would arrive on her doorstep first thing in the morning and apologise profusely for missing his appointment. For a moment or two she wondered if she had got the day wrong. Had she asked him to come back the day after his first visit or two days after? Perhaps there was nothing sinister going on. She had got the day wrong and he had gone off to explore the region, ready to return the following day.

By midnight her hopes disappeared. She knew she was just trying to fool herself. George was dead, just as his father was dead. He had died because he was a threat. He was a threat to her, to Elisa Stasi, so it was she who was in part responsible for his death.

With this admission came a certain amount of relief. She managed to sleep for a few hours. In the morning she rose a little earlier than usual but breakfasted without haste. She took a taxi to George Candless's *pensione*. She did not expect him to appear suddenly. All she wanted, and got, was confirmation that he had not returned. The *portiera* grumbled that rent was owing and she would not hold the room indefinitely. Elisa paid off the arrears and collected George's belongings which the *portiera* had already placed in a flimsy cardboard box. There was nothing else to do.

In the taxi that took her back to her house, Elisa was already beginning to plan. She spent the remainder of the morning sifting through old photographs, mostly those of her husband Giorgio. She wept. Before lunch, however, she dried her eyes and put all the photographs away. She showered, and by the time she seated herself in the dining room she almost looked her usual calm, assured self.

In the afternoon she went to church to make her confession. She wanted to tell her confessor everything but could not. She could not even confess her reticence. Instead she confessed her naïvety, her lack of knowledge of the ways of the world. Even as her confessor protested she continued; she confessed to ignorance, to closing her eyes to reality. She said she was guilty of the sin of blindness. She began to weep.

She knew that on the other side of the curtain the priest was struggling. He bid her be calm. He started talking to her about the nature of sin. He noted that there were sins of omission as well as commission but felt that the former did not apply in this case. Unless he had more details however, he could not say. He urged her to confess but she would not. He pointed out that absolution was not possible unless she made a true confession. She said that she held the truth, the truth was inside her but it could not be released. She rose and left the confessional without waiting for a reply.

She was still distressed but a little calmer when she reached home. She showered and changed and then sat in the lounge for half an hour. Two things lay in her hands. One was George Candless's passport; the other was the train ticket to Rome. She put the passport on the table and examined the ticket. It was a single ticket, open. Anyone could use it, at any time. Although not superstitious she felt that her ownership of the ticket and the manner in which she had come to possess it were signs which she could not ignore. She packed a small bag with a few essential items, left a note for Lucia who was out shopping, and took a taxi to the station.

Now she was on her way home and it was too late to turn back. It was too late to undo all the hurt she had been responsible for. She had made many people unhappy – Simon, Donald McPhail especially, and her father too. Perhaps she should include him because she had been hard on him, there was no doubt of that; she had been hard and unforgiving. True, he had been a monster both to herself and to her mother but he had changed in his later years. She was sure of that, too. Yet at that time she could not find it within herself to bend a little. She had been single-minded all her life; she had stuck to her purpose all the way through and now she realised that not only had she ruined at least two lives but she had also been responsible for the death of two men.

So now there was only one course open to her. She had to atone for what she had done, not to change what had happened – it was too late for that – but to register her culpability and pay the price for it. She realised that what she was going to do was an attempt to create peace within herself and, in a sense, that was a selfish act. She did not care. It seemed she was no longer in control of what she was doing; she was being driven and it was too late to stop. It was too late to worry about who or what she was being driven by. She was merely going to do something she had contemplated doing thirty-five years ago. In the midst of her despair, her courage had failed her then. This time, her reasons for carrying through this act were different. In a way, courage had little to do with it now. She would do it because she knew it was the right thing to do.

Although it was only three thirty in the afternoon it was already getting dark as the train approached Strathinver. Elisa put on her coat and got her small suitcase down from the rack.

At the station she put the suitcase in the care of the left luggage office and climbed into the first available taxi. She instructed the driver to go to Spaladale. Now that it was dark she felt safe but she needed everything to go quickly and smoothly. It was essential that she was seen by as few people as possible. It was hard but she even tried not to look out the window. She adopted an aloof demeanour with the taxi driver in order to discourage conversation.

The roads were covered with a light skiff of snow but the temperature had risen slightly and it seemed that a thaw had set in. As she travelled the ten slow miles to Spaladale she realised that a great number of things had to conspire in her favour if she was to carry out her plan successfully.

There were moments of horror when she thought of all the changes that might have taken place since she was last in the village. Maybe the streets had all changed and new houses had been built; maybe it would actually be impossible for her to find her way round. She decided that she would just have to leave it to chance; all these things were beyond her control.

She asked the taxi driver to take her to the manse. This was a reasonable destination and set apart from the village – at least she hoped that was still the case. She recognised the curve of the back road into the village and saw the lights of the manse and the dark shadow of the church beside it. She managed to persuade the driver to leave her at the end of the drive explaining to him that the snow had not yet been cleared from the stretch near the house itself. He was happy to comply.

She set off up the drive but when she was sure that the taxi was gone she retraced her steps and rejoined the main road. She followed it round towards the wood. There was little light as the sky was heavy with cloud and no moon was visible. However, she was able to make out the shapes of trees and the snow on the ground gave off a pale glow.

When she judged she had walked far enough along the road she clambered with difficulty over the low dyke at the side and plunged into the wood itself. If all was the same as before, she knew she would reach a track before long. She did so and a couple of minutes later she stood at the side of Loch Craig whose white frosted surface was just visible as a huge ellipse before her.

She could have stopped to do some remembering – the curling rink had been marked out over there; this was the spot where Stewart Candless's car had slipped into the loch; over there, a few yards down the path, was where she had met Donald the day before she had left Spaladale so many years ago. There were lots of things she could stop and think about but she dared not do it. She knew she could so easily be foiled in what she had to do and the main obstacle was herself. The loch began to glisten in front of her. She stepped out carefully onto the ice and then began to run forward.

TWO POSTSCRIPTS

ONE: GEORGE SANDISON

IN Rome I asked at the embassy; I went through their lists. In Naples I spoke to people at the British Council; I asked the long-stay expatriates; I hovered in bars and got into conversation with as many non-Italians as I could find. I've made all possible approaches. I've poked around and generally made a nuisance of myself.

Nothing.

So I came to the conclusion which I probably came to a long time ago but just couldn't quite admit to myself: my father is dead.

Of course, if he'd wanted to do a disappearing act as Elsie McAndrew did so successfully, then he would have made sure no one found him. He needn't have stayed in Naples, either. He could have gone to another part of Italy. And then why just Italy? He could be anywhere in the world, anywhere.

But I don't think so. I know he's dead. I'm pretty sure Elisa Stasi knows he's dead too, though she hasn't accepted it yet. But it will be confirmed to her. She won't find out who did it or when – it's too late for that – but she'll find out enough to convince her that it really did take place, whatever the finer details might be.

I'm not interested in the details. I don't want to know who, where and how. I don't want to re-open the case, to bring someone to court. This whole business has never been motivated by revenge.

But I think about him a lot, especially now that it's clear I'll never meet him. I think of him with affection. This is mainly because no one else did. There was not a soul with a good word for him. Except Stewart at the end. But maybe Stewart was trying to compensate for wronging him in the first place. My father was a victim but perhaps he took on the role himself. I don't know. He was a sad man.

All this is conjecture of course; I've so little to go on. That's why I've been walking round the city so much, wondering if at any time I've walked along a street where he walked, stood for a moment at a corner where he once stood, looking across at a church or outdoor café. And where did he stay while he was here? Probably in a *pensione* but which one? Who knows how many there are in the centre of the city. But I could go through the lot. It's not impossible. I could visit every one, spend a night in each one. Taking it further, I could stay for one night in every room of every *pensione* in the city to be sure that at least once I stayed in the same place as he did, the same room, the same bed. But could I be sure? And how long would it take me anyway – a year, five years? And what good would it do me? No, I don't think it would prove anything. It would just be an indulgence, the manifestation of obsession. I would be using method, logic, to pursue something that is not shaped by their rules. It would just be a waste of time. And money.

Not that money's a problem. After all, Stewart left me a pile.

I think about her a lot, too, this Elsie/Elisa woman. Why did she agree to see me anyway? It's difficult to know. Maybe she was just tired. Maybe she feels safe now that her husband's dead – both her husbands are dead. Perhaps she was just curious. But it was a risk. It is a risk.

Of course, I've got more chance of being where she has been than where he has been. She's lived in this city for – how long is it? – well over thirty years, anyway. So I must be constantly passing over cobbles and paving slabs that she has walked along with the occasional intrusion, like distant radio interference, of my father.

She's a good woman, too, I'm convinced of that. I think she believed me. I think she believed everything I said, Yes, I'm sure she did. Gullible.

Not that I told many lies, not many. But I'll have to stop because it becomes difficult, after a while, to remember what was a lie and what was not. This confusion makes things worthless, it makes the past a jumble of uncertainties and to make sense of it you have to rely on belief. I have always felt belief to be insubstantial.

As for my father, what have I been able to find out? I'm presented with stories about him, tales told about him by people who met him and perhaps thought they knew him. All these people were biased one way or another. Some loved him but had their love spurned; some bore grudges for his bad behaviour to them; some felt him too pushy for his own good; others saw him as a waster, a drunk, a man who threw away his talent and his money on things of no importance. Stewart thought him hard-working but obsessed by one big story that would make his name.

So, when my father latched on to Elsie's story did he follow it and follow it all the way across Europe to a city whose language and culture were new to him just because he wanted a scoop? No, I don't believe that; I'm sure there's more. But here I am dabbling in belief and that's what I want to get away from.

But still, I will have to construct my father's life from a collection of half-truths, outright lies and the uncertain tales of those who knew him and whose memory over such a spell of time is suspect. Working with such material what will I end up with?

Sometimes I wonder if it's worth it.

One thing is sure: Elisa Stasi won't lead me any closer to the truth. But she might lead herself there and that will be worthwhile, I suppose. I know now that my father was murdered and I think that she must know this too, somewhere inside. It's just admitting it that's difficult. If she does admit it, if she does find out, I wonder how she'll handle it.

But I won't be around to find out. It struck me as I left her – I'd thought of it before, but never really examined it – that I'm the threat now. In 1947 it was different of course. My father could have ruined everything. As for me, well, maybe it's all too late. Maybe Elisa Stasi's past doesn't matter any more. Her husband's dead; the influence of the Stasis has declined. Who would really be interested in some story about her early life? Who would believe it?

But then, not everyone here thinks as I do. Belief is not something shifting and unreliable; it's solid. Those who chose to believe it might feel that some response was necessary.

So, it's a risk and it's one I'm not ready to take. I came over here to Procida and I've decided not to go back to Naples even though I've left one or two things in the *pensione*. If anyone comes looking for me they might be persuaded to wait till I get back.

I'll investigate other routes to the mainland. I need to get to Rome quickly and get a new passport – I told the truth about that, at least. And I'll start again. I'll try and persuade them to give me a new name: George Sandison. It will be difficult, I'm sure, and I'll have to lie a bit to get my story right. I may even have tell a little of the truth. But George Sandison it is from now on. I can give my father this much, at least.

TWO: THE McPHAILS

THERE really was a Loch Craig, filled with newts and frogs, which I visited as a child in the company of Donald McPhail. There really was a curling brush which I converted into a walking stick. There really is a photograph of three old men and a little dog – my grandfather, my great-grandfather, the man I call Simon and a terrier whose real name was Coogan. I could go on counting off articles that existed or still exist, events that did actually happen. However, the main thing that I have to record at this point is that the story of Elsie is complete fiction. I made up her life – her lives – and her deaths are a product of my imagination. That is not to say that some truth does not attend them. You see, I have shifted ground a little from the first death of Elsie. Lies, fiction, unreality; these words are not synonymous. After all, I have gone to the very great trouble of writing about Elsie because I think she has value and is perhaps more real – no, substantial is a better word – she is more substantial than my uncertain memories of her husband. As I wrote about her and got to know her I began to lose interest in trying to justify her. This little disclaimer may not be entirely satisfactory but it is the truth.

So, Simon really existed, though his name was not Simon. My memory of him is hazy, restricted almost completely to that single visit to his house in search of the meaning of a word. No, I have built up Simon into something he was not, but then I have done the same for all of them, including the McPhails. The McPhails. I said somewhere at the beginning that I have three main memories of Donald and I have recounted two of them already. On reflection the third, which concerns the day he left the village, is of his wife more than of Donald himself. I will tell it now, with a little description of the lady we all knew as Mrs Donald, not just for the sake of completeness but because what happened that day set me on my way to discovering something about what the truth is and what it is not. I was nine or ten years old and for the first time I recognised that things were not always what they seemed or what other people would have me believe. I suppose it was the beginning of the death of my childhood.

*

The deaths of the McPhails did not upset me much. I can remember clearly hearing of the death of Mrs McPhail but I can't be sure when it was that Donald died or even if it was mentioned to me at the time. Whatever the case, it made little impression on me. My grief had been felt a few years before when they left the village.

I choose to think that it was this fact of departure, of leaving the little world of the village that represented for me then something at least as great as death. Despite what old Mrs McPhail said I knew they were not going away for a holiday. No one had told me but I knew. Their son-in-law had come up from Edinburgh and he was taking them away. I knew I would never see them again.

The McPhails' house and our house were on opposite sides of the main village street. Our houses were also the first in the village if you were approaching from the south. Now there is a new road which bypasses the village but when I was a child, when my grandparents and the McPhails were still alive, the village street was very busy and old people found it difficult to cross. Cars sped in round a long bend from the country and seemed to come upon the village suddenly, were almost at the other end before they had time to slow down. Because she was very hard of hearing Mrs McPhail found the road particularly hazardous.

I remember her as a tiny, frail, old lady. Whenever my mother or grandmother, watching from the window of the front room, saw Mrs Donald about to cross the street there would be a few moments of high tension and feverish activity. 'There's Mrs Donald!' one of them would shout. 'She's going to cross the street!' as if this were some momentous and quite outrageous act. A rush to the front door would follow and instructions would be shouted across to her, often conflicting instructions, on when to cross the road. In all this Mrs Donald was almost set apart. She seemed to be in another world, separate from the intense activity on the other side of the street. Either she could not hear my mother and my grandmother or she chose to act as if she could not hear them. She seemed only dimly aware of the cars that whizzed by. She decided upon her moment almost arbitrarily, or perhaps merely on the basis of how long she had been waiting. Then she launched herself gently from the kerb and crossed, safely, to the other side.

Relieved that Mrs Donald was safe and well after the dangerous journey she had undertaken from her house all of thirty yards away, my mother and grandmother would usher her in to sit at the large Queen-Anne table in the middle of our dining-cum-living room. Conversations with Mrs Donald, because of her deafness, were noisy affairs. People had to shout at her. Sometimes it was clear that she had misheard something that had been directed at her and she would go off on some distant tack from which it was difficult to recover her. Her own voice was quite quiet, rather crackly, and her favourite phrase was 'That's that.' 'Well,' she would say, when the conversation was clearly in a lull, 'well, well, that's that.' It had a definite finality to it and it usually signalled Mrs Donald's departure, which was attended with all the worry about her return journey that her trip over had occasioned.

Then came that day when the McPhails left the village and never came back. They were transferred from being friends and neighbours to being people talked about separately. Even on the day they left, before they actually got into the car that drove them away, they had become different. My learning about how the adult world worked was gleaned in snatches of conversation, little revelations that occurred often by chance. It was detective work, this piecing together of information let slip by adults. I heard the phrase, said of the McPhails, that they were old. It was not an explanation so much as the revealing of some sin, some crime that they had been discovered committing.

So they stood by the car saying goodbye and there was Mrs Donald more tiny and wrinkled than ever, saying to no one in particular, 'Just a month or two of course, a little holiday.' And we all said, yes, yes, a little holiday, a short break. And everyone, all of us there, our hands on the car door, my grandmother, my mother, my father, the son-in-law, the daughter, the McPhails themselves, even me, we all knew it was a lie.